"You can dream now Ryanne," Hugh said

"Someday soon your sight will return. If you woke up tomorrow morning and could see, and the threat posed by Beck miraculously went away, what would you do?"

Hugh was right. Ryanne hadn't allowed herself to dream, and she was afraid to do so now because shattered dreams were unbearably painful. But because she was wrapped safely in his arms, Ryanne let an imaginary light illuminate what her heart wanted most.

"I would want..." *to see your face, to know you were mine forever and that the darkness could never touch me again because you are my light....* The words were there in thoughts that burned brightly, but it was a futile dream, and saying it aloud would only make the hurt that much greater when it didn't come true....

ABOUT THE AUTHOR

Connie Bennett's previous book, *Thinking of You*, was recognized as one of the outstanding Superromances of 1988 in *Romantic Times* magazine. Connie, a Missouri native who came on board the Harlequin ship in January of that year with *Share My Tomorrow*, was deeply honored by the recognition. Thoroughly happy with her new career, she hopes to combine romance writing with screenwriting in the future. Harlequin is keeping Connie busy for now, though—she has four more Supers currently in the works!

Books by Connie Bennett

HARLEQUIN SUPERROMANCE

Don't miss any of our special offers. Write to us at the following address for information on our newest releases.

Harlequin Reader Service
901 Fuhrmann Blvd., P.O. Box 1397, Buffalo, NY 14240
Canadian address: P.O. Box 603,
Fort Erie, Ont. L2A 5X3

When I See Your Face

CONNIE BENNETT

Harlequin Books

TORONTO • NEW YORK • LONDON
AMSTERDAM • PARIS • SYDNEY • HAMBURG
STOCKHOLM • ATHENS • TOKYO • MILAN

FORTY YEARS OF
Romance

Published July 1989

First printing May 1989

ISBN 0-373-70364-3

To Marcia,
who sees with her heart
what most of us forget to look for

PROLOGUE

THE GUNSHOT WAS entirely unexpected, and in Ryanne Kirkland's opinion, totally uncalled for. It reverberated through the shadowed warehouse, echoing in the near darkness long after the man in the rumpled suit had clutched his chest in surprise and pitched to the concrete floor, dead. The other man—the one with the gun—calmly replaced the weapon in the pocket of his tailored worsted jacket, bent over, and then pried the briefcase from his victim's lifeless fingers. Except for the unusual, stark surroundings, the two men could have been stockbrokers conferring on a deal; a deal that obviously had gone very sour.

Hidden in the shadows watching every gruesome move the murderer made, Ryanne suppressed an insane desire to scream. She wasn't a screamer by nature. In fact, the last time she could clearly recall doing so she had been six years old and her mother had just informed her she was too young to travel across the country to see the Beatles in concert. The resulting tantrum had shaken the rafters, and it wasn't until her father had quietly emerged from his study and told Ryanne how disappointed he was in her that she had calmed down. Disappointing her father was one thing Ryanne could not bear, and that had been her last temper tantrum.

Now, however, Ryanne felt justified in screaming. It wasn't every day that she witnessed a cold-blooded murder, nor did she often find herself alone in a deserted warehouse with a stranger who had no aversion to using his very deadly gun. She was relatively certain that even her calm, practical father would have forgiven her for screaming in this instance...probably.

The scream welled in her throat, burning and begging to be released, but she somehow managed to hold it back. With or without her father's approval, she had to. No one knew she was hiding in the shadows of the warehouse of a chemical processing plant in one of the less reputable areas of Chicago. Her decision to follow Vinnie Perigrino, the man in the rumpled suit, had been an impulsive one. The man who had killed him didn't know she was here, thank goodness; his ignorance was the only thing keeping her alive. One ear-piercing scream was the quickest ticket to kingdom come Ryanne could have purchased, so she swallowed the painful yell and tried to think rationally about what to do next.

And, of course, the answer was astonishingly clear: she would stay here, hidden in the darkness, until the murderer left.

It was a simple plan that did not require her to do anything, which was good, because Ryanne wasn't sure that her legs would have held her up had she come up with a plan of action that required action. She'd been crouched behind the fifty-gallon chemical drums that read Flammable in big red letters for what seemed like ages, and her legs felt watery and trembled. Staying put was definitely the best plan all around.

The man with the gun would leave through the same downstairs door he'd come in by. After waiting a decent interval to make sure the coast was clear, Ryanne would follow. She would run to her car, parked out of sight just around the corner, and drive like a bat out of hell to the nearest pay phone. There, she would call her editor on the city desk at the *Examiner* and report what she'd just seen, then she'd call the police.

Or maybe she'd call the police and then phone her editor. Yes, police first, she finally decided. Old habits were hard to break, and for a reporter the first instinct was always the story, but Ryanne swore that if she got out of this mess, common sense would prevail and she'd give the police the first crack at the case. And while she was waiting for the police to arrive, she'd call her editor.

Patting herself on the back for having made such a rational decision at a time when there didn't seem to be a rational bone in her body, Ryanne tried to keep her breathing under control; it was showing a marked tendency to be harsh and erratic. She mentally repeated the litany *Stay calm, stay calm* and waited for the gun-toting man in the worsted suit to leave so that she could follow the scenario she'd just plotted.

Only Worsted didn't follow the script. He was supposed to leave, but he wasn't showing any signs of hotfooting it out. Instead he placed the briefcase on the floor and started dragging the body away from the clearing in the center of the room toward the wall opposite Ryanne's hideout. More drums lined that area, stacked three high and who-knew-how-many deep.

Now why on earth would he do that? Ryanne wondered. Certainly when the work crew came in tomorrow morning and found a dead body in the middle of the floor it would put a pall over the day's activities, but Ryanne doubted that Worsted was concerned about the delicate sensibilities of the workmen. If murder didn't faze him, why would he care where the body was found as long as he was well away from the scene of the crime before that happened?

Unless, of course, finding the body wasn't inevitable.

Ryanne felt a shudder of apprehension ripple down her spine and that barely suppressed scream welled again. Those bright red letters, *F-L-A-M-M-A-B-L-E*, jumped out at her and everything suddenly became clear. Worsted didn't want his victim found, and the best way to ensure that was to place the body next to several thousand gallons of highly flammable chemicals and set off an explosion. When those drums blew, there wouldn't be enough of Perigrino left to know he'd ever existed. And when Vinnie disappeared, so would Ryanne Kirkland.

Douglas Sutherland, Ryanne's city desk editor, was bound to take a dim view of one of his reporters getting herself blown up, even if there was a good story in it. It was Douglas's very pragmatic theory that reporters did a better job when they were functioning well enough to write down the facts, and in this instance, Ryanne agreed wholeheartedly with her boss. She'd grown rather fond of living these past twenty-eight years. She had good friends and a great job, her Aunt Rose seemed to have forgiven her for being an old maid, there were two gold fish depending on her as their only visible means of support and her best suit was ready to be picked up at the cleaners.

Disappearing without a trace would definitely put a crimp in her life-style.

Vinnie's dead weight was forcing Worsted to labor over his job of disposing of the body. He was getting closer to the opposite wall, and Ryanne quickly began evaluating her options. There weren't many of them, and the time to exercise them was definitely *now*. The second floor of the warehouse was a three-sided affair, like a gigantic horseshoe, and the fourth side—to Ryanne's right—was nothing more than one long drop to the lower floor.

There were two enormous, open freight elevators that were obviously used to carry the chemical drums up or down as the situation warranted, and on either side of the elevators, a safety railing led to vertical steel ladders at both ends. It was one of those ladders that had allowed Ryanne to follow Vinnie upstairs, unseen. He'd unlocked the side door and left it conveniently ajar, leading Ryanne to believe he was going to be meeting someone else in the warehouse. At the time, Ryanne had hoped that Vinnie would lead her to someone a little higher up on the syndicate ladder. Now she just wanted to get out with her hide and her story intact.

Perigrino was a small-time hood who'd fallen in with bigger-time hoods who ran an illegal gambling operation. Ryanne's best sources on the mayor's organized crime unit had informed her that the police were planning to put the squeeze on Vinnie in the hopes that he'd lead them to the uptown banker who was laundering the syndicate's ill-gotten booty. Knowing a banner headline story when one was tossed into her lap, Ryanne had used a few more contacts to find Vinnie, and had followed him to the darkened warehouse because it was Friday night and she had nothing better to do.

Taking the unlocked door as the next best thing to an engraved invitation, Ryanne had silently followed Vinnie into the warehouse, keeping to the shadows, never once pausing to wonder if she was doing the sane, logical, reasonable, *safe* thing. Like her Pulitzer prize winning father before her, Ryanne thought first, last and always of the story.

An hour ago she'd thought this one was getting more intriguing by the minute. Visions of a substantial raise in pay had danced in her head as she'd watched Vinnie step onto one of the freight elevators and ride to the second floor. When he'd disappeared, Ryanne had quietly sprinted through the shadows to one of the ladders and scrambled up like a monkey. She'd found a convenient hiding place from which to watch whatever proceedings were about to unfold, and she'd waited.

Worsted had arrived moments later. He'd ridden the elevator up, stepped off and moved directly to the center of the room where Vinnie had stood so casually he might have been waiting for the crosstown bus.

Too far away to hear more than muted murmuring, Ryanne had watched. Vinnie gave Worsted a briefcase, and they chatted some more, like old college chums at their twenty-year class reunion... until Worsted calmly, and in the most civilized manner imaginable, pulled out a gun and decreased Chicago's population by one—a body count that was very shortly going to double if Ryanne didn't act fast.

Though Worsted was facing her as he tugged the uncooperative body, Ryanne knew she'd have to take her chances. The shadows were deep and Worsted was some distance away. Also, he was understandably distracted. No matter how composed he appeared to be, lugging around a man he'd just murdered had to be a little unnerving.

Ryanne stood slowly and tested her shaky legs by flexing her knees. Normally she was in excellent physical condition, but terror had a way of making even the strongest legs a wee bit unsteady. Thankfully they felt more substantial than warm Jell-O.

The Nike running shoes she'd been known to wear with even the classiest pieces of her limited wardrobe enabled her to move quietly, and she retreated a little farther into the shadows, then began inching her way toward the ladder. A rabbit warren of corridors among the stacked drums provided suitable cover, and she merely retraced the route she'd taken when she arrived. But the make-shift tunnels soon ran out, and she stopped, peering across the room toward Worsted, who had almost suc-ceeded in draping Perigrino across the top of a chemical drum. Obviously he was leaving nothing to chance.

As though Vinnie had looked down from somewhere in the great beyond and seen what was about to happen to his former self, the dead man grew even more un-cooperative and slid off the drum with a deadening thud. Ryanne heard what she assumed was a muttered curse from Worsted, and she glanced furtively at the ladder. It was twenty feet away, and the room offered only a few paltry shadows to protect her. Why that twenty feet hadn't seemed so open and desolate when she'd been headed in the opposite direction she couldn't say; she just knew that now it did.

But there were no alternatives open to her and she glanced at Worsted one last time. Miraculously, his back was to her and she knew she'd never get a better oppor-tunity.

Keeping as close to the wall as possible, she moved out of her rabbit warren. One step at a time, flattened against the wall, her heart pounding out the cymbal crashes from the *1812* Overture, she forced herself to keep going. Another step, fifteen feet to go, then twelve ... nine ... seven ...

She might have made it if Worsted hadn't turned.

CHAPTER ONE

Douglas Sutherland
Chicago Daily Examiner
Michigan Ave.
Chicago, IL

Hugh MacKenna and Assoc.
Private Investigators
La Cienega Blvd.
Los Angeles, CA

Dear Hugh:

Enclosed are the newspaper clippings and copies of the old police reports you said you'd like to see, and I've enclosed a couple of photos as well. The gorgeous redhead in the eight-by-ten glossy is Ryanne Kirkland, and the one who looks as if she gargles with lemon juice is Judith Tremain, Ryanne's secretary. They'll be arriving in Los Angeles on Monday, and Ryanne has promised that she'll call you just as soon as they get settled into the house at Malibu. If you can take a look at the security system in the house she's sublet and make sure it's in good shape I'll be forever in your debt. Ryanne is very special to me and I'll rest a lot easier knowing you're going to be looking out for her while she's in L.A. working on her screenplay.

In regard to the clippings and the other stuff I've enclosed, I think you'll find it all interesting, probably even fascinating, but overall, the incident is a dead issue. As long as Ryanne is blind the man who left her for dead in that warehouse five years ago has no reason to try to kill her again, but I really appreciate the thorough approach you've taken to this simple favor. I like the idea that someone out there knows her history and understands what she's been through.

One word of caution, though: for both our sakes; don't let on to Ryanne that I've told you everything. She has this cockamamy notion that if people know the whole story they will pity her more than she thinks they already do. If she knew I'd told you, she'd serve my head on a platter to that guide dog of hers, so mum's the word, okay? If Ryanne wants to tell you the story, fine, but you didn't hear it from me!

Well, that's about it for now. If you have any questions please give me a call. I'll be right here, chained to the city desk as always. Take care of yourself—and Ryanne.

Love,
Uncle Doug

Uncle Doug? Hugh looked at the endearment again and smiled ruefully. Douglas apparently thought he was asking his "nephew" a pretty big favor; it had been twenty-five years, at least, since Hugh had called his father's best friend "uncle." Hugh's parents had still been married then, living the Ward-and-June-Cleaver myth in a quiet Chicago suburb. Everything had been simple and innocent. Unfortunately his parents' ugly divorce had proven to Hugh that few things were simple, and no one stayed innocent for long.

Tossing aside the letter and the unbidden memories it had provoked, Hugh reached into the manila envelope and extracted the rest of the material Douglas had sent. Ryanne Kirkland's picture was on top and Hugh looked at it objectively. Douglas hadn't exaggerated. It was a beautiful face. But then, what else would one expect given the amount of reconstructive surgery she'd had after falling off that warehouse ledge and landing flat on her face? Given that kind of challenge, how many plastic surgeons in the world would create an ugly face?

But beauty, artificially achieved or not, was still beauty, and Hugh knew how to appreciate it with the best of them. Her face was rounded in a gentle oval and her features were soft, her lips prettily bowed. The fiery mane of red hair that framed her face was attractive, too. Ultimately, though, Hugh found it was her eyes that he could not avoid. They were enormous, bright blue eyes that stared beyond the camera straight into his own.

Eyes like those could reduce a man to cinders in a matter of seconds, Hugh decided. Then he remembered that those lovely eyes couldn't see.

"New case, Hugh?" Mo Johnson stepped through his boss's open door and took a chair without benefit of an invitation.

"No, just a little background work on a favor I'm doing for Douglas Sutherland, an old buddy of Dad's from Chicago. He's got a friend moving into a house a mile or so up the beach from my place and he wants me to check out her security system and keep an eye on her while she's in L.A."

Mo quirked one eyebrow. "Normal caution against Sin City crime, or is he expecting trouble?"

Hugh leaned back, tapping the photo thoughtfully against the edge of his desk. "Maybe a little of both. Doug's the overprotective, fatherly type, but he may have reason to worry. You ever heard of Ryan Kirk?"

"The mystery writer? Sure. I never miss a book. I hear they're turning his latest into a movie."

"Not 'his,'" Hugh corrected. *"Hers."* He tossed Ryanne's picture across the desk.

"You're kidding." Johnson looked at the photograph in disbelief. "You mean to tell me this gorgeous lady is Ryan Kirk, writer of the grittiest, seamiest detective novels since Mickey Spillane?"

"That's right. Her name is Ryanne, with an *a-n-n-e*, Kirkland. Until five years ago she was a reporter, and according to Douglas, a damned good one. She didn't start writing the Cameron Lawe mysteries until after she lost her sight."

"You mean she's blind?"

"Yep." He shoved the second picture across the desk. "This is her secretary, Judith Tremain."

Mo studied the middle-aged face that might have been attractive if Ms. Tremain had learned how to smile. "Definitely not the type I'd like to meet in a dark alley."

Hugh smiled. "Doug says she's a real dragon lady."

Mo looked at the photo of Ryanne again and shook his head. "Ryan Kirk is a woman. How about that?" He returned the pictures to the desk. "How'd she go blind?"

"She was working on a story about a nickel-and-dime gambling syndicate and saw a small-time hood get waxed by one of his associates."

"So the guy blinded her to keep her from testifying?" Mo shuddered. "That's positively medieval."

"No, no. She was trying to get away from him and fell off a ledge in a warehouse. The fall smashed her head up pretty badly," he said, remembering his conversation with Douglas the previous week.

Mo made a noise that signified his disgust. "Did they get the guy who did it?"

"Nope. Ryanne had never seen him before. Doug says the police are pretty sure they know who he is, but a blind eyewitness tends to make a poor impression on juries. As far as I know, the guy was never even charged."

"Any chance she'll get her sight back?"

Hugh shook his head. "The doctors say no way. Something about irreparable damage to the optic nerve because of the fall. But I think Doug is a little nervous about Ryanne right now because she's been having headaches and has decided to go to a big specialist out here. The top neurological man in the country or something like that. Doug thinks the killer has been keeping track of her all these years and might get the wrong idea about why she's seeing the doctor. He may think there's a chance she'll get her sight back."

"And try to kill her," Mo added, though it was unnecessary because they both knew the implications of what Hugh had just said.

"It's a possibility, though I'd say a very remote one. I can't imagine this creep taking the risk of icing Ryanne unless he's got proof she's going to see again, and Doug says there's no chance of that."

"So where do you come into all this?" Mo asked.

"I'll just go over her security system and play good neighbor Sam. Make sure she gets settled in comfortably, drop in for a friendly visit from time to time."

"Sort of a one man Welcome Wagon."

"Something like that."

Mo glanced at the picture of Ryanne again and sighed. "Why is it you always get first crack at the gorgeous damsels in distress?"

Hugh pretended to be appalled. "Are you suggesting that I might try to seduce a poor little blind girl? I can feel my Boy Scout merit badges tarnishing as we speak."

"I didn't think they let subversive types like you in the Boy Scouts," Mo said teasingly.

Hugh chuckled at the jibe, but instead of taking up the gauntlet he glanced at the other photographs Douglas had sent. There was an attractive shot of Ryanne Kirkland dressed in shorts and a halter top, romping on someone's lawn with a cute golden retriever nipping at her heels, and another shot of her and the dog nose to nose that was too schmaltzy for words. The next picture brought Hugh up short, though, and he forgot to be cynical about the sentimental shots. It was Ryanne in a dramatic evening dress that bared one shoulder and clung to every curve of her fragile, slender body. Her hair was upswept, her face was glowing, and by her side, in harness, was the same carefree retriever from the previous photographs. He wasn't her pet, he was her guide dog— her eyes.

Once again, Hugh was captivated by the clear, unshadowed beauty of Ryanne's blue eyes, but something unusual caught his attention and he flipped back through the pictures. In all but the one he'd handed Mo, Ryanne was wearing glasses.

"That's weird," he muttered under his breath.

"What?" Mo asked.

Hugh handed over the pictures. "Why would a blind person wear glasses?"

"Camouflage?"

"You're a big help."

Mo ducked his head modestly. "I like my job, so I do my best to please the boss. So tell me, boss...are we going to sit around here all day looking at pictures, or what?"

Hugh grinned. "Are you trying to tell me you're bored, Mo?"

"Hey, I'm a detective. I get paid to detect."

Hugh tossed the pictures aside and pulled a slim file from his desk. "In that case, why don't you sink your teeth into this."

"Ah-ha!" Mo's eyes lit up. "What is it? Blackmail? Arson? Industrial espionage?"

"None of the above," Hugh told him. "It's a little old blue-haired Beverly Hills matron who thinks her husband OD'd on Geritol. She wants to know how he's spending his time away from her."

Mo groaned in misery. "I had to ask." He stood and moved toward the door. "She wants pictures and everything?"

"And everything."

"Oh, brother." Mumbling something about investigating employment opportunities in life insurance sales, Mo left and Hugh went back to the photos Doug had sent.

He saw a pretty lady who'd had a hard life—pretty pedestrian in his line of work—yet Hugh suddenly felt a deep foreboding that Ryanne Kirkland was about to change his life. He sluffed the idea off as maudlin claptrap, but this was one premonition he should have listened to. Closely.

CHAPTER TWO

"JUDITH!" Exasperated, Ryanne jerked her head and torso from the empty cabinet, misjudged the distance, and banged her head on the shelf above her. "Damn!" Rubbing the latest of her growing collection of bumps and bruises, she settled back on her haunches to wait. Pots, pans and a varied assortment of baking dishes fanned out around her in a cluttered but well-organized circle.

"Aren't you finished yet?"

The thickly padded hall carpet had muted Judith's footsteps so that Ryanne hadn't heard her coming, but she was much too familiar with her secretary's perpetually irritable voice to jump at the sound. Until Ryanne's "accident" as she euphemistically referred to it, Judith had been secretary to the circulation manager at the *Examiner*. Ryanne had known the older woman for years. When her new career as a novelist had taken off and it became apparent that she needed a combination secretary, assistant, and companion to help keep her life in order, Judith had been Ryanne's first choice. Despite their constant bickering, Ryanne had never regretted hiring her.

She turned toward her indispensable friend. "Never, as long as I live, will I sublet another furnished house."

"You called me out here to tell me that?"

"Yes."

"I'll make a note of it."

"In braille, please."

"Naturally."

The floor squeaked ever so slightly as Judith turned to leave, but Ryanne protested. "Wait a minute! I need your help."

Judith gave the array of cookware a dismissive glance. "It's your mess—you clean it up."

"Just tell me where that enormous stew pot is, okay? I put it right there—" she pointed unerringly to a conspicuously empty spot on the floor "—and now it's gone."

"Well, I don't see it, either. Are you sure you didn't put it back in the cabinet?"

Ryanne rubbed the bump on her head. "I'm sure," she replied tightly.

"Then it's vanished," Judith pronounced helpfully.

"Great. As if a furnished house isn't bad enough, it has to be a *haunted* furnished house as well."

"You know, if you'd just left things as they were you wouldn't be having this problem," Judith commented, bending down to the cabinet to see for herself whether or not the elusive pot was there.

"If I'd left things as they were, I'd be spending the next six months not knowing where anything is. Do you see it?"

"Nope." She moved on to the next bank of cabinets. "You probably put it in one of these thinking it was a teapot."

Ryanne sighed heavily. "Judith, I may be blind and temporarily disorganized, but I do know the difference between a three-gallon enamel stew pot and a whistling teakettle." She reached into the box sitting next to her, poked around for a moment and came up with a huge blue enamel lid. "See, here's the lid. I just need the pot it attaches to."

Judith let the cabinet door shut with a bang and Ryanne made a studied attempt not to jump at the sound. Even after five years loud noises still bothered her, and though Judith was well aware of the minor phobia, she rarely went out of her way to protect Ryanne from the small upsets. In fact, Ryanne was certain her companion leaned in the opposite direction, making loud noises deliberately. It was as though she was subtly trying to reassure Ryanne that not every bang meant imminent danger or death.

"Not in there, either? Don't tell me I'm going to have to hold a seance to find it," she quipped, ignoring the shudder down her spine that accompanied the banging of cabinet doors as Judith continued to search.

"No, but it has to be here some—" As she turned around, the dining area fell into Judith's view, and underneath the chrome-and-glass table sat the stew pot— just inches from the twitching nose of Ryanne's dozing golden retriever. "Aha! That stupid dog pilfered it. You don't need an exorcist, you need an obedience school."

"I should have known," Ryanne muttered. "Aggie came sniffing around here a few minutes ago and I shooed her away. She must have nudged it over there while I had my head in the cupboard."

"All the evidence points in that direction." Judith went to pick up the pot and moved to the sink to wash it.

"Is she asleep?"

"Under the table," Judith confirmed.

"Well, don't wake her until I get this job finished."

"Are you kidding? If I had my way I'd put her to sleep permanently."

Ryanne clucked her tongue reproachfully. "Now Judith, you love Aggie as much as I do. Admit it."

Ryanne could almost visualize Judith drawing herself up indignantly. "I'll admit no such thing. I loathe the beast."

Across the room the familiar clatter of Aggie's choke collar warned both women that the guide dog had heard herself being discussed. The canine padded across the floor and poked her nose into the back of Judith's knee. "Get away," she growled, but Aggie only wagged her tail happily and nudged her again. "Stupid dog can't even tell when she's not wanted."

"Aggie knows who loves her and who doesn't, don't you baby?" Ryanne cooed, and the dog responded instantly and predictably to her mistress's voice. Before either woman could stop her, the affectionate retriever was plowing through the cookware and planting her cold, wet nose and scratchy tongue on Ryanne's face.

"Aggie, no!" Ryanne squeaked, but the dominoes had already started to fall. Her wailed protest only made Aggie think it was playtime, and when Ryanne jerked away, trying to restrain the dog, her backward movement overturned a set of saucepans. Startled by the crash, Aggie skittered to one side, landing squarely in a well-stacked pile of cookie sheets. Her feet skidded out from under her as she tried to find solid ground again and the box of lids tumbled and clattered all over the floor.

Panting, her golden eyes wide, Aggie finally stepped back and looked at the mess she'd created. Ryanne, who'd landed squarely on her bottom, threw up her hands in abject frustration, and Judith, who had stood patiently waiting for the chaos to subside, merely smirked. "Shall I call Guiding Eyes for the Blind and tell them you want to return one slightly clumsy, extremely idiotic dog?''

"Stuff it, Judith. Clumsy or not, Aggie stays. You, on the other hand . . .''

"Yes?'' she prompted expectantly. It was unusual for her to make it through a day without being fired, so she figured it would be just as well to get it out of the way this morning.

"Can help me clean up this mess,'' Ryanne finally finished. "You wash and I'll dry and put away. And we'd better hurry. Hugh MacKenna is going to be here in less than an hour and I've got to change clothes.''

Resigning herself to the task ahead, Judith bent and began reassembling the pieces of cookware, placing them on the counter next to the sink. "I thought he was supposed to be here at eleven.''

"That's right,'' Ryanne said, groping at her feet for errant pots and pans.

"Well, if you're going to change you'd better do it soon because it's ten forty-five right now.''

Ryanne's head shot up. "You're kidding?''

Judith sighed patiently. "I've known you for most of your adult life and you still haven't learned that I never kid.''

"Omigod, Judith, what am I going to do? I can't meet a man who has a voice that sounds like smooth Kentucky bourbon looking like this! When we talked on the phone yesterday I thought I'd died and gone to heaven.''

"Don't worry about it, Ryanne,'' Judith advised. "If he's one of Douglas Sutherland's friends, Hugh Mac-Kenna has got to be at least sixty years old. He's probably as bald as a billiard ball with a gut that hangs over his belt and peeks out from under his sweaty, tattered T-shirt.''

"Don't be ridiculous. This is Hollywood, land of the beautiful. They don't even let you on the Ventura Freeway without checking for an even tan. And besides, what do I care what he looks like? It's his voice I'm in love with."

"Uh-huh. The last time you fell in love with a voice, it had a wife and two children."

"Ah, but what a voice it was. I spent many a sleepless night over that one, let me tell you." She grinned in the general direction of her companion, who was busily washing by this time. "Unrequited love has taken a rap through the centuries, but I can tell you from personal experience, it ain't all that bad. I've yet to meet a man who can match my fantasies of him."

"I don't want to hear about your fantasies," Judith informed her.

"Judith, old duck, what you need is a man of your own. Then we'll talk about fantasies."

"No thanks. I've had my turn. Romance is only for the very young or the very foolish. I am neither."

"Nonsense. Romance is universal."

"Is that why you live like a nun?" Judith asked shrewdly. "Or are you planning on letting old bourbon-breath change all that?"

"That's bourbon *voice*," Ryanne corrected. "And I doubt he'll change anything about my life because I plan on worshiping him from afar."

"Well, unless you go change your clothes, I'd make that very far, because you look like something the cat dragged in."

"I'm changing, I'm changing," Ryanne promised, heading out of the kitchen. "Just leave those things in the drainer and I'll put them away when old bourbon-voice leaves."

"All right, but next time you get down on the floor, put Agnes the Menace on her bed chain!"

"Yes, sir!"

With Aggie at her heels, Ryanne breezed confidently down the long hall, pleased that there was at least one place in this unfamiliar environment where she could move at her normal, breakneck pace. The rest of the house was one gigantic obstacle course, with tables, chairs, ottomen and other evil accoutrements that jumped out at her with annoying regularity. She'd been in the house four days, and had spent the biggest portion of her time trying to memorize the layout of the place and the whereabouts of the insidious, shin-eating furniture. If she concentrated completely, she could move fairly well through her bedroom, its adjoining bathroom and the kitchen, but the huge living room that was separated from the kitchen by an open bar, and the office Judith was still trying to whip into shape were maddeningly elusive. But before the week was out, she would conquer them. She had to—it was a matter of honor. No mere house was going to get the best of Ryanne Denise Kirkland!

Counting the doorways in the hall as she passed them, she rushed into the master bedroom, then paused to take stock. Judith had described every room to her in minute detail, and she knew the enormous suite stretched out on either side of her, with a luxurious king-size bed to her right, and beyond that, floor-to-ceiling windows and French doors that led to a cedar deck. The deck ran the entire length of the back of the house, which overlooked the ocean.

In front of her was a small, comfortable sitting room, and to her left, a walk-in closet and the door to the most extravagant bathroom Ryanne had ever encountered.

Just thinking about the gigantic whirlpool bathtub made her mouth water, but there was no time for indulgence now.

Moving slowly she resisted the temptation to run her hand along the mirrored closet doors as a guide, and instead she listened for the subtle change in air pressure that signaled the opening to the bathroom. Guided by the hollow sound, she hurried in as quickly as she dared, and stripped out of her T-shirt and cutoffs, tossing them into the hamper. She laid her glasses on the counter as she filled the marble basin with water and began washing the morning's residue of grime from her face and arms.

Ryanne knew that she was facing a mirror that ran the length of the seven-foot vanity, and as she toweled off, she wondered absently exactly what it was the mirror saw. Friends told her that her face, which had once been pretty but unremarkable, was now beautiful. Even crusty Judith had declared that it was "passable," which had to mean this new face was something special indeed. But to Ryanne, it was a mystery—even though she had memorized every line and contour with her hands. She knew her nose was a little shorter than it had been, her chin and jaw not quite as obstinate and her cheekbones a little more distinctive, but how all those elements fit together she didn't have a clue. And she never would. It was strange having to rely only on imagination to picture how other people looked, and Ryanne thought it was downright eerie to know that if she miraculously got her sight back she wouldn't even recognize her own face.

From the kitchen, Ryanne's human alarm clock shouted that it was ten fifty-four, and Ryanne retrieved her glasses and hurried back toward the bedroom. In her haste, she misjudged the location of the door and bounced off the frame like a pinball off a bumper pad.

With a muttered curse, she adjusted her position, this time giving way to the temptation to feel her way along the wall, around the corner to the closet. She had worked hard to make her movements as close as possible to those of a sighted person, and that meant using sound cues instead of touch whenever possible to determine the location of a door, a room, or an object. Since she was short on time, though, Ryanne abandoned her vanity in favor of making it to the closet in one piece.

There, her entire summer wardrobe stretched out before her, and since clothes had never been a priority in her life, it was a pretty short stretch. With her hands she quickly skimmed over the sections of blouses, pants and jeans, until she came to the small selection of dresses. Old bourbon-voice deserved something special, Ryanne figured, and she was going to give it to him. Somewhere in here was a pastel blue outfit consisting of a cap-sleeved bolero that would adequately cover the scars on her shoulder, and a calf-length sundress that would hide the black-and-blue on her shins, her constant reminders that she moved too fast and with too little caution.

Searching for the gauzy, gathered cotton set, she dismissed the first few dresses until she came to the short-sleeved bolero.

Working quickly, she removed it from the hanger, laid it carefully aside, then did the same with the thin-strapped sundress. The gathered, lace-edged half slip she wore under the dress was attached to the hanger with clothespins, and she hurriedly slipped it on. The dress went over her head next, and for once, the zipper did what it was supposed to and zipped without a snag. As the bolero went on, she bent to the shoe rack and rummaged around until a pair of delicately strapped sandals appeared under her agile hands. She slipped them on hurriedly, reminding herself that in them she'd have to walk slowly and carefully or she'd have a broken toe to match her bruised shins.

"It's eleven-o-four," Judith hollered from the kitchen. "He's late!"

"So am I!" Ryanne yelled back as she emerged from the closet. She felt her way back into the bathroom, groped for her hairbrush and gave the wild mane a quick once-over. Though she couldn't see it, her hair was one thing she had no trouble visualizing, since it had been giving her problems all her life. Knowing that without a curling iron it was useless to try to subdue it, she merely pulled it back from her face and secured the sides with tortoise-shell combs. With no time for makeup she decided she'd just have to trust that her plastic surgeon had been diligent about natural beauty.

Back in the bedroom she snatched Aggie's lead from the closet hook where the guide dog's harness was stored, and took off for the kitchen.

"All finished. How do I look?" she asked as she entered and whirled in a pretty pirouette. When Judith answered from the living room, Ryanne realized she'd been wasting her smile on the refrigerator.

She turned toward the voice that informed her, "You've looked worse."

Coming from Judith, that was high praise, but Ryanne couldn't resist a dry, "Gee, thanks."

"What do you want, a medal? You look fine, and even if you didn't, there's no time to do anything about it. Jack Daniels just pulled up in the driveway."

"Wonderful!" Ryanne moved toward the window where her sentry was spying. "Is he driving a snazzy little sports car?"

"No, he's in a nondescript black van with a gaudy logo that reads MacKenna and Associates."

Ryanne smiled at Judith's irritable tone. "So tell me, what does he look like?"

Judith peered through the blinds as she assessed their visitor. Hugh MacKenna was tall, broad shouldered and lean hipped, with just enough masculine arrogance in his long-gaited walk to make a woman—any woman—take a second look. His light brown hair was so perfectly groomed that the ocean breeze wouldn't have dared disturb it, and the expression on his handsome, classically sculpted face said he knew it. All in all, he was one of the most attractive men Judith had ever seen.

Of course, not even bamboo shoots under her fingernails would have forced her to admit it.

"Judith, come on," Ryanne prodded. "Describe him to me."

Judith let the blinds fall and turned toward her friend. "Form a mental picture of Quasimodo wearing huaraches."

A picture of Charles Laughton as the Hunchback of Notre Dame wearing an Izod sweater, cotton baggies and trendy Mexican sandals popped into Ryanne's head and she burst out laughing. Knowing Judith's perverse sense of humor, Ryanne was certain her secretary's assessment meant Hugh MacKenna was inordinately good-looking, but the mental image wouldn't go away and she struggled to bring her laughter under control. She almost succeeded, but then the doorbell chimed, sounding like a muted version of Quasimodo's cathedral bells and she started laughing all over again.

"You get it, Judith, and I'll hold on to Aggie," she instructed, fighting back laughter as she attached the dog's lead to her choke chain. *Quasimodo wearing huaraches?''* The image assaulted her again; "Come on, admit he's not that bad."

"Are you kidding," Judith scoffed, refusing to confess. "Tanned or not, they wouldn't let this guy anywhere near the Ventura Freeway."

CHAPTER THREE

LAUGHTER? Hugh glanced around as he neared the front door. Somebody inside Ryanne Kirkland's house was definitely amused about something. The burst of laughter on the other side of the door cackled and rolled, and while Hugh couldn't have said it was a pretty, musical sound, it certainly was infectious. He just couldn't keep from smiling.

"I guess I don't have to wonder if anyone's home," he muttered under his breath. "Just whether or not anybody in there is sane."

He pressed the doorbell and thought he heard another, quieter laugh, and he waited. His hand was poised in midair, ready to ring again when the door finally cracked open. A pair of grimly suspicious eyes glared defiantly at him as though trying to make him feel guilty for having had the audacity to ring in the first place.

The lines around the woman's mouth were drawn into a perpetual frown and he'd have bet his life there was no way the burst of laughter had passed between those forbidding lips. She had to be Judith. The picture Douglas sent hadn't done her justice.

"Yes?"

Hugh put his most confidence-inspiring smile in gear. "Mrs. Tremain?"

"Yes."

"I'm here to see Ryanne Kirkland. I'm Hugh Mac-Kenna."

She looked him over dispassionately. "Can you prove that?" she challenged.

"Certainly." Somewhere behind the door, out of Hugh's narrow range of vision, a chuckle was winding down, as though someone was trying to regain control of their funny bone. Hugh's questioning smile acknowledged the sound, but Mrs. Tremain remained oblivious. He reached for the slender wallet in the inside breast pocket of his jacket, noticing when he glanced down that Judith's right foot was wedged tightly against the back of the door. Anyone who wanted to get past this lady un-invited would have to break her foot to do it. A formidable woman, indeed; Ryanne Kirkland would never have to worry about door-to-door salesmen.

Judith accepted the open wallet and carefully inspected the driver's and investigator's licenses that rested one above the other.

"Do I pass muster?" he asked amiably.

Judith took a step back and opened the door wider. "You're late."

Hugh's smile didn't falter. "Yes, I apologize for that. I was out in the valley and got caught in a traffic pileup on the Ventura Freeway."

That was too much for Ryanne. Laughter bubbled over again as Hugh moved into the living room. He watched as she clutched her dog's leash in one hand and put the other over her mouth in an attempt to control her giggles.

"Was it something I said?" Hugh asked dryly.

Ryanne could feel the heat of embarrassment rising in her cheeks. "I'm sorry," she managed to gasp, knowing she was making a spectacle of herself. "Really..." She finally managed to regain control. "It was just something Judith said earlier that struck me as funny. Please forgive me. I'm Ryanne Kirkland." She stepped forward and held out her free hand toward the voice that sounded even sexier in person than it had on the phone.

"It's a pleasure to meet you." Hugh accepted her firm handshake and resisted the temptation to hold on a little longer than was necessary. The pictures Douglas had sent of Ryanne hadn't done her justice, either. The attractive features were the same, and her eyes just as crystalline blue, but no photograph could have captured the effervescence of her smile or the infectious nature of her laugh. Ryanne Kirkland was like an uncorked bottle of champagne, bubbly and beautiful. Just looking at her, Hugh felt as if the champagne cork had popped him right between the eyes.

With great reluctance he released her hand, only to find it filled again with the enthusiastic wet nose of her golden retriever. Always ready to overwhelm a new audience, Aggie lunged toward Hugh, and Ryanne gave the lead a firm snap.

"No!" she commanded, her voice low but gruff. "Aggie, sit."

"It's all right," Hugh reassured her. "I like dogs."

"Shh! Don't let her hear you say that or you'll never get rid of her," Ryanne warned him. "Unlike Judith, Aggie doesn't know the meaning of the word stranger."

"She's a beautiful dog."

"Thank you. Despite her excess enthusiasm, Aggie is a sweetheart. I don't know what I'd do without her."

Behind Hugh, still stationed near the door, Judith expressed her opinion of that statement with a loud harrumph, which Ryanne deliberately ignored.

"Why don't you have a seat, Hugh. I'll tie this monster down to keep her out of your way. Believe me, you'll thank me for it later."

"I trust your judgment." Hugh grinned and moved to the sofa.

Ryanne listened carefully as he moved and when she had accurately placed his location, she chose a seat for herself at the opposite end of the couch. She fastened the lead around the sturdy leg and Aggie pondered this new limitation for a moment before settling down on top of Ryanne's feet.

That chore completed, Ryanne turned her attention back to her guest. "Would you like coffee? I'm sure Judith would be happy to brew a pot."

Hugh took a quick look at the secretary and decided Ryanne couldn't have been more wrong. "No, thanks."

Ryanne smiled at him. "I appreciate your coming by like this. I have the feeling Douglas Sutherland coerced you into giving me the VIP treatment."

"I wouldn't say that, exactly, but he did make it clear that if I didn't do my best to see that you got settled in comfortably he'd tell my father I was being a bad boy."

Ryanne laughed lightly. "That sounds like Douglas. He and your father are old friends, aren't they?"

"They survived World War II together and haven't let anyone forget it since. Dad runs a deep-sea fishing charter on the gulf in Mississippi and they get together every year to invade the beaches at Normandy."

Ryanne nodded, smiling. "I remember Douglas's yearly vacations while I was working at the *Examiner*. He always returned with a sunburn and a fish story even Herman Melville would have envied."

"If you think Doug is bad, you should hear Dad. Nobody can weave a fish story like Webb MacKenna."

"I'll take your word for it." If only because she enjoyed the sound of his voice so much, Ryanne would have liked to question Hugh further about his family, but since she felt guilty about taking up his valuable time, it didn't seem appropriate to sit and chat. "Douglas told me you're a private investigator, Hugh. And he also said you're an expert in security installation and maintenance."

"Let's just say I do a lot of that sort of work."

"Well, I appreciate your willingness to check out the system I inherited here. I tried to tell Douglas that it wasn't necessary to bother you, but he insisted I give you a call."

"I'm glad he did," he reassured her. "It's no problem, believe me. I imagine Douglas also told you I live right up the road."

"Yes. That seemed awfully convenient to me," Ryanne said teasingly. "Considering the fact that a real estate broker friend of his in Chicago used her connections to help me get this place. I'd say one or both of us was set up."

"You think Doug is playing matchmaker?" Hugh asked wryly. The only thing that surprised him about the thought was that he hadn't considered the possibility himself. It was clear from the sudden frown that appeared on Ryanne's face, however, that that particular idea had never crossed her mind. Apparently the thought didn't please her, but she recovered quickly and managed a smile. "No, actually, I just thought maybe he was playing mother hen again. He's so overprotective sometimes that I want to strangle him. It would be just like him to appoint a watchdog to keep track of me out here."

Hugh laughed as though the thought was farfetched, yet he mentally saluted Ryanne. She was obviously a keen judge of character. To keep her from carrying her watchdog theory any further, Hugh changed the subject smoothly. "Yesterday on the phone you mentioned that the owner of this house subscribes to the Malibu Security Watch System, isn't that right?"

"Yes. Before Mr. Reston left for Europe he sent me copious instructions on the system," she answered, noting that Hugh's conversational transition had been a little too brisk. Obviously she'd been right about Douglas— he *had* appointed Hugh MacKenna as her guardian. She'd have to do something about that, and soon. For the time being, though, she'd play the game and see where it led. She smiled sheepishly. "I've been practicing activating and deactivating the system, and I have to tell you, I'm really impressed with the security officers who respond to the alarms. They're remarkably forgiving when you accidentally set it off. Being blind does have certain advantages at a time like that. They may think I'm an idiot, but they wouldn't dare say it to my face."

Hugh chuckled appropriately at the bit of self-deprecating humor, but Ryanne could tell it was nervous laughter. It was always that way in the beginning, she had discovered. Until people got to know her they were never really sure whether or not there was an edge of bitterness to her references.

"Have you committed the Security Watch phone number to memory in case of an emergency?" Hugh asked.

"Yes," Ryanne confirmed. "And I'm a whiz at 911 for police or an ambulance."

"Good." He looked at her, wondering if she could tell he was returning her bright, impish smile. Her face was turned precisely toward him, their eyes nearly meeting. She was so good at looking directly at him that until she'd reminded him he'd nearly forgotten she was blind. "Frankly, Ryanne, the Security Watch System is about the best protection you can have in this neighborhood."

"That's nice to know."

"The only real problem with the system is that the sensors tend to go bad pretty quickly because of the sea air around here. As I'm sure you've already discovered, most of the houses on Malibu Beach are only a stone's throw from the ocean at high tide and the sand and salt spray can really get to them. I'll check out all the alarm sensors inside and out and if there's a problem Security Watch will send out a maintenance man to fix it."

"I appreciate your help."

"As I said before, it's no problem."

Ryanne heard Hugh stand and she followed suit. Aggie, never one to be left out, jumped up as well. "Is there anything I can do to help you?" Ryanne asked, realizing as the words came out of her mouth that it was a stupid question. Even if she could see, she still wouldn't have the vaguest notion of how to assist him.

But Hugh didn't seem to think it was a dumb question—or at least he didn't let on that he thought it was. "No, thanks. It's a pretty simple job, really. I'll just get my equipment kit out of the van and call Security Watch to let them know what I'm up to." He stepped around the glass-and-chrome coffee table.

"I'll leave Aggie tethered to the sofa so she won't pester you to death, and if you need to know where anything is, just ask Judith," Ryanne suggested.

"Fine." Hugh started toward the door, then stopped. "By the way, one of my associates, Mo Johnson, is a big fan of yours. When he found out I was coming here today he asked me to tell you that in his humble opinion your Cameron Lawe mysteries are some of the best detective novels being written today. He says you write gritty, realistic violence like nobody he knows.''

For just a second Ryanne's pleasant smile slipped. "Tell him that's because I've seen a lot of violence. Close up and firsthand.''

A small, dismal silence fell over the room, but before Ryanne had the chance to kick herself for what she'd said, Judith took charge. "It's almost noon," she announced. "Are you going to get this over with or am I going to have to fix lunch for you, too?''

Hugh looked at the secretary. Her face was set in a belligerent frown, but her eyes were firmly focused on Ryanne. They were filled with a concern Hugh was certain she'd rather not have anyone else see, and he decided that despite Mrs. Tremain's rude, obnoxious behavior, he liked her a lot. "This is going to take a while, ma'am," he informed her placatingly. "Please just go on with whatever you have planned and don't pay any attention to me.''

"Easier said than done," she muttered, moving toward the door to open it for him. "Just ring when you're ready to do the inside—and try not to track in any sand, would you?''

CHAPTER FOUR

WHILE HUGH WORKED, Ryanne tackled the mess she'd left in the kitchen and Judith retreated to the office, muttering unkind epithets about men under her breath.

True to his word, Hugh's inspection did take quite a long time, and it wasn't until Ryanne finished the cupboards that he finished his rounds upstairs. What with all the clanging of pots and pans, however, Ryanne had lost track of his movements through the house, so when he suddenly spoke to her from the hall entrance to the kitchen she jumped.

"Hi. Have you finished reorganizing?" he asked.

Ryanne put her hand over her pounding heart. "Are you part Indian or something? You didn't make a sound coming down those steps."

"I'm sorry if I startled you."

"Don't apologize. But if you keep it up I'm going to have to hang a bell around your neck."

Hugh grinned. "That would give a whole new meaning to the phrase, 'I'll be there with bells on,' wouldn't it?"

"I suppose so." Ryanne chuckled. "Could I tempt you with a cup of coffee now?"

"That sounds good."

While Ryanne searched for a mug she heard Hugh move to the end of the Manhattan-style bar and pull out one of the stools. "So, tell me about this security system

I inherited,'' she suggested, then turned her attention to the coffee.

"You'll be happy to know it's in fairly good shape."

Ryanne turned toward him and narrowed her eyes comically. "Why do I not like the sound of *fairly* good?"

Hugh laughed again. "Don't worry, it's no big deal. The system checks out fine except for the west window in the master bedroom and the doors to the upper deck. The pressure sensors there aren't nearly as responsive as they should be and they need to be replaced, that's all. I'll call Security Watch and have them send someone out. I'd do the work myself but they get a little testy when unauthorized personnel start replacing their equipment."

"That's okay, really, Hugh. You've done more than enough already. I'll call them later and request the repairs."

Hugh started to protest that it was no trouble. He knew it could be days before Security Watch got someone out on call unless a little pressure was applied, but Ryanne had a stubborn look that he knew better than to challenge. She was an independent lady who had to depend on others too often because she was blind, so she made up for it by doing as much as she could for herself. He felt his already considerable respect for her go up another notch. "All right," he acquiesced. "But if you have any trouble or get any flack, please let me know. The owner is a friend of mine and he owes me a favor or two."

As they had talked Hugh had watched Ryanne, mesmerized by the ease with which she had managed to fill the two coffee cups with exactly the same amount of coffee—and not spill a single drop. The only clue he had that she couldn't see was the way she moved slowly toward him with the back of her free hand held slightly in front of her body so that it came into contact with the bar. She swept her hand gently over the tabletop next to him, making sure the space was empty before setting the cup down.

"Thanks."

"You're welcome." Ryanne moved back to the opposite counter for her own mug. "It's not as good as Judith's coffee, but it's drinkable."

"Your secretary is very..."

"Rude?"

Hugh chuckled. "Formidable was the word that came to mind."

"You should try for a career in the diplomatic corps," Ryanne suggested. "Don't take her attitude personally. It's just her way of keeping the world at arm's length. You get used to her after a while."

"You'd have to. I got the impression from Doug that they don't get along too well."

Ryanne waved an airy hand. "That feud is all for show. They're both so overprotective of me that they constantly disagree about what is or is not in my best interests." Since Hugh seemed in no hurry to leave, Ryanne changed the subject, wanting to find out a little more about him. "Tell me more about your work, Hugh. Somehow you don't fit the normal image of a crusty old private eye working out of a seedy upstairs office. What kind of cases do you handle?"

"Oh, the usual. We get a few divorce cases, but mostly it's security installation and corporate espionage. I have a computer expert on staff who specializes in computer fraud cases and I handle personnel security clearance for several large firms around the country."

"You travel a lot, then?"

"Some," he admitted. "Enough to make it cost efficient to keep my own jet hangared out in Burbank."

"You make it sound very routine."

"Most of the time it is."

Perched on a stool around the corner from Hugh's, Ryanne plied him with more questions about his work and finally got him to admit that he did occasionally handle unusual, even dangerous cases. Hugh wasn't the first private investigator Ryanne had ever met, but she quickly discovered he was one of the most interesting.

Part of her mind was focused fully on everything he said, but the purely feminine side of her was listening intently to the way he said it. His voice was rich, almost hypnotic, and there was a warmth to it that exuded trustworthiness. Without her sight to guide her, Ryanne had learned to depend on voices to tell her what she needed to know about a person. After she'd known someone for a while, their actions spoke louder than words, of course, but in the beginning, she trusted her instincts about voices, both what they said and what they didn't say. And Hugh MacKenna's voice was speaking directly to Ryanne's libido right now.

Given what Judith had said about his Quasimodo looks, Ryanne was certain Hugh was a very attractive man; she certainly hoped so at any rate. Fate played funny tricks sometimes, as Ryanne was acutely aware, but it just wouldn't be fair if a voice like Hugh's didn't have a face and form to match it.

"Well, have I bored you to tears yet?" Hugh asked when Ryanne temporarily ran out of questions.

"Hardly. You try to downplay it, but you really do lead a fascinating life." Ryanne slipped off the stool and picked up her cup. "Would you like some more coffee?"

"Just half, please." He placed the mug in her outstretched hand and watched her as she moved. Again she poured their coffee with amazing effortlessness, and before he even realized the words were out, he asked, "How do you do that? No, wait, I'm sorry. That was rude," he apologized, unable to believe he'd spoken without thinking. He wasn't accustomed to saying anything that wasn't carefully thought out in advance, but Ryanne Kirkland was having an unusual effect on him. Already more than once he'd had to force his thoughts back into line when they'd wanted to wander off and concentrate on the wisps of red hair that teased her forehead and framed her lively eyes behind those mysterious glasses.

Ryanne could tell he was embarrassed by his own question and that he wasn't a man accustomed to being embarrassed. If there was one thing she'd learned how to do well, though, it was ease the discomfort people felt at asking such natural questions. "Don't be silly, Hugh. You can ask anything you like. I can't pretend not to be blind, and you can't pretend not to notice."

"All right, then, how do you do it?"

Ryanne could hear the easy smile in his voice. "The same way you learned to come down creaky stairs without making a sound, I suspect. Lots of practice and knowing the right technique. First of all, I know exactly how much coffee is coming out of the spout and how much the cup will hold. And also, I can feel the heat on my fingers as the coffee level rises. My favorite technique, though, is just listening. Any vessel has a hollow sound when it's empty, and as you fill it with liquid, that sound rises in pitch. Try it sometime with a glass of water, but unless you want to embarrass yourself the first few hundred attempts I'd advise you to practice when you're alone."

"I'll give it a try," he promised.

Ryanne returned with their coffee. "Any more questions?"

"Even personal ones?" he asked, his voice softer, his smile no longer evident.

Ryanne had heard that tone too many times not to know what was coming, and she sobered as well. "How did I become blind?" she asked for him.

"Yes."

"What did Douglas tell you?"

She heard him shift on the stool before he answered. "Only that you were a reporter until you were blinded in an accident five years ago," he replied, hating himself for not being able to tell her the truth. Yet instinctively he knew that Doug was right about Ryanne. She would not appreciate knowing that Hugh was aware of her whole, tragic history. In fact, he suspected that if she did know she might withdraw from him completely, and he most definitely did not want that. Something about Ryanne was drawing him like a magnet and Hugh, who had always found himself attracted to smart, independent, savvy women, wanted to get to know this one better.

Ryanne leaned back on the stool and crossed her legs, carefully adjusting the full skirt over her bruised shins to give her time to think about what to tell him. She had pat answers on this topic—one for every occasion. All she had to decide was whether to tell him the simple cleaned-up-cocktail-party version of her story or the *Reader's Digest* condensed version that was grim but not gory. There was, of course, the unvarnished truth, which included how it felt to know she was going to die, a description of the searing pain of Worsted's bullet as it entered her shoulder, and a recounting of her long, torturous road to recovery. But no one had ever heard the unvarnished truth, and probably no one ever would. It was a living nightmare that replayed endlessly in Ryanne's head, one that she couldn't share.

In this case, though, the cleaned-up version didn't strike her as appropriate, so she opted for something in between versions one and two. "Actually it happened while I was sticking my nose in where it didn't belong," she began. "I was following the subject of a police investigation and one of his cohorts took exception to the fact that I saw him commit murder. In my attempt to make a fast getaway I fell off a steep ledge in a warehouse loft. I'm convinced the only thing that saved my life was the fact that I fell on my head—it's far too hard to allow any life-threatening damage."

"And the fall caused your blindness?"

"Uh-huh." She pointed vaguely toward her head. "Neurological damage to the optic nerve."

She said it casually, without bitterness or recriminations, as if she were just stating a simple fact. Hugh had known women who spoke more passionately about a broken fingernail than Ryanne did about her blindness. Was it a front? he wondered. How could she not be bitter? "Did they catch the guy?" He already knew the answer, of course, but Ryanne didn't know that and if he didn't ask questions she was likely to get suspicious. And, too, Hugh wanted to hear the story from her so that he could see if she was coping with the tragedy as well as it appeared.

"No. The police are pretty sure they know his identity, but I'd never seen him before so they couldn't make a case. All I could give them was a description that matched Worsted's—and about a million other men in the Chicago area."

"Worsted? That was his name?" Hugh asked, pouncing on the piece of information that hadn't been included in the sketchy reports Doug had sent him.

Ryanne chuckled. "No, that's not his name. I labeled him that at the time because he was wearing a worsted business suit, and the name just stuck." She turned her head away from Hugh's slightly and he realized that she wasn't as casual about the topic as she pretended. "I know it sounds silly, but it's easier for me if I call him Worsted rather than his real name."

"Why?"

She shrugged. "Somewhere in Chicago there's a man who would sleep a whole lot sounder if I was dead. I'm never going to get my sight back, but I can't imagine that he's one hundred percent positive of that. In a small way, I'm still a threat to him."

"So you think of him in the past tense and refer to him by a name you made up because it makes him seem a little less . . . real."

"Exactly." Ryanne turned her face to him again, amazed that he'd caught on so quickly to what she meant and how she felt. "So . . . any more questions, or have I depressed you enough for one day?"

"Just one more . . . for now." The way he said it let Ryanne know that since there was a *now* there would definitely be a *later*. Strangely, the idea was a lot more appealing than she would have liked.

"Ask away," she invited.

"Why do you wear glasses?"

The puzzlement in his voice was so acute that Ryanne couldn't help but laugh. "Philodendrons," she replied, then waited for the inevitable.

"Philodendrons? Why on earth—"

"Think about it," she insisted. "Where do you usually find philodendron and other annoying potted plants?"

Though he was certain there was a connection between her eyeglasses and potted plants, Hugh still hadn't made it, and he didn't like being in the dark. "I don't know.... In houses, restaurants, lots of places."

"And *where* in houses and restaurants are they usually to be found?" she prodded.

"On tables, in hanging baskets... Oh." The light finally dawned and he laughed.

"Exactly." Ryanne laughed with him. "When I first got out of the hospital and was stumbling around like an idiot I moved back home because I figured if my family couldn't be counted on to feel sorry for me and allow me to wallow in self-pity, who could? Unfortunately my aunt who raised me after my parents died had other plans. And she had *plants*, too. Dozens of them hanging everywhere. Walking through her house was like navigating a macrame obstacle course. I never knew when some branch was going to whip out and poke me in the eye."

"You mean she didn't take them down?" he asked, astonished that anyone could be so cruel to a woman who'd just suffered a major trauma. He also wondered what had happened to her parents, but now didn't seem like the right time to ask.

"On the contrary. She left them right where they were and told me to get used to it. And when I finally snapped and began yelling at her to take them down or I'd rip them down with my bare hands, she calmly said—" Ryanne raised her voice a pitch in imitation of her Aunt Rose "—'Is that how you're going to live your life, Ryanne? Making the rest of the world alter itself to suit you, or are you going to make alterations and learn how to fit the world?'"

Her voice returned to normal. "The next day I started wearing sunglasses, but when I realized they fit the stereotype of a blind person with a white cane I switched to regular glasses with shatterproof plastic lenses. I thought I'd try wearing the shades here in L.A., though."

They both laughed, and Ryanne leaned forward as though about to confide a secret. "In case you hadn't noticed, Hugh, the world has been booby trapped. When you least expect it, up pops a hanging plant, an untrimmed hedge, a low hanging branch, an open cabinet door..."

Or a man who tries to kill you, he added silently, trying to squelch the pity he knew Ryanne wouldn't want. Aloud, he commented only, "So you practice self-defense against the booby traps."

"Exactly."

Her hands were lightly clasped together, resting on the bar as she leaned forward. Her face was glowing with life and humor, and Hugh couldn't resist the impulse to reach out to her and cover her hands with his own. "You're a remarkable woman, Ryanne Kirkland," he told her softly, his voice intimate and filled with respect.

Ryanne felt the strength and warmth in his firm hands; heard those same qualities in his voice, and for a moment she was stunned. Mostly to irritate Judith's puritan ethic and to amuse herself, Ryanne joked about men and fantasies often, but it had been over five years since she'd let a man get close enough to touch her. Oh, Douglas and one or two of the reporters she still kept in contact with occasionally gave her a hug or patted her on the shoulder, and because she knew she could trust them she looked forward to that type of casual contact.

But this was different. Hugh MacKenna was a virtual stranger, and no matter how pleasant Ryanne seemed on the surface, always lurking underneath was the knowledge that the next stranger she met could be Worsted. He could walk up to her, engage her in conversation, laugh at one of her jokes—and put a gun to her head without her even realizing that the man who haunted her dreams was blowing her brains out.

That kind of fear and an instinct for self-preservation had been Ryanne's constant companion for five years now, and to prevent disaster she made it a habit to avoid being alone with strangers. As time passed the danger lessened, but an ingrained habit had been formed. The only reason she'd let her guard down with Hugh was that Douglas trusted him implicitly and had instilled some of that trust in Ryanne. She'd been prepared to like Hugh because of Douglas, and she had no objection to swooning a little over his gorgeous bourbon voice. Letting him touch her like this, though, making her heart beat faster because she liked his touch . . . that was out of the question. Hugh was just feeling sorry for her and pity was one thing Ryanne couldn't tolerate.

Stiffening, she pulled her hands abruptly out of his and seized on his compliment as a way of discouraging him. "Just what is it, Mr. MacKenna, that makes me so remarkable?" she asked with flat practicality, slipping off the stool. "Is it because I can do parlor tricks and pour coffee without making a fool of myself? Is it because I'm blind, and any blind person who doesn't sit cowering and weeping in a corner is to be commended? Just what makes me so remarkable?"

Hugh knew he'd made a mistake the moment he'd reached out to her. He'd felt the tensing of her body—an instinctive, repulsed response to the touch of a stranger.

He regretted the action, but not his compliment. Whether she knew it or not, blind or not, Ryanne Kirkland *was* remarkable.

He kept his voice even and calm when he told her, "What makes you special, Ryanne, is the way you light up a room when you smile. And the fact that you've been through so much and have survived with that light still shining—that's remarkable. But I'm sorry if I offended you."

He was so sincere, his voice such a compelling caress, that Ryanne couldn't hold on to the defensive anger she was using as a shield. "No, I'm sorry, Hugh," she said after a moment. "I usually leave the barking to Aggie and the biting to Judith. I didn't mean to take a piece out of your hide."

"Don't worry about it," he reassured her with a little laugh. "My hide is as tough as your head."

"Wanna bet?" Ryanne challenged. She held out her hand. "Give me your mug and you can have one more cup of coffee for the road."

CHAPTER FIVE

"ARGH!" Frustrated, Ryanne plopped her forehead on the top of her typewriter and resisted the urge to smash all the keys down at one time.

"What's *your* problem?" Across the room Judith swiveled around from her word processor and scrutinized her employer. "You're supposed to be writing, not resting. There's a difference, you know."

"Yes, I know," Ryanne said, lifting her head. "Unfortunately this stupid screenplay isn't cooperating."

Ryanne heard Judith's heavy sigh. "What is it this time?"

"I'm trying to transform the shoot-out in chapter six into a viable movie scene and it just isn't working! What made the scene so gripping in the book is that the reader knows everything Cameron is thinking—that he really doesn't care if he comes out of this confrontation alive. But in the screenplay all I've got is action—just a lot of bullets and blood."

"Then you've got to find a way to illustrate how reckless Lawe has become."

"That's right," Ryanne snapped, "but how do I show that? Ooh, I hate writing movies! Why on earth didn't I just tell them to let someone else adapt the book?"

"Because you wanted to maintain the integrity of your creation, you wanted the challenge of writing a movie script and you wanted a free trip to Hollywood. Not necessarily in that order," Judith replied testily. She'd lived through too many of Ryanne's creative temper tantrums to take this one seriously. "Why don't you get out of here for a while so I can get some work done? It's no picnic for me to transfer what you write into this complicated screenplay format, you know. Go take a walk on the beach or something. I'm sure your pitiful excuse for a guide dog could use some exercise, and I could certainly use some peace and quiet."

Ryanne nodded. "That's a good idea. Maybe I'll get inspired."

"There's a first time for everything," Judith said dryly. Her chair whined as she swiveled back to her computer, not so subtly telling Ryanne she'd been dismissed.

"Come on, Aggie. Let's go for a walk." The guide dog, resting at Ryanne's feet under the table, jumped up eagerly as Ryanne stood, and together they took off down the hall.

Ten minutes later, Ryanne had changed shoes, harnessed her dog and the two of them were tramping briskly down the beach. The ocean sounded gentle today, she noted, just a whispered sigh as the waves whooshed in, and she relaxed almost immediately. She'd been in Malibu for a week now and because she and Aggie had walked the smooth stretch of beach every day she was confident her guide dog would not lead her astray. Out of long practice, part of her mind kept track of how far they'd wandered from the house, but another part was free to focus on the problems she was having with the adaptation of her book.

She'd met with the producer and director of the movie several days ago, so she knew what they wanted and she knew what she wanted. It was just a matter of getting it on paper without losing that indefinable something that made the Cameron Lawe mysteries so special. Judith was two-thirds correct about Ryanne's reasons for wanting to do the script herself. The trip to Hollywood had been far from free, but it was important to Ryanne that the integrity of her creation be maintained, and she relished the challenge of doing something new and different.

Of course, with that challenge also came the fear of failure, but Ryanne had long ago learned that fear was something to be faced and conquered. As a child, she had been so afraid of the dark that she'd had to keep a nightlight burning in her room to chase away the monsters that came out of the closet to watch her sleep. Now darkness was all she knew, and the monsters were no longer imaginary. The fear she lived with was real, but she met it head-on every day and managed to survive because there was no alternative.

Ryanne estimated that she and Aggie had been walking for nearly a half an hour when the guide dog stopped abruptly as though waiting for instruction or warning her mistress that something was impeding their progress. The sound of the waves coming into the shore had changed, informing Ryanne that they had reached the breakwater—a little peninsula of stones that jutted out into the ocean. With Judith's help, Ryanne had studied the beach and taught Aggie that this particular spot marked the end of their hiking trail. Aggie was telling her it was time to turn around and head back down the beach.

"Good work, Aggie!" Her voice full of praise, Ryanne reached down and patted Aggie lovingly on the head to reinforce the dog's training. "That's very good! Okay, we'll go home now." She turned the dog around. "Beach house, Aggie. Hup-up."

"Ryanne! Wait up!"

Startled, Ryanne stopped and turned back up the beach. Even from a distance the deep, whiskey-smooth timbre of Hugh MacKenna's voice was unmistakable. A smile that was half surprise, half pleasure spread across her face and she waved. "Hugh?"

"Hello, Ryanne." Only slightly winded, Hugh jogged up to her.

"Where did you come from?" Ryanne asked, wondering if her delighted smile looked as idiotic as it felt. She hadn't heard from Hugh since he'd stopped by to inspect her security system four days earlier, and she had mixed emotions about his absence. Her logical self had told her she didn't have time to waste on whiskey-voiced private investigators, but her purely feminine side had been disappointed that he hadn't found an excuse to call or come by for a visit. This wasn't a chance meeting, she was certain, and her feminine side was delighted.

"I called your house and just missed you," he explained. "Judith reluctantly told me you'd gone for a walk up the beach, so I decided to jog down and join you. Unless you'd prefer to be alone."

"Don't be silly," Ryanne said a little too quickly. "Of course we'd like your company. Aggie and I were just about to head back, though."

"No problem." Together they turned back down the beach.

"How near here do you live?" Ryanne asked.

"About a mile and a half on up the coast. I'm just outside the Malibu city limits."

"Then you must know this beach fairly well."

"Like the back of my hand. There's a stretch of rocky shoreline just north of my house that has some interesting tidal pools. I'd be happy to show them to you if you ever get tired of this endless expanse of sand."

Ryanne laughed. "Is that the L.A. equivalent of 'come up to my apartment and I'll show you my etchings'?"

"Precisely." Hugh chuckled. "Until I moved to the beach I never realized what an aphrodisiac the ocean could be. One look at my tidal pools and all the women fall breathless at my feet."

Or into your bed, Ryanne thought. After Hugh had left her house the other day Ryanne had cajoled Judith into giving her an accurate description of Hugh, and now she knew that his voice wasn't Mr. MacKenna's only astonishingly attractive feature. She'd learned that his hair was a soft, satiny brown and his eyes were an odd shade of amber and gold. She'd already determined for herself that he was quite tall, but according to Judith he had an athletic physique that was very impressive. Judith had said his features were as firm and classically sculpted as the rest of him, and the picture that had ultimately formed in Ryanne's mind was that of Michelangelo's David, not Victor Hugo's Quasimodo. Listening to his voice now, feeling his magnetic presence beside her, and remembering Judith's description, Ryanne suddenly wished that Michelangelo had been a little more modest and provided David with a pair of trousers.

"So tell me, Ryanne, has Security Watch fixed your faulty sensors yet?" Hugh asked.

Considering her keen physical awareness of him, Ryanne was tempted to tell Hugh that there was absolutely nothing wrong with her sensors, but then she'd have to explain the pun and she didn't think it was particularly wise to let him know the detour her thoughts had taken. Instead she answered, "As a matter of fact, they haven't. I called them right after you left and they never showed up. Yesterday I sicced Judith on them and even that didn't get results."

"They're probably too intimidated to show up now," he joked. "Would you be offended if I offered to give them a call for you?"

Ryanne smiled at him sheepishly. "No, actually, I'd be grateful. If I hadn't been so stubborn the other day you could have played Sir Galahad then and saved me a lot of bother. Do you mind çalling?"

"Of course not. I wouldn't have volunteered otherwise. I'll call as soon as we get back to your place. As I told you, the owner owes me a favor or two."

"If you get results, I'll repay you with the libation of your choice," Ryanne promised. "My larder is now fully stocked—I have coffee *and* tea."

Hugh's voice lowered fractionally. "Actually I had something a little more substantial in mind as payment."

His seductive tone had warning bells ringing in Ryanne's head. She stopped abruptly, tilting her head coolly toward Hugh. "Oh?"

"I was hoping you'd allow me to escort you on a tour of Los Angeles."

"Oh." She relaxed and laughed lightly.

"What did you think I was going to suggest?"

"Something wicked and thoroughly indecent."

"Who me?" he cried, feigning injury. "What kind of a cad do you think I am, anyway?"

"A very nice one," Ryanne answered, resuming her walk down the beach.

"Then you'll accept my invitation?"

She sighed. "Oh, Hugh . . . I don't think so."

"Why not? You can't spend a few months in Hollywood and not see the sights—" His voice died abruptly. "Sorry. That was a stupid thing to say."

Ryanne stopped again and Aggie gave a patient, heaving sigh as though she wished her mistress would make up her mind. This time she sat on Ryanne's command and waited.

"Hugh, the word 'see' doesn't bother me. It's so much a part of everyone's vocabulary that I'm really not even conscious of it anymore. I still 'see' things, you know. I just don't see them the way everyone else does."

Hugh looked at her closely, admiring her courage and the simple sincerity she used to put people who said stupid things at ease. He also admired the long, shapely curve of her newly tanned legs and the way her slender, feminine figure filled out the shorts and camp shirt she was wearing. So much so, in fact, that he was beginning to feel like the lascivious cad she'd almost accused him of being. He forced his attention back to their conversation. "You have a very philosophical way of looking at it, Ryanne," he told her softly. "I'm not sure if I could be quite so... accepting if I were in your position."

Ryanne considered that for a moment. "No, you wouldn't be. Not at first, at least. I certainly wasn't. But eventually you learn to adjust, to adapt. Being blind doesn't mean that you stop enjoying life or caring about people. It doesn't diminish ambition or curiosity or any of the things that motivate people to move forward with their lives."

"Really?"

"Yes, really," Ryanne said, a little surprised that Hugh would question what she thought was a statement of obvious fact.

"Being blind doesn't curtail curiosity?"

"No."

"Then in that case, how can you possibly turn down my invitation to tour Hollywood? Aren't you the least bit curious to see the Walk of Fame and Grauman's Chinese Theatre?'' He leaned close enough that Ryanne could smell the faintest trace of his musky cologne and lowered his voice to a deliberately tantalizing, seductive whisper. ''If you'll go with me I promise to let you stand in John Wayne's footprints.''

Ryanne squelched her laughter and matched his tone. ''You're using the wrong bait, MacKenna. If you'd offered to let me stand in Harrison Ford's footprints I might have been tempted.''

Hugh snapped his fingers. ''Shucks. I don't think they've gotten around to cementing him yet. Would you settle for R2D2 and C3PO?''

Ryanne laughed. ''It's not quite the same. I do have to thank you, though. You could have simply told me they were Harrison's footprints and I'd never have known the difference.''

Ryanne felt Hugh's swift change in mood even before he spoke, his voice low and sincere. ''I'd never lie to you, Ryanne. Or mislead you. It's not a good way to earn someone's friendship and respect.''

''No, it's not,'' she agreed quietly, inordinately pleased that Hugh wanted those things from her because she realized that she wanted them, too. But being friends implied placing a certain amount of trust in another person and that was something she found very difficult. Particularly when that other person was a charming, attractive male. She decided the best course was to change the subject. ''Tell me, Hugh, what brings you out to the beach in the middle of the business day? Are you playing hooky or has MacKenna and Associates fallen on hard times?''

Hugh recognized an evasive tactic when he saw one and he decided not to press the point—yet. ''I'm playing hooky—it's the boss's prerogative. I finished a missing husband case this afternoon and decided to take the rest of the day off so I could check in on my favorite new neighbor. How's the screenplay coming?''

Ryanne moaned and threw her head back in misery. "You had to remind me."

"That good, huh?"

"Oh, don't pay any attention to me. I'm not happy unless I've got something to complain about."

"What seems to be the problem? Maybe talking about it to an impartial observer will help."

Pleased to have a willing listener, Ryanne recounted the problems she was having adapting her novel into a viable screenplay. Though he hadn't read the book, Hugh seemed to understand, and he was surprisingly good at helping Ryanne get to the heart of the trouble. He had an instinctive grasp of what was important and what wasn't, and Ryanne was impressed with his insight into the business of screenwriting. With his help, she soon had a clear picture of what she needed to do to make the difficult scene work.

"Are you sure you're not a writer masquerading as a private investigator?" Ryanne asked suspiciously. "You're very good at this."

"I've had a little practice," he admitted. "A couple of my cases were used as the basis for a TV pilot a few years back."

"Really? What series?"

Hugh named one of the most popular detective shows on television and Ryanne whistled appreciatively. "I'm impressed."

Hugh laughed ruefully. "Don't be. I still act as a consultant to the writers from time to time, but believe me, the life of the series hero bears very little resemblance to my everyday life."

"You mean 'Any similarity between persons living or dead is purely coincidental'?" Ryanne quoted.

"Precisely."

The brisk pace Aggie set had carried them quickly back to Ryanne's place. As they drew up to the beach house Hugh started to tell Ryanne she had arrived home, but Aggie beat him to the punch. Knowing exactly where she was going, the golden retriever executed a sharp turn that sent Ryanne barreling into Hugh's chest. She stumbled and Hugh grabbed her, steadying her with one arm around her waist. She felt so delightful pressed against him that Hugh was grateful for the dog's error. Ryanne, however, was far from pleased.

"No!" she said sternly as she dropped Aggie's harness and gave the lead a sharp tug.

"It's all right, Ryanne. No harm done," Hugh insisted.

"No, it's not all right. Aggie's job is to keep me from colliding with persons, places and things, not *cause* collisions, and she knows it. Would you mind helping me reenact that to teach her a lesson?"

Not exactly sure what she had in mind, Hugh nonetheless agreed. "What should I do?"

"Just stand there and I'll bump into you again lightly."

"Hmm...that has possibilities," he mused aloud, and Ryanne tried to ignore the wicked smile she heard in his voice, concentrating instead on her dog. She backed up a step, leaned her shoulder against the hard wall of Hugh's muscular chest, and gave Aggie a firm, sharp, "No!"

Aggie's tail, normally so happily active that it was almost a lethal weapon, dropped dejectedly at the sound of her mistress's displeasure. The movement was so pathetic it was an effort for Hugh to keep from laughing.

Obviously as far as this dog was concerned the sun rose and set on Ryanne Kirkland. Somehow, Hugh didn't find that the least bit hard to understand.

Backing several steps away from Hugh, Ryanne ordered Aggie to come to her. The dog obeyed instantly, and when Ryanne picked up the harness and commanded, "Aggie, beach house," Aggie stepped forward smartly, making an exaggerated, wide arc around Hugh, and stopped, as she should have in the first place. Ryanne tapped her foot forward, automatically checking for an obstacle, and finding none, she commanded, "Aggie, right, right."

The retriever responded, navigating Ryanne around Hugh. Ryanne praised her accomplishment so lavishly that Aggie's feathery tail began its happy wagging once again. Now, Hugh did laugh, and he followed Ryanne up the stairs to the enormous deck.

Ryanne lavished more glowing praise on the dog as she removed Aggie's harness and tethered her to the rail. Hugh leaned against the wall opposite her, watching Ryanne's deft movements. Her lustrous red hair curtained her face as she leaned down, and he longed to gather it into his hands and savor the texture. For three days now he had found thoughts of Ryanne Kirkland catching him unawares at the oddest moments. The memory of her effervescent smile and sparkling blue eyes had left him feeling pleasantly anxious and a little out of breath.

It had been so long since Hugh had been this intrigued by any woman that he'd found himself wanting to see her again just to make certain she was as real as the attraction he felt for her. If his missing husband case hadn't taken him on a three-day jaunt through Las Vegas and Lake Tahoe he'd have called on Ryanne much sooner.

Now that he was back, Hugh intended to make up for lost time.

"I'll have to give Aggie a good brushing before I let her back into the house," Ryanne informed him as she moved slowly around the deck searching for the patio table. Before she'd left for her walk, she had placed Aggie's grooming comb on the table so she wouldn't have to track sand inside to retrieve it, but now the table was proving elusive.

Hugh watched her grope around, wondering what he should do. It was obvious Ryanne had lost her bearings; she was moving away from the table rather than toward it. For the first time since he'd met her, Ryanne seemed vulnerable, and the reality of her blindness was driven home. It made Hugh's heart ache. For a second he considered simply retrieving the grooming equipment himself and handing it to her, but he quickly reconsidered. He couldn't treat her as though she were helpless. Yet he couldn't just stand and do nothing, either.

"The table's behind you, Ryanne," he said finally. "About five feet or so."

Ryanne smiled as she moved in the direction he indicated. "Obviously I need to grow eyes in the back of my head," she quipped. With a sweep of her hand across the table she located the comb, then turned to Hugh and looked at him seriously. "Thank you. Nine out of ten people would have just handed it to me."

"I didn't think you'd want that," he told her, matching her quiet, sincere tone. A kind of understanding passed between them that made Hugh feel as breathless as he felt when he saw her lovely smile.

She gave him a softer version of that smile now, but it was no less effective. "You're right. There are so many things I simply can't do that it's important to me to do for myself the things I·can."

"I figured that out the other day when you wouldn't let me call Security Watch."

Ryanne laughed. "And look where that got me."

"Would you like me to make the call now while you're brushing Aggie?"

"That would be great. The phone is on the bar in the kitchen."

Hugh knocked the sand off his sneakers but before he could reach the door Judith appeared and sent him a quelling glance. "I see you found her."

"Yes, thanks to you," he responded politely.

Judith didn't seem to appreciate being reminded that she'd done something nice. She looked away from him and spoke directly to Ryanne. "Right after you left, *he*—" she jabbed an accusing finger at Hugh "—called, and right after that the Security Watch people finally showed up. Needless to say, I haven't gotten any work done."

"But the security system is fixed?" Ryanne asked hopefully.

"So they said."

"Wonderful!" Ryanne smiled happily at Hugh. "I guess you don't get to play Sir Galahad after all."

He snapped his fingers. "Drat the luck! Now I don't have any leverage to coerce you into spending Saturday with me."

Ryanne started to comment, then changed her mind. Instead she turned to her secretary. "Judith, since your workday has already been shot, would you mind fixing Hugh and me something cold to drink? He's going to keep me company out here while I brush Aggie and I know you'd rather I didn't track sand into the house."

Judith sighed. "All right. What do you want? There's a pitcher of iced tea already made."

"That would be fine, thank you," Hugh answered as he moved to the table and sat in one of the cushioned deck chairs.

"Me, too, Judith. And bring a glass for yourself."

The door slid shut and Ryanne knelt beside her dog to begin combing the sand out of Aggie's silky golden hair. Hugh could tell that something was bothering Ryanne, but her inconsequential small talk gave him no clue as to what it was. Judith returned shortly with a tray bearing a pitcher of iced tea and two glasses. She placed them on the table in front of Hugh, giving him a strange, hard look as she did so. Her frown was even more disapproving than usual, and Hugh wondered why she seemed so displeased until he remembered his comment about coercing Ryanne into a date. Apparently Judith didn't approve.

"Aren't you joining us, Judith?" Ryanne asked as she unfastened Aggie's lead from the deck railing and rose.

"No, thanks. Some of us have work to do in the middle of the afternoon."

"In that case," Ryanne said patiently, "would you mind taking Aggie in for me? I'm sure she could use a drink, too."

Judith sighed and took the lead and grooming comb Ryanne held out to her. "Why not? Come on, beastie." Before she went inside, she stepped back toward the table and tapped the back of the chair beside Hugh's. "The chair's here," she informed Ryanne, tapping it again.

Grateful for the sound cue that kept her from groping around like an idiot again in front of Hugh, Ryanne moved toward the tapping. "Thank you."

Judith grunted and took Aggie into the house. As the door slid shut, Ryanne swept her hand over the table until she encountered the tray. She filled both glasses, placed one in front of Hugh, and settled back. "Now, where were we?"

"We were making small talk until we could be alone and you could say whatever it is you wanted to say to me."

Ryanne chuckled. "You're very perceptive."

"It's an occupational hazard that sometimes spills over into my personal life," he told her seriously. "Do you want to explain why it bothers you so much that I invited you out on a date?"

"Oh, Hugh..." Ryanne took a deep breath and released it as a wistful sigh. "Even under normal circumstances I don't date much."

"What do you mean by normal circumstances?"

"Back in Chicago, on my own turf, working within my regular routine," she explained.

"Why not?"

Ryanne shrugged. "It's just more of a hassle than it's worth. I go out with friends occasionally, but the 'You Tarzan, me Jane' dating ritual is something I don't particularly enjoy. I never have."

"I see," Hugh said thoughtfully. "What if I promise I won't do my Tarzan yell even once and swear that our date would be strictly platonic?"

Ryanne's gaze was so direct that Hugh was almost convinced she was seeing straight through him. "If you promised that," she said softly, "you'd be lying and I'd be very disappointed." Embarrassed by her own bluntness, Ryanne averted her head. "Sorry. I probably shouldn't have said that. I may be reading this situation all wrong. For all I know, you're just trying to be congenial to me because Douglas asked you to."

"No, Ryanne," Hugh said gently. "You're not misreading the situation and I'm not just doing Doug Sutherland a favor. You're an intelligent, beautiful, witty woman and I am very attracted to you."

"And I'm attracted to you as well, Hugh," she admitted. "But the fact remains that for me dating isn't a very good idea."

"But why not?" Hugh pressed, then pulled back. "Sorry. Look, Ryanne, I'm not trying to railroad you. I admit that taking no for an answer is not something at which I excel, but if you want me to take a hike, I will. If that's the case, though, I'd like to understand why." He hesitated a moment before asking. "Is it because you're blind?"

Ryanne's esteem for Hugh rose several notches. Except for Judith, nearly everyone Ryanne knew was uncomfortable with her blindness and tried to pretend it didn't exist. Hugh on the other hand seemed to accept it as a matter of fact, something to be acknowledged and then dealt with as gracefully as possible. She liked that attitude a lot, because it told her he wasn't feeling pity for her as she'd first suspected. And she liked Hugh a lot, too. Which was one of the reasons she didn't want to go out with him.

"Quit while you're ahead" was Ryanne's motto where men were concerned. Right now, Hugh liked her. He was attracted to her. But if she spent the day with him as he'd suggested, all that would change. Once he got a good dose of what it was like to date someone who was blind, the attraction she sensed emanating from him and the regard she heard in his voice would vanish, and Ryanne would be left feeling inadequate and disappointed.

She couldn't say that to Hugh, of course, but neither could she lie to him. "My blindness has a lot to do with it, yes," she admitted, leaning forward intently, hoping to make him understand. "Hugh . . . have you ever had a blind date? I mean a real *blind* date? It isn't a carefree picnic in the park. In fact, it can be damned inconvenient at times. I don't know my way around Los Angeles, and neither does my guide dog. Aggie and I both would be almost totally dependent on you. *My* restricted mobility would be a restriction on you. You've only seen me in settings where I'm comfortable—where I know my way around. Once you see me out in the real world I'm afraid you'd be very disillusioned."

Hugh considered her words carefully, but she hadn't said anything that discouraged him. "I'm willing to take that chance if you are."

But I'm not *willing to take that chance,* she wanted to shout. She'd been down this road before, had given in and accepted invitations from people she'd dated before her accident, people she should have been comfortable with. The result was always the same. The moment the novelty of her blindness wore off, disappointment set in. Things became awkward and strained, and the date ended in disaster. And if that was the way it happened with old friends it was bound to be much worse with Hugh, this handsome, charming man who was little more than a comfortable stranger.

Every instinct for the self-preservation of her heart and her ego cried out to Ryanne to say no. Inside her head, though, another tiny voice of hope was saying *Maybe this time it will be different.* And Hugh had issued her a challenge of sorts. Perhaps the only way to prove to him that it was a mistake for them to spend Saturday together was to take the risk and let him see for himself.

Praying she wouldn't regret her decision too much, Ryanne sighed. "What time should I be ready?"

"How does 10:00 a.m. sound?" he asked, smiling.

Ryanne heard his smug tone and wondered if his smile was as delightful as it sounded. "Ten will be fine." She paused, then said, "Do you always get your own way, Hugh MacKenna?"

"Most of the time."

Ryanne sighed again. "Let's hope this is one time you don't live to regret it."

CHAPTER SIX

"Now, you've got plenty of change for a pay phone, and you've memorized the number here, right?" Judith pressed, watching Ryanne like a hawk as the younger woman finished dressing.

"Yes, Judith, I do," Ryanne said tightly, trying not to lose her temper. Ever since Judith learned Ryanne had accepted Hugh's invitation she had made her displeasure obvious, and Ryanne's nerves were strung as tightly as a violin string. She was simultaneously excited and terrified about her date with Hugh, and her companion was only making things worse. "And I'm wearing my most comfortable walking shoes, Aggie has had her breakfast and she's been outside. Except for a few minor details, I'm as ready as I'll ever be, so please stop worrying."

Judith sighed audibly. "Don't get flip with me, Ryanne. This is not Chicago."

"What's that supposed to mean?" Ryanne snapped, turning to face Judith, arms akimbo.

"It means you don't have a home-field advantage. You're going to walk out of here with a man you hardly know—"

"He's a friend of Douglas's—and a private detective, to boot. What could be safer?"

"Staying home."

"Well, I'm not, so would you please get off my back!" Instantly remorseful, Ryanne apologized. "Oh, Judith, I'm sorry. I didn't mean to yell at you. I know you're just worried that I'll be hurt if this date goes badly, but—"

"Your wounded psyche is the least of my worries," Judith returned sharply. "You're not *home*, Ryanne. You don't know where anything is. L.A. is different from Chicago, but it's still a big city and there are a lot of dangers out there. All it would take is Hugh MacKenna carelessly turning his back on you for one minute and you could get so lost we'd never find you. There's not a cop standing on every street corner, you know."

Judith had a valid point, one Ryanne had considered several times herself. Aggie was the perfect example of Newton's law of inertia; once the dog started moving she would continue in a straight line until someone told her to stop, or an obstacle blocked her path. It wouldn't take much for Ryanne to get separated from Hugh and become lost. But Ryanne had calculated the risk involved and decided it was worth it. Now confronted with the issue, she calmed herself and sat on the edge of her bed. "Judith, L.A. isn't a foreign country. English is still the primary language here. If I do get separated from Hugh I'm reasonably sure someone will be able to tell me where I am and direct me to a pay phone. Frankly, though, I don't believe that will happen. I trust Hugh. I think he's capable of being responsible for my welfare."

"It's not a matter of trust or responsibility, Ryanne," Judith argued. "It's a matter of not being familiar with your particular needs."

Ryanne managed a smile. "Then he'll either learn, or get so frustrated and disgusted that he'll call it a day, bring me home and I'll never see him again."

"Which will be very painful for you."

"Aha!" Ryanne jumped up, laughing. "You *are* worried about my wounded psyche!"

There was a long pause and Ryanne suspected that Judith was trying not to laugh with her. When the other woman refused to acknowledge the accusation, Ryanne told her, "Don't worry about me, please. I've got a firm grip on what's happening with Hugh. I think he's just attracted to me now because I'm something a little different from what he's accustomed to. He'll squire me around today until he realizes that I'm more trouble than I'm worth, and that will be the end of it." Her voice was light, but a little stab of hurt accompanied her words.

"And you can handle that kind of rejection?" Judith asked quietly.

Ryanne shrugged. "I have before."

"All right." She turned to leave. "I'll be near the phone all day if you need me."

"Thank you, Judith."

The secretary left Ryanne's bedroom without further comment and Ryanne checked the time, lifting the crystal on her watch and feeling for the position of the hands. Nine forty-five. She had to hurry. She was dressed and had already finished applying her makeup, but she still needed to do something with her hair. On the other hand, Hugh seemed to like her hair loose. Ryanne moved to the bathroom vanity and expertly brushed and fluffed her long, thick tresses. Then, she lightly touched her blue trousers and floral print shirt, staring sightlessly into the mirror and wondering if Hugh would approve. This date with him had become important . . . far more important than Ryanne wanted it to be. She wanted to be casual about the whole thing, wanted to feel as though it didn't matter to her if Hugh ultimately became disillusioned with her. Other people went out on first dates all the time, discovered they weren't compatible and never saw each other again. But most other people didn't have two strikes against them from the outset, either.

Maybe I made a mistake, not dating more, Ryanne thought. It might have been easier if she'd given herself more chances to adjust to and overcome the feelings of rejection and inadequacy she'd experienced on her few previous dates.

Maybe it won't happen that way this time, she dared to hope. Maybe Hugh would be different. It had been such a long time since she'd been involved with someone that the idea of feeling that wonderful man-woman attraction again was very seductive. She knew instinctively that Hugh MacKenna was a man who could make her feel like a woman, make her feel wanted and desirable. And even though their relationship could last only for the brief period she'd be in Los Angeles, Ryanne was honest enough to admit that she'd take that over nothing.

The doorbell rang and Ryanne put her expectations and her fears aside. She was going to go out with Hugh, enjoy herself while it lasted and take whatever happened—good or bad—as it came.

"THE FAMOUS Grauman's Chinese Theatre has changed ownership since its heyday in the forties," Hugh informed Ryanne in his best professional tour-guide voice. They were walking down Hollywood Boulevard's Walk of Fame, and his running narration included descriptions of the famous buildings they passed, the movie star plaques imbedded in the sidewalk, as well as the colorful people they encountered. "There are more crazies per square inch on Hollywood Boulevard than anywhere else in the world," Hugh had already informed her, and having heard the guitars of street musicians clashing with the chanting of traveling, robed religious groups, Ryanne was inclined to believe him. Now, though, they had crossed Highland Boulevard and seemed to have arrived at a section of the famous street where the sounds around were more normal—city traffic and gaping tourists.

"It's Mann's Chinese now," Hugh continued. "But fortunately, the architecture hasn't changed one bit. It's still as gaudy and delightful as it was the day Betty Grable sat down and immortalized in cement America's most famous pair of legs." He touched Ryanne's arm lightly and slowed down. "We'll make a right turn here," he informed her.

"Aggie, right, right," she instructed. The dog obeyed and Ryanne could tell immediately that they had entered an enclosure, yet she still had the sensation of the sun shining down on her. The concrete suddenly became rough and uneven, and Ryanne stopped. "Is this it?" she asked, grinning from ear to ear. "Whose famous footprints am I standing in?"

Hugh looked down and laughed. "Actually you're standing in George Raft's famous *hand*print."

Ryanne moved her feet quickly. "Sorry, George," she quipped. "Where are Humphrey Bogart's prints?"

"Over here, I think." Moving slowly, Hugh directed Ryanne around the courtyard, all the while reading the signatures inscribed in the jigsaw configuration of cement blocks. He also described the classic black, red and gold pagoda architecture that towered above them, and Ryanne was enthralled. Hugh's descriptions were so detailed and vivid that she felt she could almost see the building herself. His knowledge of movie star lore was also impressive, and Ryanne spent the entire morning laughing. She was enjoying herself more than she had in longer than she could remember.

They found Rin Tin Tin's paw prints, which did not seem to impress Aggie in the least, and when the crowd for the noon matinee began lining up they decided it was time to move on.

"Aggie, follow Hugh," Ryanne instructed. He led them through the crowd and back out to the sidewalk. "Where to now?" she asked when they stopped just beyond the line of moviegoers.

"Are you hungry?"

"Starved."

"All right. We'll go back to the car now and head down to Farmer's Market. There's a sandwich stall there that serves the best gyro west of Chicago. We can picnic at the La Brea Tar Pits."

"The Tar Pits?" Ryanne looked skeptical. "That sounds...interesting."

Hugh laughed. "Oh, it will be, I promise."

Allowing Aggie to set her usual brisk pace, they quickly reached Hugh's convertible, which was parked in a lot just off Hollywood and Vine. As they moved into the flow of traffic, Hugh kept up a running commentary of their location and Ryanne began to form a mental picture of a well laid out city. It was a far cry from the picturesque, winding mountainous road they had taken from Malibu to reach Hollywood.

Los Angeles was certainly a city of contrasts, Ryanne decided. Wooded hillsides overlooked palm tree lined suburban streets, and square city blocks were evidently close to a prehistoric landmark where saber-toothed tigers and mammoth elephants once disappeared in an oozing mire of tar.

They reached the Farmer's Market on Fairfax much more quickly than Ryanne had expected and Hugh led them through the winding labyrinth of covered stalls. The smell of food interested Aggie far more than Rin Tin Tin's footprints had, and Hugh began to wonder if it had been a mistake to bring Ryanne in here. The walkways in the market were narrow and crowded, and it was a struggle to keep Ryanne close while her guide dog weaved right and left, scavenging for bits of food that had been lost or discarded by the lunch crowd.

When Ryanne realized what was happening she disciplined the dog sternly, but Hugh was relieved when they finally reached the Greek sandwich stall. He read Ryanne the menu and when they had their meals in hand, he led her out of the market via a different route. With no food to distract Aggie the dog's performance improved drastically. On the way to the car they browsed the souvenir stands, and Ryanne, with Hugh's help, chose a selection of postcards to send friends back home. Then they inspected the wares at a shop specializing in imported Mexican sculptures and jewelry. Despite Ryanne's protests, Hugh bought her a beautiful pair of carved abalone shell earrings, and asked Ryanne to help him pick out a gift for Judith, as well. He claimed it was a peace offering for the irascible secretary, but Ryanne accused him of trying to buy Judith's affection. They settled on a bracelet of silver and turquoise. Hugh hoped that if the trinket didn't persuade Judith to like him, it would at least provide her with a reason not to slam the door in his face next time he came by.

He lost count of the number of times that strangers—adults and children, alike—approached Ryanne curiously and stopped to pet her lovely dog. Each time, Ryanne patiently repeated the same speech, informing the stranger that a guide dog in harness should never be petted, spoken to, or distracted in any way. She explained that petting the dog, whose natural inclination was to seek approval and affection, diminished Aggie's ability to do her job properly. It astonished Hugh that after the fifth or sixth time someone stopped to admire the dog that Ryanne could still recite her admonition so gently. Hugh was certain that if he'd been in Ryanne's position, he'd have been barking, "Leave the dog alone, dammit!"

Despite the distractions, though, they made their way back to the car. They piled in again, with Aggie at Ryanne's feet and Hugh behind the wheel, and this time their journey was even shorter. They had gone barely three or four blocks by Ryanne's estimate when Hugh rejoiced at discovering a convenient parking space on Sixth Street.

"Well, here we are," he proclaimed, shutting off the engine.

"The La Brea Tar Pits?" Ryanne asked, her voice once again doubtful. To her right, she heard what sounded like a breeze rustling through the leaves of nearby trees. "A prehistoric tar pit surrounded by trees—in the middle of the city?"

"That's right," he replied cheerfully, climbing out of the car. "Wilshire Boulevard is just one block south of us."

"The tar pits are on Wilshire?" Ryanne asked, incredulous. "I had always imagined that they were somewhere out in the desert."

Hugh chuckled as he opened and held the door for Ryanne. "Not only are they *on* Wilshire, sometimes they are even *in* Wilshire. Every now and then the tar bubbles up and breaks through the pavement. It plays havoc with the traffic."

"I can imagine." Ryanne and Aggie joined Hugh beside the car and waited patiently while he unlocked the trunk. Obviously he had come prepared. He explained what he was doing as he extracted a cooler with soft drinks, and a serviceable blanket.

"Where did you put the bag I brought along?" Ryanne asked as he closed the trunk. "I should give Aggie a drink of water while we're having lunch."

"I've got it right here, too," he informed her, juggling the cooler, the blanket and Ryanne's canvas bag, which contained a gallon of fresh water and a stainless-steel bowl. Ryanne insisted he allow her to carry something, and eventually Hugh relented and handed her the bag containing their sandwiches.

With Hugh in the lead and Aggie commanded to follow, they moved off down the wide sidewalk. Soon they moved onto a paved path amid a grove of trees, and as they wandered in a seemingly aimless zigzag pattern, Hugh described the replicas of gigantic prehistoric sloths. The most remarkable part of the park, though, was the actual tar pit itself, a large black pit that smelled to Ryanne like fresh asphalt heated by the sun. Hugh described the life-size replica of a saber-toothed tiger crouching on a rock that jutted out over the pit, and at the other end of the enclosure, two mammoth elephants seemed to be trumpeting frantically because their baby was mired in the tar. Promising to take Ryanne to the underground museum later, Hugh led the way back to the edge of the grove and found a quiet, shady spot at which to spread out their blanket.

While Ryanne attended to Aggie's needs, Hugh put their sandwiches on paper plates and distributed napkins and a soft drink for each of them.

"You're very domestic," Ryanne complimented him facetiously as she settled across the blanket from him.

"Being a bachelor does that to you."

"You've never been married?" she asked, then took a bite of her sandwich.

"Never."

"Never found the right woman, or are you just allergic to the institution in general?"

"Severe allergy. Deadly, in fact," he told her with mock gravity. "What about you?"

"I've never taken the plunge, either."

"Why not?"

Ryanne shrugged and devoted an undue amount of attention to her gyro. "I was always so single-mindedly devoted to being a reporter that I didn't have a lot of time for developing long-term relationships. And then after I lost my sight . . . well, it just didn't seem too practical."

"Blind people do get married, Ryanne," he reminded her gently.

"Of course they do," she allowed. "Many have families and lead full, productive lives. But that particular life-style is just not one I envision for myself."

She could have gone on to explain that finding a man willing to encumber himself with a blind wife wasn't exactly easy. And she could have told him about her own reluctance to risk the disappointment she would inevitably suffer if she allowed herself to want to find that man. The dreams of a home and family were ones that Ryanne had forced herself to abandon. Instead she had built a new life and a new career on the premise that her independence was the most important thing in the world to her.

Uncomfortable with their discussion, Ryanne changed the subject, drawing Hugh out first with questions about his father, then carefully probing his life before he settled in Los Angeles. He told her about his restless, vagabond mother who had divorced his father when he was nine. From there, he described the succession of cities, stepfathers and "uncles" he'd been subjected to until he was finally old enough to put his foot down and insist on being allowed to live with his father.

The stories he related about his mother's exploits were all told humorously, but the picture of his childhood that emerged was less than ideal. Apparently Hugh's mother was in love with the idea of being in love, and her constant search for something that always seemed to elude her grasp had made her son's life miserable.

"You must have been a very lonely child," Ryanne commented a little sadly, remembering her own lonely years.

"It forced me to grow up a little faster than I might have liked," he admitted. "But I was born with a streak of independence a mile wide, anyway."

"Where is your mother now?"

Hugh laughed. "I got a postcard from her last Christmas that was mailed from somewhere in the Caribbean. She and husband number six—or maybe seven—were honeymooning there."

"Did your father ever remarry?"

"No. After Mother and I moved away from Chicago, Dad sold his Army surplus stores, bought a couple of fishing boats on the Gulf and became a crusty old sea-faring bachelor." Hugh realized how skillfully Ryanne had elicited information from him and he laughed ruefully. "You must have been one helluva reporter, Ryanne. I haven't talked this much about myself in a long time."

Ryanne ducked her head. "Sorry. I have an insatiable curiosity about people and what makes them tick."

"And yet you hate to answer questions about yourself," he noted slyly.

It was Ryanne's turn to laugh. "Oops. I'd forgotten how perceptive you are." The remnants of their lunch had already been cleared away and Ryanne lay down on the blanket, facing Hugh with her left hand propping up her head.

"Perception is about seventy-five percent of my job," he said, reclining to mirror her position.

"What's the other twenty-five percent?"

"Dogged persistence and knowing when someone is trying to divert my attention. Like now, for instance."

She grinned sheepishly. "Sorry. I like asking questions more than I like answering them."

"Then I won't ask if you'd rather I didn't," Hugh told her seriously.

Ryanne shook her head. "No, it's okay. But you see, Hugh, you have a stock of humorous stories that paint a vivid picture of what your childhood was like. You can laugh now at how one of your stepfathers deliberately lost you at a carnival when you were twelve, and if I choose to I can take your humor at face value. Or I can look beyond the laughter to the pain you must have suffered, and get a clearer understanding of some of the forces that made you the man you are today."

"Not many people do that, Ryanne," he told her quietly. "Most are content to laugh at the stories without realizing there's anything behind them."

"And you prefer it that way, don't you?" she asked shrewdly.

Hugh cleared his throat uncomfortably. "As a general rule, yes. With you, on the other hand...well, somehow I have the feeling you'd get down to the truth no matter what I said."

"Don't give me too much credit," Ryanne warned him. "I don't have any mystical powers."

"Or funny stories about your childhood?" he asked gently, steering the conversation back on course.

Ryanne shifted her position, rolling onto her stomach so that her weight rested on her elbows. Clasping her hands she said, "No, I don't."

Hugh moved, too, stretching out on the blanket so that their shoulders were almost touching. "You mentioned once that after you lost your sight you went home to live with your aunt." He paused a moment, then asked gently, "What happened to your parents, Ryanne?"

"When I was twelve my father was killed in a hit-and-run accident. A year later my mother died of cancer."

"I'm sorry."

Ryanne sighed heavily. "So am I. Aunt Rose and Uncle Charley were wonderful to me, but I don't think I ever fully got over that sense of betrayal I felt because my parents deserted me."

"All children feel that way when they find themselves alone, Ryanne. Surely you must know by now that they didn't have a choice."

She frowned and her voice took on a faraway quality. "No, Hugh, they both had choices. Daddy's decision I can understand, but not Mother's. After Daddy died she just gave up on life. When her cancer was diagnosed she refused treatment, not because she was frightened of the surgery, but because she just didn't want to live any longer. Having a daughter who needed her wasn't a good enough reason to fight."

If that were true, Hugh could understand how Ryanne might still feel betrayed by her mother's death, and he told her so. He wanted desperately to reach out to her, but he held that desire in check, fearing she might pull away. Somehow he sensed that if he moved too quickly, presumed too much about this relationship that was still so very fragile, he would lose her.

Reminding himself to go slowly, he concentrated on something she had said that puzzled him. "What did you mean when you said your father had a choice, too?"

Ryanne gave him a crooked smile. "Did I say that?"

"Yes, you did," he affirmed seriously, refusing to be diverted. Something wasn't right and he wanted to know what it was. "How can you blame your father for being in a hit-and-run accident?"

"He didn't have to walk out into the street, did he?" she quipped with morbid humor.

"Ryanne!"

"Sorry," she apologized unremorsefully. She had no intention of talking about how her father had died. It struck her far too close to home. "Look, Hugh, could we drop this, please? Let's just say that both of us survived our somewhat unpleasant childhoods and go on from there."

She sat up and Hugh followed suit. "All right. What's next then?" he asked.

"Well, let's see...." Ryanne thought for a moment, an impish grin replacing the look of sorrow that had marred her face moments earlier. "We could sit here a while longer and keep poking around at each other's deep, dark secrets, or we could complete your guided tour."

"Oh, the tour, definitely. Our secrets can wait until another time."

CHAPTER SEVEN

"Is THERE ANYTHING I can do to help?" Ryanne asked
when Hugh came out of the kitchen and joined her on the
deck. She was exhausted from their day on the town, but
she felt a little guilty about sitting with her feet up while
Hugh did all the work.

"Not a thing. Here." He handed her a fluted wineglass and sat in the cushioned deck chair beside her. "The
grill's almost ready, the table is set and everything else is
just waiting. How do you like your steak cooked, by the
way?"

"Medium rare." She sipped her wine and smiled.
"You're going to spoil me rotten with this Julia Child
impersonation. Judith and I usually share the cooking
chores."

"Are you a good cook?" Hugh asked with interest. It
was rapidly becoming a consuming passion to know
everything there was to know about the fascinating
woman beside him.

"I'm terrible. Aunt Rose used to cringe when I put
water on to boil. She badgered me all the time I was in
high school and college to take home economics along
with my journalism courses, but I was still living at home
then, and I didn't realize that reporters had to feed
themselves."

Hugh chuckled, watching Ryanne's animated face.
Just above the horizon the sun hung like a gilded med-

allion. It bathed Ryanne in amber light and turned her hair to molten gold. She was unbelievably beautiful and he wanted her. Badly. It was a struggle to keep his mind off that growing need and keep track of their conversation. "Earlier today you mentioned something about being single-minded regarding your career," he reminded her, thinking of the quiet, unrevealing hour they'd spent sharing a blanket in the park. "What made you want to be a reporter so badly?"

For an instant Ryanne's expression took on that sad, haunted look he'd witnessed in the afternoon, but she answered him promptly. "My father was a journalist. I can't remember ever wanting to be anything else."

"Because you liked the job, or because you wanted him to be proud of you?" Hugh asked gently.

Ryanne turned her face toward his, capturing his eyes so unerringly that for a moment Hugh forgot she couldn't see. "No," she corrected him, her voice soft. "I wanted to be like him. His life stood for something—he had ideals. He believed in things like honesty, truth and decency at a time when those things were even less fashionable than they are today. He believed in fighting for what he thought was right." *And it killed him,* she added silently, turning her face toward the sunset. "Sounds hokey, doesn't it?"

"I don't think so," Hugh said, touched by the depth of emotion he heard in her voice. "I can only imagine how proud it would make him to know his daughter remembers him with such respect. He left quite a legacy behind. It must have been hard for you to have to give up being a reporter."

Ryanne nodded, pushing away the knife-sharp grief that pierced her whenever she thought of everything she'd lost five years ago. "It was. I loved it all—the interviews, the vague leads that led to big stories, chasing down elusive city officials . . . seeing my byline under a front-page headline and knowing I was doing something important. I thrived on it." She paused for a moment, her expression becoming wistful. "After the accident Douglas offered me a job on the desk, transcribing stories that came in over the phone from our field reporters, but I'd have gone crazy in less than a week."

For just a moment Hugh glimpsed the enormity of the vacuum blindness had created in Ryanne's life. He felt sorry for what she'd lost, but more importantly, he felt a deep respect for the way she'd put her life back together after what must have been nearly total destruction. "So you decided to write mysteries instead," he concluded.

She smiled. "Yep."

"Do you ever dream about being able to go back to reporting?"

Her smile faded. "No. That's an indulgence I can't afford." She slipped off her glasses, closed her eyes and turned her face toward the horizon again. "The sun's down now, isn't it?"

Hugh looked out over the ocean, letting himself be swept along by the quiet, languid mood that fell over them. "Mm-hmm. It just slipped out of sight. This is my favorite part of the sunset," he told her, rising to walk to the deck rail. "The bright glare is gone and all that's left is a splash of color and fading light. Smog may not be healthy, but it does spectacular things to L.A.'s sunsets."

"Describe it to me," Ryanne requested. He complied, describing the vivid line of scarlet that painted the horizon, then blended upward into hues of magenta and purple. Golden clouds hovered in the foreground and the ocean below grew dark and mysterious. As he described each detail, Ryanne added to the picture in her mind until she had an image that was breathtakingly beautiful. She visualized Hugh as well, imagining his tall, broad-shouldered silhouette in the foreground of the magnificent sunset. She'd ascertained from the sound of his voice that he'd turned toward her. He'd fallen silent, too, and the knowledge that he was watching her caused Ryanne's pulse to quicken.

They were motionless for a moment, caught in the tableau of the silent sunset. It was Ryanne who spoke first, trying to break the tension that suddenly hung thickly in the air, but her voice failed her. It came out as little more than a hushed, seductive whisper. "Are you tired of having to describe everything to me?"

"Not at all," Hugh replied, his voice as soft and smooth as satin. "You make me look at things in a way I never have before—as though I were seeing them for the first time."

Mesmerized by his voice, Ryanne remained silent. She heard him move away from the rail, but she stiffened in surprise when he sat on the edge of her lounge chair, facing her. "There are some things I just can't describe to you, though, Ryanne," he said finally.

There was a hint of a teasing smile in his voice that Ryanne couldn't help responding to. She relaxed and played along. "Such as?"

"Such as the expression on my incredibly handsome face," he said with mock seriousness.

Ryanne struggled to hide a smile. "And what expression is that?"

Hugh leaned closer, resting one hand on the opposite side of her chair. "This is my come hither, smoldering-with-sensuality look."

Ryanne pressed one hand over her heart. "Oh, my! Should I be swooning?"

"Most women do," he replied matter-of-factly.

"Okay." Ryanne threw her head back melodramatically and went limp. "How's this?"

"Your swoon needs practice."

She straightened. "Sorry. I'm not accustomed to receiving smolderingly, sensual looks from incredibly handsome faces."

"I find that hard to believe, Ryanne. Most men probably just aren't smart enough to describe their looks to you."

"Or humble enough."

"That, too."

Ryanne laughed, thoroughly enjoying their playful flirtation. Hugh was teasing her, and yet he wasn't. By making fun of their mutual attraction he was easing the fears she would normally have experienced having someone so close to her. He was making her feel wonderful, and she didn't want that feeling to end. "You know, Hugh, I think the problem is that I really don't have a clear mental picture of a smoldering, sensual look." Boldly she raised one hand and touched his face. "Let's try the visualization by touch method. Give me that look again."

"I never stopped," he informed her, keeping his voice light despite the sudden sharpening of his senses as her gentle, agile fingers lightly caressed his face.

There was a light stubble of beard on the long line of his jaw, Ryanne noted, and he had a small, Kirk Douglas cleft in his chin. Her fingertips brushed his full lower lip and darted away quickly, moving upward before she could allow herself to imagine those lips pressed to hers. His eyes were deep set and his lashes seemed incredibly long. On his forehead she discovered deep vertical lines and one eyebrow was noticeably higher than the other. It took her a moment to realize he was leering at her comically, his face shamelessly contorted. She withdrew her hand and schooled her own face into a reproachful mask.

"If this is what smoldering sensuality looks like I'm almost glad I can't see it."

Hugh straightened as though he was thoroughly insulted. "Obviously you failed to notice my striking resemblance to Robert Redford."

"That's true," Ryanne agreed. "What I got was more like Donald Duck."

"Donald Duck!" He gasped with indignation. "Just for that I ought to kiss you thoroughly and erase that fowl image."

Ryanne's heart began racing but she never gave a thought to escaping. "But sir, I've never been kissed by Donald Duck, therefore, I wouldn't know whether you kiss like him or not."

"Have you ever been kissed by Robert Redford?"

"No."

Without warning, Hugh slipped his arms around Ryanne, pulling her so close that his breath was warm against her face. "Then I can't possibly lose, can I?"

Ryanne's laugh was smothered when Hugh's lips touched hers. A delightful, erotic shock wave coursed through both of them and all playfulness left Hugh's kiss. He drew her even closer, teasing her lips with his tongue, exploring and tasting, just as he'd wanted to from the moment he met her. Stunned by her own eager response, Ryanne placed one hand at the back of Hugh's head while the other tested the breadth and strength of his chest and shoulder. The kiss deepened and ignited fires in both of them, but a cold, wet nose abruptly extinguished them. Aggie, who had been resting peacefully beside Ryanne, took exception to being excluded from this interesting new game and she pushed between them excitedly.

Hugh drew back and looked at the dog trying to crawl onto Ryanne's lap. "I thought they were trained to *guide* their owners, not *guard* them."

Ryanne grinned and ordered Aggie to sit. "They're not. That playful curiosity is just a fringe benefit."

"This could pose a serious obstacle to the development of our relationship, Ryanne," he told her jokingly, but Ryanne took his comment seriously.

"Do we have a 'relationship,' Hugh?"

Lightly, Hugh brushed a lock of hair away from Ryanne's forehead. "We could have. If you want it as much as I do."

"You mean I haven't managed to scare you off yet?"

Her voice was light, but something in her tone betrayed her. "Have you been trying?" he asked in response.

She shrugged and shifted so that there was a little more distance between them. "Frankly I figured I'd accomplish that just by being myself."

Frowning, Hugh stood, retrieved both their glasses and refilled them from the bottle of wine on the serving cart next to the French doors. "Then you were either underestimating yourself or me, Ryanne. I'm not quite sure which."

He touched the wineglass to the back of her hand and Ryanne took it from him, subdued. All their former playfulness had evaporated. "You're angry, aren't you?"

"Angry? No," he said, sitting on the edge of her chair again. "Just confused. You know, the other day you said something about being afraid I'd be disillusioned after I'd spent some time with you.''

"That's right.''

"Well, we've spent time together now, and I haven't been disillusioned in the least.''

"Are you sure?'' she asked, wanting to believe him because his friendship had become so important to her.

"I'm sure, Ryanne. If I had gotten tired of you or fed up, or whatever else it is you expected, why would I have invited you here for supper? Why didn't I just drop you off on your doorstep, say *adiós, muchacha*, and beat a hasty retreat?''

Ryanne lowered her head and fidgeted with her wineglass. "Maybe you brought me here for the payoff,'' she suggested, hating herself even as the words came out. She didn't believe Hugh was like that, but she had to be sure.

"The *payoff*,'' Hugh repeated disgustedly. He stood and moved away from her toward the deck rail. "Ryanne, in case you haven't been keeping up on current events, let me clue you in. The era of the quick seduction and the one-night stand is over. Women aren't the only ones looking for so-called meaningful relationships anymore.''

He took a sip of wine, then continued. "Now I will admit that this poses a few problems for confirmed bachelors like myself, but just because I have no desire to get married and settle into suburbia doesn't mean that I don't crave feminine companionship—not just sex, but real intimacy and friendship, too. I happen to have a particular weakness for attractive, intelligent, fun career women and you fit all those categories very well. Maybe too well.''

Ryanne smiled. "What do you do if one of those attractive career women gets a little too serious and wants to replant you in suburbia?"

Hugh pushed himself away from the rail and returned to sit beside her. "That happens a lot less often than many people would think. Usually most of my relationships dissolve by mutual agreement. You'd be surprised by the number of women out there who are just looking for a simple, uncomplicated friendship with a male while they focus on their careers."

Ryanne nodded, understanding what he was trying to tell her. He was laying out the ground rules, and inadvertently explaining one of the reasons he found her attractive. Long-term, lifetime commitments were something he would always avoid, but Ryanne was only in town for a few months. Once her screenplay was finished she would head back to her life in Chicago and Hugh knew it. He was offering her a comfortable, friendly relationship while she was in Los Angeles, and when she left he would no doubt expect them to say "So long" and part with a friendly kiss.

Ryanne was amazed that she found the idea so attractive, but then, she couldn't recall anyone who'd ever attracted her the way Hugh MacKenna did. She had dated regularly in college and during her first years as a reporter, but she'd been too career oriented to involve herself in a serious romance. With the blind optimism of youth, she had always assumed that a husband and children would eventually come along, but she'd been in no rush. And because of the moral values her parents, and later her aunt and uncle, had instilled in her, she didn't believe in sleeping around. Her only affair had been with a good friend in college, someone Ryanne had liked and respected, but whom she had known instinctively would never demand more from her than she was ready to give.

And then she'd had the "accident" that had forced her to abandon her nebulous dreams of a warm, loving man to share her life. She hadn't counted on charming, funny Hugh MacKenna coming along and offering her a short-term, no-strings romance, but Ryanne knew already that she wasn't going to reject the proposition. She would have to guard her heart, of course, and not do something stupid like falling in love. But so far, Ryanne had managed to avoid that pitfall for all of her thirty-three years; surely she could continue that record for another few months. The opportunity to be wined and dined, courted, romanced and made to feel like a woman by an attractive, desirable man was something she couldn't pass up. More importantly, she didn't *want* to pass it up.

There was still one last issue, though, that had to be gotten out of the way once and for all. "Hugh, it really doesn't bother you that this—" she pointed to herself "—purportedly attractive, intelligent, funny career woman just happens to be blind?"

Hugh reached for Ryanne's left hand and turned it palm up. Gently his thumb caressed the small, callused ridge that her guide dog's harness had put there. "It bothers me, Ryanne, because it's made you doubt yourself. It's made it hard for you to believe that a man could find you special enough that knowing you, being close to you, would be worth whatever problems or inconveniences your blindness might cause."

Ryanne could tell that it was dark now—the sun was no longer warming her face—and she didn't think Hugh had put on any lights yet. She hoped that the evening shadows were hiding the tears that pooled in her eyes. Leaning forward, she reached out gingerly and cupped Hugh's face in her hands. Her thumbs lightly brushed his mouth, then her lips followed suit. She let them linger there for a moment, and Hugh accepted the kiss for what it was.

"Thank you," she whispered, smiling shyly as she pulled away.

"Thank *you*." More than anything, Hugh wanted to pull her into his arms for a fuller taste of the sweetness he'd glimpsed so briefly, but he knew it was not the time. This wasn't a relationship he wanted to rush—it was too special for that. "Are you hungry?"

"Does the sea rush to the shore?"

"I guess that means I should put the steaks on now." Hugh stood, taking hold of Ryanne's hand and pulling her to her feet.

"If you don't I may start eating the chair cushions," she warned him.

"Well…that may not be such a bad idea," he said, his voice tinged with remorse.

"Why?"

Hugh tucked her hand into the crook of his arm. "Because I neglected to tell you that *I* can't cook, either."

THE NEXT DAY, in Chicago, a man named Del Michelon looked down at the busy street twenty-seven stories below his office window and contemplated the foolhardy error he had made bringing Arlen Beck into the organization. Behind him, he could hear Beck squirming in the plush chair like a worm on a hook—which was only appropriate. Beck was a stupid, clumsy fool, and Michelon didn't like "employees" with those particular characteristics. Now, more than ever, he wished he had simply disposed of the banker two years ago instead of absorbing Beck's illegal gambling syndicate into his own.

Michelon's silent treatment and that broad back planted firmly opposite him was unnerving, and Arlen finally cleared his throat tentatively. "Mr. Michelon—"

"Shut up, Arlen," Del snapped, not bothering to turn around. "I've got to decide what to do about cleaning up your stupid mess."

"Do you want her killed?" Beck asked.

Michelon finally turned. "No, I don't want her killed, you idiot. This is not the 1920s and I'm not Al Capone. Murder is a messy business and I try to avoid it unless it's an absolute necessity." Michelon eyed Beck critically. "If you'd realized that five years ago we wouldn't be in this position now."

Arlen lowered his head. "I know, sir. But Perigrino had to be disposed of—there was no other choice at the time. He had already made a deal with the district attorney—"

"I know, I know," Michelon snapped. "But you should have contracted the job out—and made sure there were no witnesses. If that girl gets her sight back—"

"But maybe she won't," Beck said, cutting him off hurriedly.

Michelon shot him a withering glance. "Why else would she be going to one of the best specialists in the country?"

"I don't know," he mumbled. "How are we going to handle it?"

Michelon hated hearing Beck say "we." He wanted to tell the glorified punk that it was his own problem, not the organization's, but Del couldn't do that because if Arlen Beck was arrested for arson, murder and attempted murder it would put Michelon's entire empire in jeopardy. In exchange for leniency, Beck would probably give them the head of Chicago's biggest gambling syndicate on a silver platter, and Del Michelon hadn't gotten where he was by losing his head—literally or figuratively.

Grimly he turned his back on Beck again. "*We* are going to wait and see what happens," he said finally. "Is your man in L.A. reliable?"

"Yes, sir. He's one of ours."

Michelon frowned and turned. "Not someone who can be traced to me, I hope?"

"Of course not."

"Good. When is the girl's appointment with that specialist?"

"June twenty-ninth at 11:00 a.m. Six weeks from Monday."

Michelon nodded. "By 9:00 a.m. on the thirtieth I want to know exactly what the doctor said."

"The doctor's reports will be confidential—"

"Then have your man bribe someone in the doctor's office, or have him break in and steal the file! I don't care which. If she's going to see again, I want to know it!"

Beck shrank from his boss's anger. His voice was small when he asked, "And if they can operate on her or something?"

"Then we won't have a choice, will we? We'll have to kill her *before* she gets her sight back and can identify you. Can your man out there take care of it?"

"Yes, sir."

Michelon stared at Beck coldly. "Good. And Beck...if it comes down to murder, see that it's done right this time. I wouldn't want to be in your shoes if you botch it again."

"That's not going to happen," Beck promised fervently, rising. "If there's even the slightest chance she'll see again, Ryanne Kirkland will be dead. You can count on it."

CHAPTER EIGHT

"Oh. It's you." Judith stood at the front door, staring at Hugh through narrowed, suspicious eyes.

"It's nice to see you, too, Judith," he said good-naturedly. It had taken a while, but Hugh had finally gotten accustomed to the secretary's peculiarities. On the outside she was as crusty as the barnacles on one of his father's boats, but inside she was as soft as a marshmallow—particularly where Ryanne was concerned. He even suspected that Judith was developing a soft spot for him, but he couldn't be sure. In the month that he'd been dating Ryanne, he and Judith had developed a friendly animosity that kept them both on their toes. "May I come in?"

"I'm expecting the caterers," she informed him firmly.

Hugh nodded as though that explained everything and rephrased his request. "May I come in if I promise not to scare them away when they get here?"

She sighed heavily and stepped back. "I suppose so."

Hugh moved past her into the living room. "Judith, may I ask you a personal question?"

"Only if you absolutely have to."

"Is there anyone in the world you like?" he said teasingly.

Judith closed the door and looked at him dispassionately. "I like caterers."

"Oh. Next time I come by I'll bring food, then."

"In your case it wouldn't help." She moved off toward the kitchen and Hugh followed her, chuckling.

"You're a tough nut to crack, Judith." Aggie came bounding at him down the hall and Hugh bent to scuff her ears. "At least Aggie is pleased to see me," he told Judith with a grin.

Judith's answering look told him how little that endorsement meant to her. "I thought you were meeting your father at the airport today."

"Not until noon. I had an hour or so to spare so I thought I'd drop by and see if you or Ryanne needed any last minute help with the party. Where is she, by the way?"

Judith's disgruntled look turned to one of concern and Hugh swatted Aggie lightly on the rump to send her off. He straightened and moved to Ryanne's friend. "What's wrong?"

"She's in her room—asleep, hopefully. She got another one of those damned headaches this morning."

Hugh frowned. Doug Sutherland had mentioned something about Ryanne's recurring headaches when they'd first talked on the phone more than a month ago, but until a couple of weeks ago that bit of information hadn't really sunk in. He had taken Ryanne to a charming little Italian restaurant out in the valley, and halfway through the fettuccini Ryanne had turned white as a ghost and nearly fainted. It had been obvious that she was in severe pain and Hugh had spirited her home and into bed. Deeply concerned, he'd wanted to stay with her, but Judith and Ryanne had both protested.

"It's just a little headache," Ryanne had told him, trying to make her voice strong and reassuring but failing miserably.

"Ryanne, *little* headaches don't make people pass out."

"I didn't pass out. I just got a bit dizzy, that's all."

"Tell that to the waiter at Viva Italia. He nearly called the paramedics, and I probably should have let him! Ryanne—" he sat on the edge of the bed and took her hand "—obviously this has happened before. Have you seen a doctor?"

Ryanne shook her head and winced from the effort. It had been clear to Hugh that it was costing her a lot just to keep track of what he was saying, but he was too worried to let the matter drop. "Not yet."

"Her headaches just started a few months back, not long before we came out here," Judith told him as she placed a cold cloth on Ryanne's forehead. Then she gave her charge a couple of aspirins and ushered Hugh out of the bedroom and down to the kitchen before completing the explanation. "They were mild at first, but when they started getting worse we decided she should see someone about them."

"Are they related to the fall that caused her blindness?"

Judith shook her head helplessly and poured them both a cup of coffee. "We don't know that yet. The doctor who treated Ryanne after the attempt on her life has retired since then, but she called him anyway. When he found out she was coming to L.A., he referred her to a doctor out here who specializes in neurological disorders. Supposedly he's one of the best in the country."

"Why hasn't she seen him yet?"

"Because he's booked for months in advance, that's why. She's got an appointment on the twenty-ninth. That was the earliest they could work her in," Judith explained waspishly. Obviously she wasn't any happier about the delay than Hugh was.

Hugh's frown deepened as he sipped his coffee. "Why didn't she tell me about this?" he asked, more of himself than of Judith.

"Why should she?" Judith snapped. "Ryanne is convinced they're just plain tension headaches or something. She refused to believe that it's anything more serious. And she's probably right."

At the time Hugh had agreed with Judith's assessment, mainly because he couldn't bear the possibility that something might be seriously wrong with Ryanne. In the weeks that had passed since then, she had had two more bouts with the pain that was so intense it sent her off to bed for hours at a time.

The unfairness of it made Hugh want to strike out at something, but there was nothing to strike, which frustrated him all the more. Ryanne had dealt with so much in her life—her parents' deaths, an attempt on her life that had caused her to lose not only her sight but also the job she loved—and now there was this excruciating pain and the ever-present worry that she might be seriously ill. Ryanne had never admitted that fear, of course, and neither had Judith, but Hugh knew they felt it because he felt it, too.

Ryanne had become so important to Hugh in such a short time that it scared him, yet he couldn't bring himself to back away. She brought him a kind of happiness—a peace and contentment—he'd never known before, and he was determined to allow that feeling to run its natural course.

She was so easy to be with. During the week she worked on her screenplay and had long meetings with the film's director and producers, but many of her evenings were spent with Hugh. They took long walks on the beach or just sat quietly on the deck and shared the sunset. They entertained each other with accounts of the day's frustrations. Ryanne's recounting of the problems she was having with the movie people kept Hugh in stitches. With considerable aplomb, she dealt with their pompous, overblown egos, their daily demands for changes and even an amorous advance or two from the film's associate producer. Hugh had taken the time to read all four of her Cameron Lawe books, and Ryanne had invited him to read her screenplay. He believed her when she told him repeatedly that his insight helped her greatly, not only with her script problems, but with the business of private investigation as well.

The evenings they spent together were simple and pleasant, made up of uneventful moments Hugh had come to cherish. They livened things up on the weekends, though, and Hugh had never enjoyed Los Angeles as much as he did when seeing it through Ryanne's perspective. One weekend he took her to a glamorous star-studded restaurant, and the next they ate hot dogs while standing in line for hours waiting to see the opening of a new science fiction film. Ryanne had followed the story fairly well and had been caught up in the audience's excitement, but Hugh was convinced her greatest enjoyment of it came later when he'd been able to explain the dazzling special effects and describe to her the bizarre aliens that had inhabited the movie.

After that day, Hugh had taken Ryanne to other theaters, to see other major films so that she could experience the pleasure of being part of the crowd. In Hollywood, moviegoing was an event, and audiences applauded and cheered as though they were witnessing a stage production. Nowhere else in the world was watching a film quite the same, and Hugh wanted Ryanne to enjoy the furor. More often than not, though, they watched rented movies on the video cassette recorder at Ryanne's house, where Hugh could stop the action with the remote control and explain any important details she had missed.

Business had called Hugh out of town for an entire week, and the time had moved so slowly for him that he'd thought he would go stir-crazy. His body had been in Boston, but his mind had been firmly attached to the beautiful redhead he'd left behind in Los Angeles. When he'd returned, they had picked up as before, but their time together had taken on a new intensity, as though they both realized what a wasteland their week apart had been. They attended a play at the Mark Taper Forum, and the next night, a concert in Griffith Park. Last week he'd convinced her to take a day off in the middle of the week and they'd left Aggie behind and headed for Disneyland. The guide dog would have been welcome in the park, of course, but she couldn't have accompanied them on the rides, so Hugh became Ryanne's eyes. With her on his arm, Hugh had seen the wonderland with the unadulterated pleasure of a child.

In all the time they had spent together during the past month, though, Hugh hadn't taken Ryanne back to his beach house. Considering his growing hunger for her, he knew that if he took her there again she wouldn't be going home until morning. Ryanne was so precious to him, that he was determined not to rush her into something she might later regret.

"Hugh? Judith, did I hear Hugh's voice?" Ryanne came down the hall moving a lot slower than usual out of deference to the pain in her head.

"I'm right here, Ryanne." He went to her and touched her arm so that she would know he was close. She placed one arm around his waist and Hugh gently drew her to him, kissing her lightly on the forehead. "Judith told me you had another headache."

"The worst of it has passed," she told him, giving in to the desire to lean her head against his shoulder and absorb his warmth and strength. "I thought you'd be on your way to the airport."

"I just stopped by to see if I could run any last minute errands for the party—speaking of which, are you sure you're going to be up to playing hostess tonight? Maybe you should cancel."

Ryanne shook her head gingerly and moved away from Hugh to the bar. "No, I'll be fine in another hour or so." She sat on one of the tall stools and Judith automatically handed her a glass of iced tea. "The food's been ordered, the guests are invited, the bartender has been hired and I'm going to celebrate the completion of the first draft of my screenplay, even if it kills me."

Hugh moved behind Ryanne and began massaging her neck and shoulders. "Well, I must say, Dad is really looking forward to it. He's never been to an honest-to-God Hollywood party before."

Ryanne hooted with laughter and immediately regretted it. She leaned back against Hugh, letting her head loll forward to allow him better access. His hands were strong, yet incredibly gentle, and it felt wonderful to have him touch her. "I hope you told Webb that this is not really a 'Hollywood' party. There's no theme, no tent and no ice sculptures—it's just going to be a few people over for a friendly get-together. Frankly I'm surprised Ted and the other movie people accepted my invitation. Tonight may be a little tame by their standards."

"There you go underestimating yourself again, Ry," Hugh accused lightly. "Who could possibly resist the opportunity to spend an evening with you?"

"You want a list?" she joked.

"No, thanks. I'll just consider myself fortunate that I don't have to fight off a bevy of ardent suitors in order to have you all to myself."

They ignored Judith's disgruntled snort and settled into a discussion of the party. Hugh had willingly agreed to act as host, and Ryanne had already warned him that she wouldn't be able to do much circulating because she tended to trip over people in a crowded room. The guest list was an odd mix, but she really didn't care. Despite their eccentricities, Ryanne enjoyed Ted Braxton, the producer of *Cameron Lawe*, and Malcolm Rissling, the director. When Malcolm had insisted she meet a few of the other preproduction people, Ryanne had decided to throw a small get-acquainted party. Then Hugh had told her that his father, Webb, would be flying in for a week's visit and Ryanne had gladly included Hugh's father. She had even invited a couple of Hugh's associates from the agency. She'd heard so much about their adventures that she could hardly wait to meet them.

All in all, Ryanne estimated that her small get-together had grown to a full-fledged party of some thirty people or so, but she wasn't worried. Hugh and Judith would be there to help her, and she really wanted to share some of the happiness she was feeling these days.

It didn't take any soul-searching to recognize the source of that happiness. It was Hugh MacKenna, pure and simple. She was enjoying the work on the screenplay, but even the fulfillment she got from meeting that challenge was nothing compared to the way Hugh made her feel. He was considerate and charming, intelligent and intuitive. He was as comfortable to be with as an old shoe, but at the same time he made her feel dizzy and breathless—as if she was on a roller-coaster ride. Most of all, he made her feel like a woman, and Ryanne was learning to relish that treatment for the first time in her life.

She joked a lot about being anxious to get her screenplay finished, but in reality she was grateful that she was a long way from having a finalized script because when she did have one there would be nothing to keep her from returning to Chicago. The thought of that always brought a pang of deep sorrow that almost felt like grief, yet Ryanne refused to dwell on the errant emotion. She couldn't afford to. Hugh had made it clear that their relationship was only temporary, and Ryanne had managed to convince herself that was the way she wanted it, too. She simply couldn't let herself fall in love; to do so would mean betraying the pact she and Hugh had agreed to that first night at his beach house. If Hugh ever suspected that she cared more for him than she should, he would end their relationship immediately, so Ryanne kept her growing emotions under control.

It wasn't easy, of course. Ryanne had never met anyone like Hugh. His strength was tempered with kindness and his playful sense of humor was a constant delight. He was caring, compassionate and endlessly patient with the inconveniences Ryanne's handicap caused him, yet never once had he made her feel inadequate or clumsy. In short, he made Ryanne want all the things out of life she'd thought she'd never be able to have.

But allowing her thoughts to move in that direction was dangerous, and Ryanne spent little time dwelling on the future. Regardless of how Hugh made her feel, she had no future with him, and Ryanne had to constantly re-

mind herself of that fact. She told herself that returning
to the security of her life in Chicago was vitally important, that her friends were in Chicago and she missed
them, that her mobility was hampered by her unfamiliar
surroundings, and that the sprawling city of Los Angeles would never feel like home. If she tried hard,
Ryanne could come up with a dozen reasons why a long-
term relationship with Hugh MacKenna would never
work.

Most of those reasons went right out the window when
she was with him, though. It took a great deal of effort
to live strictly in the present. To reassure Hugh she was
keeping their relationship in perspective, Ryanne
constantly alluded to her eventual return to Chicago. She
fervently hoped he never realized that the repeated gesture was also a desperate attempt to remind herself of the
inevitable.

The caterers finally arrived and Hugh left for the airport, promising to return with Webb that evening before
the other guests showed up. By the time he kept that
promise the house was ready for a party and so was
Ryanne, but Judith was still upstairs changing.

"I've got it, Judith!" Ryanne called to her when the
doorbell rang. She hurried to the foyer and paused at the
door. "Hugh?" she called out. Even her excitement
about the party couldn't negate five years worth of caution. Not until Hugh answered did she unlatch the door
and step back to admit him. "Good evening, sir."

Hugh stood in the doorway, momentarily speechless.
Ryanne was stunning. Dressed in a khaki-colored jump-
suit that was adorned with epaulets and gold buttons, and
was tapered at the ankles, she would have looked ready
for a safari if not for the way the soft, clingy fabric
shimmered and adhered to her every curve. A small

cluster of diamonds glittered at her throat, and her fiery red hair framed a face flushed with excitement. What got to Hugh most, though, was the smile that invariably made his heart turn over in his chest.

"You are gorgeous," he said, stepping forward. He took her hands and bent to kiss her, letting his lips linger over the greeting.

Behind Hugh, Webb MacKenna smiled broadly and cleared his throat. "Don't mind me, you two. I'll just stay here in the door and stand guard."

Her face flaming with embarrassment, Ryanne hurriedly broke away from Hugh and extended her hand. "I'm so sorry, Mr. MacKenna. Please come in."

"Dad, in case you hadn't already guessed, this is Ryanne Kirkland. Ryanne, my father, Webb MacKenna."

"It's a great pleasure to meet you, Ryanne. You're everything my son told me you were, and more. I particularly agree with the part about how gorgeous you are." He tucked Ryanne's hand into the crook of his arm and together they strolled into the living room while Hugh closed the door and followed.

"Thank you." Ryanne smiled up at him. Webb wasn't quite as tall as his son, but his voice was just as warm, and his manner equally as open and friendly. Ryanne made a mental note to corner Judith later tonight and ask her if the two men favored each other. "Hugh has told me a great deal about you, as well. Please, have a seat," she invited him.

"No, no. I came to work. Hugh took the liberty of appointing me assistant host for the evening's festivities."

"Wonderful! What exactly does an assistant host do?"

Hugh eased Ryanne away from his father and took her into his arms. "He bails out the host occasionally so that I can spend more time with the host*ess*."

"Oh, how nice!" Ryanne turned her million-dollar smile on Hugh's father. "I hope you're very good at your new job, Webb."

Since there was nothing to do until the guests came, Ryanne insisted they sit for a few minutes so that she and Webb could get acquainted. The bartender Judith had hired arrived and Hugh directed him to the bar while Ryanne and Webb fell in love with each other.

Standing across the room, watching them, Hugh felt an enormous swell of pride. For all his sixty-three years, Webb MacKenna was still a youthful, vigorous man, brimming with life and good humor. He had the uncanny ability to make friends everywhere he went, which probably accounted for the popularity of his charter business. And Ryanne was—well, Ryanne was Ryanne. There was simply no one else like her.

"Did Ryanne finally get smart and dump you for someone older and wiser—not to mention better looking?" Judith asked quietly as she came up behind him to inspect the young bartender's setup.

Hugh turned to her, ready with the snappy retort he knew she'd expect, but when he looked at her his voice failed him for the second time. Dressed in a casual pastel blue suit with a tapered skirt and unconstructed jacket, she looked like a different person. Her hair, normally a nondescript mass of severe, permed curls, was styled so that it was loose and full, and as a result, all the angles of her face were softened. She had even made a concession to the occasion by wearing a light application of make-up. It took Hugh a moment to take in the dramatic changes and finally find his voice.

"Judith, I hardly recognized you. If you'd learn how to smile I could guarantee that you'd be the second most beautiful woman here tonight."

"Forget it," she said flatly. "If I smiled, the shock would probably give you a heart attack."

"Quite likely," Hugh agreed.

She paused to consider that for a moment. "On second thought, it might be worth the effort, after all."

"Judith, you are one in a million." Hugh laughed and before the secretary could protest he planted a swift kiss on her cheek.

Startled, Judith pulled away quickly and tried not to look pleased. "You do that again, buster, and I'll break both your lips."

"Do I hear my son being threatened?" Webb asked good-naturedly, rising as he noticed Judith. Hugh took Judith's elbow and ushered her across the room. "What has he done this time?"

"He's getting as fresh as a June apple—and just about as sweet," Judith told him sarcastically. "Didn't you ever consider teaching him any manners?"

"*You've* got to be Mrs. Tremain," Webb guessed, chuckling. Ryanne made the formal introductions and the elder MacKenna asked, "Should I take the boy outside and give him a sound thrashing?"

"You should have thought of that thirty years ago." Judith sat and the men followed suit.

Twenty minutes later the guests started arriving, and for the first hour or so Hugh kept Ryanne at his side, her hand resting lightly on his arm as he guided her through the room. Finally, though, Malcolm Rissling captured her for a lengthy conversation about the problems the art director was having finding a suitable location for the movie's primary action sequences. When Malcolm spirited Ryanne away to the settee in the corner, Hugh drifted over to Mo Johnson and his attractive date.

Candy, a tall, leggy blonde who'd started the evening with Rissling, attached herself to Hugh, and though she was exceedingly beautiful, Hugh found the ingenue's conversation a little on the vapid side. He had never been particularly attracted to women who affected Candy's brand of helpless charm, and after a while, her attentions became cloying. He would much rather have been with Ryanne, enjoying her insights into the people around them, her sharp wit, and her own particular brand of seductive allure that was unintentional and unaffected.

When Ben Rosenthal, another of Hugh's partners at the agency, joined them, Hugh quickly turned Candy over to Ben and went off in search of his father. He found him in the kitchen with Judith, arguing over the arrangement of a plate of canapés, and they were having such a good time trading insults that Hugh couldn't bring himself to interrupt. He watched them for a moment and concluded that Webb MacKenna might finally have met his match in Judith Tremain—or vice versa. He wasn't sure which.

Hugh meandered back out to the bar, ordered a scotch and soda, and started mingling again. Ryanne was surrounded by a group of the movie people she'd hoped to get acquainted with, and Hugh wandered in and out of her conversational circle for the rest of the night until the party began breaking up shortly after midnight.

When Ryanne closed the door on the last guest, Hugh and Webb declared the evening a rousing success, and Ryanne collapsed against the door, exhausted but happy. "If it *was* a success, it's all thanks to the host, the assistant host, and the assistant hostess, Judith. Thank you all."

"It was our pleasure," Webb replied.

"What did you think of your first Hollywood party?" Ryanne asked him, forgetting for a moment that it was her first as well.

"A little tamer than I expected, but overall it was quite nice."

"What about you, Judith?" Hugh asked as she started toward the kitchen with a tray of glasses.

"I'm glad it's over. Now things can get back to normal—whatever that is."

Ryanne pushed away from the door. "Speaking of normal, is the house an absolute disaster area?"

"It's not too much the worse for wear," Hugh told her. "We can have it cleaned up in no time."

"No, no," Webb protested, picking up an empty hors d'oeuvre tray with one hand and a full ashtray with the other. "Judith and I will take care of this mess. You two just go out on the patio and get out of our way."

"Webb's right," Judith chimed in. "We can get this done a lot quicker without you two underfoot."

The glasses clanked as she left with the loaded tray, and Ryanne shrugged expressively. "I guess she told us."

"And *I* don't have to be told twice," Hugh replied, taking Ryanne's hand. "Come on. Let's get out of here before they change their minds."

Willingly, Ryanne let Hugh lead her out into the balmy night. Somewhere down the beach another party was still in full swing and a live band was entertaining the entire Malibu Beach colony with Glenn Miller classics. The smooth strains of "Moonlight Serenade" greeted Ryanne and Hugh as they stepped to the rail.

"Finally I've got you to myself," Hugh said fervently. "I thought for a while there I was going to have to get a crowbar to pry little Chuckie Braxton away from you."

Ryanne grimaced, thinking about the amorous associate producer she'd been fending off for weeks. "I told you the producer's nephew had the hots for me."

"And you weren't kidding. He's not the least bit subtle, is he?"

"I don't think Chuck knows the meaning of the word. He's harmless, but he's really becoming a pest. He seems to have the idea that I'm some poor, helpless invalid who needs his protection."

Hugh laughed at that. "Obviously he's not much of a judge of character. You're the least helpless woman I've ever known."

Ryanne smiled, slipped her arm around Hugh's waist, and leaned her head against his shoulder. "That's idle flattery, but I don't mind hearing you say it."

He pulled her closer. "You *aren't* helpless, Ryanne. You manage to be strong and competent, but at the same time, feminine and exciting. I certainly can't fault Chuckie's taste."

Ryanne whispered a thank-you, and turned her face up to Hugh's. He took advantage of the gesture and claimed her lips in a kiss that was as gentle and undemanding as the ocean breeze and the soft music floating around them.

"Dance with me, Ryanne," he murmured, turning her into his arms so that their bodies molded together perfectly.

"I'm not much of a dancer," she warned him, fitting her hand into his.

"Just move with the music," he advised, his voice caressingly low. "This is only an excuse to hold you close."

"You don't need an excuse for that, Hugh." Dreamily content, Ryanne snuggled her head onto his shoulder and they swayed slowly, sensuously, letting the night enfold them. When the jazz band down the beach switched to a lively version of "Little Brown Jug" Ryanne and Hugh ignored the upbeat tempo, but not the physical stirrings that brought them even closer. Hugh sought Ryanne's lips and their slow dance stopped completely. She opened to him without coaxing, and they were both lost.

He gently caressed her back with one hand while the other held her firmly against him, and their kiss quickened, deepened. Ryanne moaned softly as her hand drifted up the broad, lean expanse of his chest and came to rest at the back of his head.

Every kiss is different. The thought registered somewhere in the back of her mind, sharing space with the fever Hugh's embrace always created. His every touch, every word, every movement this past month had told Ryanne how much he wanted her, and every time he held her like this he only made her want him more. Molded against him she could feel the stirrings of his body; they matched her own. She revelled in the delightful tightening of her breasts, the delicious ache between her thighs and the sinking, swirling feeling in the pit of her stomach where she felt the evidence of Hugh's desire pressing against her.... A hunger more fierce than any Ryanne had ever imagined came over her every time Hugh held her, yet she was beginning to fear that she would never know the fulfillment of that desire.

For weeks now, he had come close, then backed off as though some invisible barrier had suddenly sprung up between them. The frustration was driving Ryanne mad; and she knew that tonight would be no different from the other times he'd held her, touched her, kissed her, then left her aching.

"The music's stopped," Hugh murmured, forcing himself to release her. He had to quit now or become completely lost in the passion Ryanne evoked. He took her hand and moved back to the deck railing, too preoccupied with controlling his own fires to notice that Ryanne was fighting an internal battle of her own.

"So it has," she commented tightly, pulling her hand away from Hugh's and crossing her arms in front of her.

"Are you cold?"

Hardly! she wanted to shout, but restrained herself and lied. "Just a little."

"Maybe we should go in, then."

"Fine." Ryanne turned toward the house, but before she could step away from him Hugh touched her arm lightly, forcing her to stop.

"Ryanne, are you all right?"

Am I all right? Of course, I'm not all right, she wanted to shout. *My heart is racing, my palms are sweating, and I want to make love with you so desperately that it hurts. How could I feel like that and be all right?* The heated words were on the tip of her tongue, but she just couldn't allow them to escape. Hugh wanted her. She was convinced of that, but apparently he had a lot more self-control then she did. Somehow she just couldn't envision embarrassing herself with a breathless, "Take me, I'm yours!" And besides, now was hardly the time or the place, here on deck with Judith and Hugh's father just inside.

Thinking back, Ryanne realized that in all the weeks they'd spent together there hadn't been an appropriate opportunity for lovemaking—since the evening they'd spent at his house, anyway. She couldn't help but wonder why. Was Hugh giving their relationship time to develop, or was he handling her with kid gloves because he thought of her as blind and vulnerable? He'd told her she was the least helpless person he knew, but did he really believe it? If Hugh was going slowly because their relationship was important to him, that was one thing; if he was afraid of taking advantage of her because she was blind—well, that was quite another.

"Ryanne?"

She turned to him and managed a smile. "I'm fine, Hugh."

"No, you're not. Something's bothering you." He took her into his arms. "Please tell me what's wrong."

All of Ryanne's senses were focused completely on Hugh, on his deep, soft voice and the way their bodies fit together. Being in his arms felt so right, how could it be wrong to tell him she wanted to make love with him? It wasn't wrong. In her heart, she knew it, but she just couldn't make herself say the words, not when there were still questions to be answered.

"I'm sorry, Hugh. I—"

"Well, Judith has kicked me out of the kitchen," Webb announced as he joined them on the deck. "Ryanne, as soon as you finish with your screenplay I want you to bring that woman down to the Gulf. We'll spend a couple of days out on the *Mary Ann* where I can boss *her* around."

With a halfhearted laugh, Ryanne stepped away from Hugh and moved to his father, grateful for his interruption. "I don't know, Webb. From what I heard tonight you seem to be holding your own with Judith. You may not need a captain's authority to get the better of her."

"She is an opinionated soul, isn't she?" Webb looked at his son. "Judith told me in no uncertain terms that it was time for us to go home so that Ryanne could get some rest."

Hugh looked indecisively at Ryanne, torn between wanting to clear the air between them and allowing her to get some rest. The look of exhaustion on her lovely face finally pushed him in the right direction. "All right, Dad. You head on out to the car and I'll join you in a minute."

Webb thanked Ryanne for the party and bade her good evening with a chaste kiss, then disappeared back into the house.

"Ryanne—" Hugh took her hands in his "—we'll finish our talk later, all right?"

"Of course." She smiled and touched his face, gently brushing his lips with her fingertips and then her lips. "Thank you for being here tonight."

"I wouldn't have wanted to be anywhere else. I'll call you sometime this week and we'll go out to dinner."

Ryanne nodded in agreement. "If Webb doesn't object, I'll see if I can get Judith to join us. We can have an old-fashioned double date."

"Oh, I don't think Dad will object at all." Arm in arm they sauntered through the house to the front door and Hugh finally, reluctantly, kissed Ryanne good-night.

Once he was gone, Ryanne tried to help with the last of the cleanup, but Judith insisted there was nothing that couldn't wait until tomorrow. Ryanne went off to her room where Aggie was sound asleep, tethered on her bed chain. She woke up as soon as her mistress entered the room and Ryanne took the dog outside one last time for the evening, then quickly changed clothes and fell into bed.

She was exhausted, almost drained, in fact, but sleep just wouldn't come. She kept thinking of Hugh and the kiss they'd shared, and she wondered how many more restless, frustrating nights she would spend alone.

CHAPTER NINE

THE HOUSE WAS dark and silent as Hugh stepped through the French doors onto the deck. Behind him his bed was a twisted, tangled mess from all his tossing and turning. He wished he could follow the example of his father, who was sound asleep in the guest room. Hugh couldn't seem to find that same peace, probably because the release he craved was down the beach, fast asleep in her own bed— alone. Even a cold, stinging shower hadn't eased Hugh's craving for Ryanne tonight, and he knew that nothing would change until he finally ended this torture and brought her to his bed.

Unbidden, the thought of Ryanne and the way she always came to life in his arms played over and over in his mind, and his body ached with frustrated desire. For a long time Hugh had treated sex casually—as a basic biological urge to be recognized and satisfied. He'd learned, though, that a quick toss in the hay with a faceless stranger was far less pleasurable than the familiarity of a partner with whom he shared something other than the passion of the moment.

That first coming together with a woman who had been courted, who recognized as he did that holding that desire at bay made the moment of completion sweeter, was always exciting. There was a sense of exploration and discovery that heightened the passion, but Hugh enjoyed equally what came later—the camaraderie, the pleasure that came from knowing what made his lover gasp with delight or writhe with ecstasy beneath him. Sexually Hugh gave the woman in his life one hundred percent of himself, using all the skill and control at his command to bring her the same degree of pleasure he derived. Emotionally, though, he'd never learned how to offer the secret parts of his mind or his heart to that woman. He cared, but never loved; not completely, without restraint.

Sensing that, his lover usually withheld that same part of herself from him. The minute either slipped over that fine line where liking turned to loving, Hugh took steps to end the relationship gently. He knew he could never reciprocate, and that to continue would be unfair and eventually painful. And since the women he dated were, for the most part, intelligent and self-respecting, they usually realized further pursuit was hopeless. Hugh could then tell himself the break-ups were "mutual." He'd lived that way for years and had never questioned the validity of his life-style.

Until now.

The warm ocean breeze caressed Hugh's face, reminding him of the way Ryanne touched it—gently, softly, like a sigh. He thought of her beauty, her courage, and her smile, and Hugh felt a desire to possess that was stronger than anything he'd ever felt before. But it wasn't just her body he wanted to lose himself in; it was her soul and her spirit, the essence of everything that made her so remarkable. He sensed that Ryanne would be a passionate lover, and the only thing that had held Hugh back, that had forced him to control his intense need to have her, was the fact that this time he wanted it all, not just Ryanne's passion and companionship, but every part of her—all the things he'd never wanted from a woman before.

He'd moved slowly with her these past few weeks, building their friendship, earning her trust, hoping that somewhere along the way she'd begin to want the same kind of relationship he wanted.

That hadn't happened. Every time Ryanne casually mentioned returning to Chicago Hugh knew that she was still taking to heart the unspoken but mutually understood rules he'd established that night he'd brought her home. Enjoy each other, but don't look for forever after. Keep it light and simple—don't start to fall in love.

He found it bitterly ironic that this time he was the one who'd broken the rules.

HUGH CALLED the following week, and Ryanne was amazed at how little persuasion it took to convince Judith to join her with the MacKenna men for an evening on the town. Hugh insisted they dress casually and they dined on delicious, gooey spare ribs at a little eatery out in the Valley. Afterward they discussed which movie to see, but with scores of choices in Hollywood, the discussion waxed into a heated argument and finally Ryanne settle the issue.

"Miniature golf?" Hugh asked skeptically.

"What's the matter, Hugh? Are you afraid you'd lose to a mere woman?" Ryanne said teasingly, barely managing to keep a straight face.

"Your being a woman has nothing to do with it," he protested. "But if the guys at the office ever heard that I got whipped by a *blind* woman I'd never hear the last of it."

Hugh's casual reference to Ryanne's blindness threw Webb, until he realized that Ryanne treated her disability as a fact and appreciated it when everyone else did the same. Since that was the case, Webb knew he had to do his best to comply.

Though Hugh hadn't said so directly, Webb could tell that his son was falling in love—probably for the first time in his life. Webb blamed himself and his ex-wife, Sherry, for their son's perpetual state of bachelorhood. Though Hugh had always had a steady girlfriend, even in his teens, Webb knew of no one who'd ever gotten under his skin. The way Sherry skipped blithely from one "true love" to the next hadn't set much of an example for Hugh, and Webb realized that his own example had been little better.

Sherry Catlow MacKenna had been a consuming obsession with Webb, and even their devastating divorce hadn't lessened his need for her. It had taken years for the pain of losing her to go away, and he hadn't had the guts to risk another heartbreak like the one Sherry had dealt him. Nowhere in Hugh's life had there ever been a model of what a marriage could be for two people who had that indefinable magic that made a lifelong commitment work. Despite his own dismal failure, Webb was enough of a romantic to believe things like that did happen, and he wanted desperately for his son to be one of the lucky few. With Ryanne Kirkland, Webb thought Hugh might just have that one in a million chance, because she was a one-in-a-million lady.

"I've got a suggestion," he chimed in. "Since Hugh is so worried about his macho image, why don't we team up. Judith and I against Ryanne and Hugh." He clapped his son on the shoulder. "That way, when you lose—and you will, my boy—you can always claim that you were just trying to spare your old man's feelings."

The taunt was as good as a gauntlet in Hugh's face, and the issue was immediately settled. They piled into the car with Judith shaking her head at the insanity of men, and fifteen minutes later they arrived at a large fantasy land of castles, moats, fountains, waterfalls and four separate eighteen-hole golf courses. The interior of the castle was taken up with a teenager's paradise of arcade machines and video games, but once they had passed through that hazardous maze they emerged into the night, and into a cool, green garden where the four courses teed off. At Webb's insistence he paid for their game, and while they waited for a free course, Hugh pulled Ryanne to one side.

"Okay, how are we going to tackle this?" he asked, handing her a putter.

She hefted the club, testing its weight. "You'll have to describe each green to me, point me in the right direction, and then give me a sound cue—tap your putter in the hole or something. Believe it or not, I used to be very good at this."

"That's great," he told her enthusiastically, "because I am the world's worst."

"Just stick wid me, kid, an' I'll make ya a star." Laughing, they joined Webb and Judith just as their turn came up on course number two.

What followed was an exercise in pure hilarity. Not only did Hugh give Ryanne the sound cues she needed in order to putt her way through the eighteen holes, but he also used every underhanded trick in the book to distract Judith and Webb when their turns came around. He stomped and coughed and clapped his hands together to keep them warm. Judith kept pointing out that the temperature was in the eighties, but that didn't deter Hugh.

He gave unsolicited advice every time Webb lined up a shot, and in general drove everyone crazy.

They laughed and argued playfully, and were generally so boisterous that Ryanne was glad she'd left Aggie at home. Disciplining her dog in the midst of all the chaos would have been nearly impossible. Also, a guide dog was only invaluable when its owner knew where she was going and what commands to issue. In this zigzagging maze Ryanne was completely lost, and Hugh was far more help to her than Aggie could have been. He was constantly at her side, giving her a feeling of unparalleled security, happiness and contentment.

With Hugh's help, she got a hole in one on the treacherous windmill hazard, but overall her scores were atrocious. Despite Hugh's attempts to even things up with his outright but good-natured cheating, he and Ryanne still lost the match by an embarrassing margin. What they lacked in skill, though, they made up for in fun, and by the time they returned home, even Judith had to admit that it had been an enjoyable evening.

The couples spent two more nights together that week, and by Sunday, when it was time for Webb to return home, Ryanne suspected that Judith was going to be very sorry to see him leave. Despite their constant bickering, a real bond seemed to have formed between them. Ryanne thought it was a shame there hadn't been more time for a little romance to develop as well. Judith had been alone for so long she deserved the attentions of someone as special as Webb MacKenna.

The day of Webb's departure Ryanne invited them over for a farewell luncheon. It took quite an effort on everyone's part not to get maudlin over the occasion.

"I'm really going to miss you, Webb," Ryanne told him as they left the dining-room table Judith and Hugh had just cleared. Webb put his arm around Ryanne and she gave him a hug. Aggie wanted in on the action and jumped up excitedly until Ryanne finally subdued her.

"I'm going to miss you too, Ryanne," Webb told her. "This has been the best vacation I've had in years. I almost hate to go, but I do have a business to run. I want you to know I was serious about that invitation I made last week. Hugh's promised to get you and Judith on that little jet of his and bring you down for a visit."

"I can't speak for Judith, but I'd love to."

Across the room Judith gave a little snort of disgust. "He'll probably get us lost in the Bermuda Triangle and we'll spend the rest of our lives floating around in limbo."

Webb moved to her. "That may be, Judith, my dear, but at least you'll be in good company."

Judith looked past Webb to his son. "I see you come by your enormous ego honestly. Your father obviously had plenty to spare."

Webb grinned. "Judith, you've got all the personality of a barbed wire fence, but I'm going to miss you just the same. Come on. I'd like to spend my last hour in Malibu on the beach. Let's go for a walk."

Judith protested that she had dishes to do, but Webb wouldn't take no for an answer, and finally they left with Aggie yapping playfully at their heels.

"Do you think they'll drown each other?" Hugh asked, taking Ryanne's hand and pulling her with him onto the sofa.

"I doubt it. Despite all their fussin' an' feudin' I think they really like each other. I certainly haven't seen Judith this happy before." Ryanne snuggled into Hugh's arms, resting her head on his shoulder.

"If that's how she acts when she's happy, I'd hate to see her when she's upset." Ryanne chuckled at that and Hugh asked, "Is Judith divorced? I've never heard a mention of her husband."

"No, she's a widow. Toby died about ten years ago. Until she came to work for me she was secretary to the circulation manager at the *Examiner*."

Hugh lifted the long strands of silky hair that cascaded to Ryanne's shoulders and pressed his lips to her throat, causing her pulse to race. "Ryanne?" he mumbled.

"What?"

"Why are we talking about Judith? We haven't had a minute alone since the party and I can think of something I'd much rather be doing."

With one hand at her waist, Hugh urged her to turn toward him, and though Ryanne complied, she couldn't bring herself to melt against him for the kiss he'd hinted at. His mention of the party brought back all the questions and frustrations she'd tried to forget, and Hugh sensed her hesitation.

"That look is back, Ryanne," he told her. "It's the same one you had last week."

Ryanne lowered her forehead to his shoulder. "I'm sorry, Hugh."

"Don't be sorry. Just tell me what's bothering you. Is it something I've said? Something I've done?"

Ryanne raised her head and gave him a rueful smile. "Actually it's more to do with something you haven't done."

With gentle fingertips, Hugh stroked her cheek lovingly. "I can't fix it if I don't know what's broken."

"I know." Sighing, Ryanne slipped out of his arms. "It's just very difficult to talk about."

"Please try." He frowned, steeling himself for whatever was to come. He tried not to think the worst—that she was going to tell him she didn't want to be with him any longer—but a painful twisting in his gut betrayed that effort.

Concerned with her own confusing emotions, Ryanne didn't hear the strain in Hugh's voice. "In a way, it's very silly—not to mention embarrassing." She stood and moved across the room hoping that a little distance would make it easier. "Hugh, last week you told me I was one of the least helpless people you'd ever known. You even said something about my being strong and competent—"

"I said those things because I believe they're true."

"Do you, Hugh? Really?"

"Yes," he answered without hesitation, growing more confused by the minute.

Ryanne sighed again. "All right, then, answer this. I'm sure you don't keep a record or have a standard routine, but . . . think back to the women you've dated in the past few years—back to the beginning of your relationships with them."

Hugh remembered the direction his thoughts had taken the previous week, when he'd been alone on his deck. Had Ryanne sensed that he was starting to care for her too much? Was she upset because she thought he was becoming too serious? He knew she considered their relationship just a temporary thing, but he couldn't allow himself to believe she was ready to end it now. "Why would you want me to think about other women, Ryanne?"

"Because I want to know how long you waited . . . that is, when you . . . If you waited. . . . I mean—"

Hugh felt the tension drain out of his body. She wasn't trying to say goodbye. "Does that very attractive blush on your cheeks mean you're trying to find a polite way to ask me how long it usually takes me to get a woman into my bed?"

"I wouldn't have put it quite that way, but yes. That's what I want to know. Hugh, we've known each other for almost two months now, and we've been dating for well over half that time. I'm not trying to push you, believe me, I'm not. I don't want you to think that ... well ..." She floundered again and Hugh refused to bail her out this time.

"Yes?"

Ryanne pursed her lips to hold back an embarrassed smile. "You're really enjoying this, aren't you? God, I feel like an idiot!"

Laughing, more out of relief than amusement, Hugh rose and crossed to her, but Ryanne backed away, holding up one hand to keep him from coming closer. "No. It's not funny, Hugh. I don't care about the other women you've been with, or how long it took you to get them into your bed. What I do care about is us and your attitude toward me."

Hugh could see that she was serious and upset. His smile vanished. "Ryanne, you have to know that I want you."

"Of course I know it, Hugh. I haven't had a wealth of experience in this department, but I'm not some naive Victorian virgin. Without actually saying so you tell me in a hundred little ways every time we're together that you find me desirable. And you can't possibly know how happy that makes me. But you're holding back, and I don't know why. You have to know that I want you, too. You take me in your arms, but you allow me to get only so close and then you pull away, as though I'm some fragile, vulnerable little thing who might faint at the first sign of real passion.

"You're handling me with kid gloves, Hugh," she continued frankly. "And I'm afraid you're pulling away from me because you think you'll be taking advantage of a poor, helpless blind girl who can't take care of herself. If I'm wrong, then I'm sorry. Heaven knows I don't want to pressure you into an intimate relationship if you're not ready to take that step, but I can't bear the thought of being treated like an invalid."

"Oh, Ryanne..." Deep in thought, he stepped away from her, examining the reasons he'd treated her with such extraoidinary care. It wasn't her blindness, he was certain of that. He didn't think of her in terms like helpless or frail, or even handicapped, because she wasn't. Again he recalled everything he'd thought about that night on his deck. She *was* special—not because of her blindness, though. She was special because she'd touched Hugh in a way he'd never been touched before. He'd taken their relationship slowly partly out of a need to guard his own heart. Hugh had never been on the short end of a one-sided love affair before, and he had been hoping beyond hope that Ryanne's feelings would eventually match his.

As much as he wanted to, he couldn't allow himself to believe that her willingness to make love with him was the sign he'd been looking for. All he knew for sure was that it was time to stop pulling away.

Ryanne stood waiting for him to respond, growing more agitated with each second that passed. Had she said too much? Had she been too forward? Had speaking out so boldly cost her Hugh's respect? He was quiet for so long that Ryanne lost track of where he had moved to and she suddenly felt almost as vulnerable as the poor little blind girl she was trying to convince him she wasn't.

"Hugh? Are you still there?" she asked finally, unable to bear the silence a moment longer.

"I'm right here, Ryanne. I . . . was just trying to figure out whether or not you were right."

"Was I?"

"No. If I've been treating you differently or specially, it's because you are special to me. I look at you, think about you, hear your voice, or see your smile, and I want you so badly sometimes that it hurts. But you're right, I have been pulling back from that...desire. I suppose it's because I wanted us to be friends before we became lovers."

"I wanted that as well, Hugh," she told him softly. "And we are friends, I think. I can't believe how important you've become to me in these past weeks. But I'll be completely finished with my screenplay in a month or two and it will be time for me to leave. I don't want to rush into anything, but I don't want to go back to Chicago knowing that I wasted a lot of precious time, either. I want us to be friends *and* lovers, Hugh," she finished, her voice barely stronger than a whisper.

She heard Hugh's footfall on the plush carpet, but when he neared she needed no sound cue to judge his location. She could feel his presence, his warmth, that incredible electricity he created, and she raised her arms to him.

Wordlessly Hugh embraced her and buried his face in her luxuriant mane. Though he hated himself for it, for just a moment he was grateful she was blind so that she couldn't see the haunted expression in his eyes. He'd been only seconds away from telling her he was falling in love, but he couldn't do that now. Ryanne obviously wasn't ready to hear that yet or she wouldn't be talking about returning to Chicago.

Until Ryanne, all of Hugh's relationships had been finite. In her mind, this one was, too. Hugh wondered what it would take to convince her otherwise, and he decided that the first step toward proving to her that she was his would be taken tonight.

"I'll pick you up about eight," he promised.

CHAPTER TEN

AFTER HUGH and Webb left for the airport, the full impact of what she'd said to Hugh hit Ryanne like a ton of bricks. She'd forced the issue and cleared the air, but she'd also committed herself to making love with Hugh—tonight. She didn't regret her decision, exactly, but she didn't feel particularly comfortable with it, either. In fact, she was a nervous wreck.

She wanted Hugh, wanted to make love with him desperately, but as the afternoon crept by and she tried to keep busy and remain calm, everything began to seem planned, calculated. Tonight she would be in Hugh's arms—in Hugh's bed—for the first time, and afterward she wouldn't be able to tell herself that it had been an impulsive act or that she'd been swept away by the passion of the moment.

Feeling like a coward, Ryanne wondered if Hugh would forgive her if she backed out. He probably would, she decided. He was too kind and understanding to sling recriminations at her, but would she be able to forgive herself? The bottom line was that she'd meant everything she'd said to Hugh about desiring him and not wanting to go back to Chicago knowing that she'd wasted precious time.

The thought of leaving Los Angeles created a by-now-familiar pit in Ryanne's stomach, but she refused to think about the eventuality or the feeling it gave her. Neither she nor Hugh believed in long-term relationships, and it was entirely possible that their romance wouldn't even last through the months it took her to finish her screenplay. The mutual attraction could burn out at any time and that would be the end of it. Unfortunately that reasoning offered little more comfort. So instead of dwelling on the future or the past, she focused on the moment—on tonight—and tried to remain calm.

There were some practical arrangements that had to be worked out, and Ryanne dreaded the confrontation that would arise when Judith discovered she was planning to spend the night at Hugh's. Ryanne knew that she had to tell the older woman. It would be unfair to stay out all night without warning her; she would worry. And there was also the problem of what to do with Aggie. She couldn't let the dog wander around loose in Hugh's house all night, and it just wasn't practical to have the inquisitive, excitable animal tethered beside Hugh's bed while they were...occupying it. Aggie would have to stay home, and Judith would have to take care of the dog's needs tonight and tomorrow morning.

There was also another consideration, a very important reason Judith had to know what was going on, and Ryanne dreaded the embarrassment that it would cause both of them. It couldn't be avoided, though, and Ryanne plucked up her courage and went into the living room where Judith was watching an old James Cagney film.

"Judith, may I talk to you for a minute?" Ryanne asked.

"Sure." She turned off the set with the remote control. "All that rat-a-tat-tat stuff was giving me a headache, anyway. What's up?"

Ryanne moved to one of the chairs flanking the sofa and perched on its arm. She had to clear the nervous lump from her throat before she could begin. "Hugh is picking me up later this evening, and I don't think I'll be taking Aggie with us."

Something in Ryanne's tone alerted Judith to her friend's discomfort and she refrained from making her customary wisecrack about the dog. "Fine. If you'll feed her before you leave, I'll take her out and put her on the bed chain before I turn in."

"Thank you, Judith, but...you may also need to take her out in the morning."

"All right," she replied without missing a beat. "Should I feed her, too?"

Ryanne frowned in confusion. "What do you mean, 'All right'? Don't I get a lecture? A warning? A sigh of disapproval? Something? Just 'All right'? Judith, I'm spending the night with Hugh."

"And that's supposed to surprise me?" Judith chuckled. "Honey, the only thing that surprises me is that you've waited this long."

"You approve?" Ryanne asked, incredulous.

"It's not my job as your secretary or my place as your friend to approve or disapprove, Ryanne."

"But that never stopped you from expressing an opinion on any topic before."

"You're a big girl now, and Hugh MacKenna is a very nice man. He cares about you—any fool can see that. In the beginning I was afraid he was on some sort of macho ego trip—that being with you made him feel like the manly protector, but he's not like that. And if you're ready to make the commitment of bringing sex into your relationship, then I know you've thought it through, weighed all the pros and cons, and have decided that being with him is what's right for you." Judith reached out from the corner of the sofa and placed her hand on one of Ryanne's. "You're a pretty sharp cookie, Ryanne. I know you're not going to get in over your head."

Ryanne wondered just how true that was, but she didn't comment on it. Instead she smiled in relief. "Thank you, Judith. I thought you'd be disapproving, or at the very least, a little surprised at me."

"Surprised? How could I possibly be surprised after you typed 'contraceptive sponges' on your shopping list last week? You stuck it in there very casually between 'cotton balls' and 'spray deodorant,' but I noticed it, believe me."

Ryanne laughed, covering her face with both hands. "I suppose that would have been a clue. I didn't realize you'd already filled that list."

"I guess that means you didn't find them, then. I put a braille label on the box and set it in your toiletry basket on the vanity."

"That was very thoughtful of you. Thanks. But no, I didn't run across it. Actually... that was the other thing I needed to discuss with you. You see, years ago I was on the pill for a while, but my gynecologist had me stop, and well... I haven't had any reason... I mean, I've never used these new sponge things before, and... well..."

"You need me to read the instructions to you."

Ryanne shook her head in amazement. "Judith, why is it that you're handling this so well and I'm tripping over my tongue like an embarrassed idiot? For crying out loud, you're twenty-five years older than I am! We're from two completely different generations. You're the one who should be embarrassed about discussing contraceptives, not me."

Judith considered that for a moment. "Well, I'm not the one who's going to be needing them tonight."

Ryanne felt her blush deepen. "You have a point. Come on, let's get this over with." She stood and started down the hall with Judith right behind her.

Together they took care of the practical issue of birth control, and Ryanne was once again left at loose ends with nothing to do but worry about what was going to happen that evening. Would she please Hugh, or would he think she was clumsy and inexperienced? Sex had never played much of a role in her life. She'd certainly never met anyone who affected her the way Hugh did, who made her want to get as close as two people could possibly get.

That intense physical longing scared Ryanne. She kept trying to convince herself it didn't mean she was falling in love; but she knew that she was—that she had. Just a little, at least. Hugh was so wonderful it would have been impossible to do otherwise, and because he was only going to be hers for a short time, Ryanne wanted to savor every aspect of their relationship. Forty years from now, when she was a spunky, gray-haired old maid, she'd be able to reflect back on the wonderful, heady summer when she'd lost her heart to a handsome private eye. Of course, she wouldn't have grandchildren to tell the story to, but she'd have a heart full of wonderful memories, just the same.

The image of the future Ryanne had projected made her smile, but it didn't do a lot to alleviate her mounting fears about the coming evening. And she found herself wondering how on earth she was going to keep Hugh from sensing that she was, in fact, falling in love with him. As the day crept by, she tried to imagine what would happen and how, but that didn't help much. When Hugh picked her up, she asked herself, would they both try to act nonchalant and pretend that this date was as casual as their others had been? Would he make a joke, treat it lightly, and try to put her at ease? When they reached his home would he take her into his arms and whisk her off to bed, or would they sit and try to make small talk? She had no idea.

She tried to imagine Hugh's lovemaking, but that was certainly nothing new. For weeks she'd thought about little else. It was different now, though, because it was about to become a reality. After tonight she wouldn't have to fantasize about what his flesh would feel like next to hers or how his mouth would feel against her breasts. After tonight she would have memories of Hugh, not dreams, and it was this that finally calmed her somewhat.

She wasn't going to the arms of a stranger tonight; she was going to Hugh. Whether her lovemaking was awkward or naive, Hugh would never judge her and find her lacking. He would be patient and kind, gentle and loving. If she told him she was frightened, he would kiss away her fears and replace her timidity with the passion that only he had been able to evoke in her. Above all, he would never hurt her. She knew that as surely as she knew that the sun would rise tomorrow morning, and that she wouldn't be able to see the dawning.

Calmer, filled with a sense of anticipation rather than fear, Ryanne finished getting ready for the evening. She put on a blouse of dark burgundy silk with short, puffed sleeves and tucked the tail into a pair of lightweight black pleated trousers. Her bare feet went into a pair of burgundy sandals and she spent a considerable amount of time taming her hair, brushing it and smoothing out the unruly curls with a curling iron until it fell in soft layers around her face and onto her shoulders.

"Ryanne?"

Ryanne stepped away from the vanity and moved into the bedroom. "Yes, Judith?"

"Hugh's here."

Ryanne's mouth went dry and the moisture rematerialized on her palms. "Oh. Good. I didn't hear the doorbell."

"That's because he came in the back way."

"Up the beach?" she asked, incredulous.

"Yep. And I think he expects to return the same way."

Ryanne laughed and leaned against the door frame. "In that case, I won't be needing these, will I?" She slipped off her shoes and threw them into the huge canvas purse she'd planned to carry. She gave Judith a few last minute, unnecessary instructions about Aggie, said a quick goodbye to the dog, then headed down the hall to meet Hugh.

He greeted her affectionately, taking her into his arms. "You look wonderful."

Ryanne slipped her arms around Hugh's waist and all her earlier fears vanished. This was where she wanted to be. "Thank you. You *feel* wonderful." She hugged him a little tighter and placed her cheek against his throat. "You smell pretty good, too."

Hugh chuckled. "That's my new after-shave cologne. The clerk who sold it to me promised it would make me irresistible."

"He was right," Ryanne told him, tilting her face up toward his.

"Why would you assume it was a 'he'?"

She smiled mischievously. "It had to be. A woman would have known immediately that you don't need any enhancement to make you irresistible."

"Tonight, my darling, flattery will get you anywhere," he murmured, lowering his lips to Ryanne's for a light, teasing kiss. The slight contact was too much of a temptation, and the kiss quickly turned into something more. Judith came down the hall, coughing melodramatically to announce her imminent arrival, and they reluctantly separated. As she passed them she mumbled something about wanting a little privacy, and Hugh took the hint.

"I understand we're on foot tonight," Ryanne said, taking hold of Hugh's hand.

"Uh-huh. I thought you might enjoy a quiet walk up the beach."

"It sounds lovely." She shrugged. "I'm ready when you are."

"What about Aggie?"

"I thought I'd let my conscience be my guide tonight," she told him softly and Hugh groaned at the bad pun.

"In that case, may I offer you my arm, m'dear?"

"Oh, thank you." They bade Judith good-night, received a halfhearted grunt in response, then slipped out onto the deck and down to the beach.

"Judith seemed awfully quiet tonight," Hugh commented as they began their leisurely hike.

"Uh, well...I guess that's because I put her in a rather awkward position when I told her I was planning to spend the night with you."

Hugh moaned. "I imagine that went over like a lead balloon."

Ryanne had one hand tucked in the crook of his arm and she placed the other one there as well. "Actually she was wonderful about the whole thing."

Hugh's pace slowed as he looked down at her, his voice filled with disbelief. "You're kidding? I'm amazed she didn't lock you in a closet and throw away the key."

Ryanne chuckled. "That's sort of what I was expecting, too, but she wasn't surprised at all."

"She did know you were talking about me, right?"

"Of course! She even said some very nice things about you."

Hugh stopped dead still. "Ryanne, I think we'd better go back," he told her seriously. "Something is obviously wrong. A mad scientist has kidnapped the real Judith and replaced her with a reprogrammed clone. My God, I've heard stories about this kind of thing, but I never thought it could actually happen to someone I know personally."

Ryanne bit her lower lip, trying to keep a straight face. "Do you think we should try to get the real Judith back?"

"Oh, definitely. This is Hollywood—it's required. Judith must be saved!" he cried, adopting what Ryanne could only imagine was an absurdly heroic pose.

"But Hugh . . . *this* Judith likes you," she reminded him.

"Oh. I see your point," he answered thoughtfully, then started up the beach again. "Obviously the mad scientist is not an evil genius, but rather a great humanitarian bent on doing good deeds to benefit mankind."

"You mean if he thinks you're all right, he can't be all bad."

"Exactly. He may be insane, but he's got good taste."

Ryanne finally gave in to her laughter and wondered why she'd foolishly wasted time worrying. Being with Hugh was as easy as breathing.

They walked slowly, talking or sharing companionable silences that neither felt compelled to fill. The sun was low on the horizon and the serious sunbathers had retired for the day, so they encountered very few people. Occasionally an evening jogger thumped past them, and where the houses sat close to the water, Ryanne could hear music or the intermittent sounds of television. For the most part, though, it was idyllically peaceful, as though she and Hugh were the only two people in the universe.

They left Malibu Colony behind and crossed a short stretch of public beach. Finally the shoreline began to curve outward, and the terrain turned rocky. Hugh stopped, looking down at Ryanne's bare feet.

Realizing the problem, Ryanne starting digging into her purse. "Let me slip my sandals on."

"I've got a better idea." Without ceremony he lifted her into his arms and started up the rock incline that led to his house.

"Hugh! You can't do that!"

"I hate to argue with you, Ryanne, but I think I just did."

"But you'll hurt yourself."

"Humor me, please. I don't get to do my Rhett Butler impersonation very often. Speaking of which, did I ever tell you that I bear a striking resemblance to Clark Gable?"

"Oh, really?" Ryanne asked skeptically, lacing her arms around Hugh's neck. "I thought you looked like Robert Redford."

"Him, too."

"My, my, that's quite a potent combination," she observed, relaxing so that she could enjoy the ride. "Robert Redford *and* Clark Gable."

"And don't forget Donald Duck," he reminded her.

Laughing, Ryanne let her head fall to his shoulder. "I don't know, Hugh, you may be more than I can handle. Why is it that I haven't had to beat a hundred other women off you with a stick to keep you to myself?" she asked just as they reached the deck.

Hugh lowered her onto solid ground but refused to release her. Instead he pulled her close, molding the length of their bodies together. When he spoke, all traces of playfulness left his voice. "That's because I haven't even looked in another woman's direction since the day I met you."

Ryanne felt a flush of heat everywhere their bodies touched, and she could hardly draw a breath to tell him, "Then I'm a very lucky lady."

"Luck has nothing to do with it, Ryanne," Hugh whispered, lowering his head to hers. Eagerly he plied her lips, tracing the bowed upper curve with his tongue until Ryanne shivered involuntarily. She opened to him but drew back her head when he would have deepened the kiss. Instead she met his tongue with her own and mimicked his movement, painting his mouth with delicate strokes until that same shiver of sensation she'd felt rippled through Hugh as well. Only then did she let her head fall back, inviting him to plunder at his leisure.

Ryanne's gesture of surrender inflamed him almost as much as her obvious desire to reciprocate every pleasure he gave her. He pulled her against him tighter, one hand molded to her hips, the other at her back, sealing their bodies together. He plunged deep into her mouth, tasting and teasing, coaxing her tentative tongue to match the fervor of his own. A piercing shaft of heat flooded his loins, and without thinking, he clasped her hips and shifted her upward until she cradled the hardening ridge of his manhood.

Ryanne moaned but the sound was lost in Hugh's kiss. She gripped his shoulders and ran her hands fervently down his back. Then she shifted, arching into him as her own fires ignited and began scorching her with the intensity of her longing. The knowledge that tonight Hugh would finally quench the fire, that she would not go to sleep alone and aching made Ryanne bolder than she'd ever dared dream she could be. Her hands mimicked Hugh's, falling to his hips, letting him know that her heat matched his own.

It was Hugh who moaned this time. The rumble started deep in his chest and rose until it meshed and blended with Ryanne's. Weeks of holding back, of denying himself this pleasure brought Hugh to the brink of his control, and finally, with a wrenching gasp, he tore his mouth away from hers. His chest heaving, brushing against the hardened peaks of Ryanne's breasts, he tried to think rationally, but the effort was nearly in vain.

"This wasn't what I'd planned, Ryanne," he told her brokenly, his lips catching hers between words.

In answer, she arched, seeking the fullness of his mouth, and they were both lost. With a growl of impatience, Hugh lifted her into his arms again and carried her swiftly into the house. In the huge, sunken living room a low, square coffee table had been laid out with two place settings, waiting only for the candles to be lit and the food to be brought in from the warming oven in the kitchen. The intimate dinner, the soft music and the wine were all forgotten. Instead Hugh moved swiftly up the steps to the hall and into his bedroom.

Trying to conquer her uneven breathing, Ryanne buried her face in Hugh's throat, her lips testing the corded sinew. She felt his own ragged breathing—which she knew had nothing to do with carrying her—and when he finally let her feet slide to the floor she brought her hands to his chest and felt for the buttons of his shirt that were keeping her from touching him the way she needed desperately to touch him—to see him.

The first few buttons fell away quickly and Ryanne felt a dusting of hair against the back of her hand. Eagerly she spread the shirt apart and let her hands trace the ridge of muscle and bone across his chest. The contrast in textures—the hardness of muscle, the heat of his skin, the softness of that fine mat of hair—made Ryanne tremble. With a kind of reverence, she explored the beautiful symmetry of his body, and Hugh ground his teeth together, praying for the control he would need to bring Ryanne the same pleasure she was giving him. He tugged at her silk blouse, pulling it out of her trousers so that he could feel her flesh against his hands. Her skin was warm and as soft as the silk of her shirt, but that contact wasn't nearly enough. Impatiently his hands moved to the buttons down the front, but Ryanne suddenly pulled away, grabbing his wrists gently as she raised her face to his.

"Hugh...has the sun set?" she asked, her voice raspy and breathless.

"The sun?" He glanced out the French doors at the glow on the horizon that painted the room a faint amber. "Almost."

"Can you close the light out with a curtain?"

Hugh pulled back and studied her face. Was she afraid someone might be watching them? he wondered. There was nothing beyond the doors to the deck but miles of ocean, but if it would ease Ryanne's mind he didn't mind closing the drapes. Reluctantly releasing her, he crossed the room and shut out the fading sunset, then returned to her. He reached for the switch of his bedside lamp, but Ryanne sensed his intent and reached for him, urging him toward her so that she could gently cup his face in her hands. Her thumbs traced his full lips and her voice trembled with barely contained emotion when she whispered, "No light, Hugh, please. Just for tonight, just this once . . . let us be equal. Share the dark with me."

"Oh, love," Hugh moaned, dragging her into his arms, fighting back the tears that suddenly burned behind his eyes. He held her close, fiercely, as though he'd never let go, and then finally, he released her.

He moved away and Ryanne choked back a sob, hating herself for having brought them back to reality. She followed his movements and when she heard the muted click of a door being closed her despair turned to a swell of love so strong it brought tears to her eyes. Another door closed, another curtain slid shut. Hugh was blocking out every trace of light from the room, voluntarily entering her world—not a world of shadows, but a world of blackness.

When he came to her again, Ryanne went into his arms knowing that her heart had already passed the point of no return.

CHAPTER ELEVEN

NORMALLY RYANNE'S PERCEPTION of time was excellent, but wrapped in Hugh's arms, her back pressed snugly against his chest, she had no idea how late it had grown. All sense of time and place had been suspended while they had made love, and now Ryanne was content to float. Hugh's deep, even breathing was as comforting as his arm, which was encircling her and keeping her close to him. His hand lightly cupped her breast as though to claim possession, and Ryanne smiled at the vague, restless movement that had his thumb gently caressing the still-hardened crest. Even in his sleep, he had the power to arouse her.

Ryanne blushed at the memory of how their gentle embrace had blossomed into a passionate fire that had threatened to consume them both. Sharing the darkness, they had undressed each other slowly, exploring and savoring. Ryanne had never experienced such tenderness, and their first joining had been a long, slow, achingly beautiful journey into a maelstrom of sensation that had left her feeling as though she'd flown too close to the sun.

Hugh's arm tightened and he moaned softly. The sound rumbled deep in his throat and Ryanne knew he had awakened even before he buried his lips in her hair. He turned her in his arms and brushed her hair away from her throat, clearing a trail for a leisurely foray across her bare shoulder, up her neck and onto her cheek until he finally found her lips. Ryanne opened to him, welcoming the lazy kiss.

"Are you all right?" he asked, nibbling his way back down her throat.

Ryanne stretched languidly. "Define 'All right.'"

Hugh chuckled as he shifted lower, making an unhurried descent toward her breasts. "Let's see... Actually it means several things. Like, are you comfortable?"

His words were muffled as he applied teasing pressure on her already overheated flesh, and Ryanne had to concentrate in order to answer. "How can I be comfortable when you're doing...that..." She sighed with pleasure when his lips finally closed over the swollen crest of one breast and created a delicious combination of friction and suction. "Any other...silly questions?" she managed to gasp.

"Well, are you at least...content?" he asked, his own breathing growing uneven. He shifted her like a rag doll so that he could give equal torment to her other breast.

"Not for long." She moaned, reveling in the heat that once again began coursing through her, settling into a magnificent ache between her thighs.

"How about happy?" he suggested.

"Deliriously."

"Sated?"

A chuckle found its way to the surface. "I was until you woke up."

Hugh stopped what he was doing and raised himself, wanting to see Ryanne's face and feeling guilty for desiring something he knew she could never experience. When he spoke again, his voice was soft and serious. "Are you disappointed?"

"Oh, Hugh," Ryanne said, sighing. She reached out, found his shoulder and let her hand trail lightly up to his face. "No one else has ever made me feel the way you do."

And no one else ever will, he told himself fiercely, fighting to keep from saying the words aloud. He had made the rules and he had to play by them—for the time being, at least. He would go slowly with Ryanne, winning her love a little at a time, if necessary, but he knew he was never going to let her go. "I'm glad," he said simply, turning his head so that he could kiss the palm of her hand.

Ryanne turned away and pressed her back against him so that they were lying the way they had been earlier, and Hugh held her close, losing himself in the sweet smelling silk of her hair. Wordlessly he began arousing her again, running his hands down her side, along her flanks, lightly brushing the soft curls of hair at the juncture of her thighs. His fingers ventured further, stroking her intimately and Ryanne arched as a shaft of pleasure pierced her. She groaned and tried to turn to him, desperate to touch Hugh and share the gift he was giving her, but he held her fast until she could think of nothing but the wave after wave of intense heat that rocked her.

Her movements against Hugh and the hoarse sounds of pleasure that whispered in her throat ignited his own fires. He thrust his hips against her thigh and pressed fevered kisses on her back and shoulders, nipping at the sensitized flesh, then soothing it with his tongue. She cried out, begging him to come to her, to take her completely, but he stopped suddenly, leaving her aching and bereft.

Ryanne froze as Hugh's hands moved to the shoulder he'd been exploring so thoroughly with his mouth, and

her passion died a withering death. Hugh uttered a muffled curse and leaned away from her, switching on the
bedside lamp. She bit down on her lower lip, already
swollen from Hugh's kisses, and waited.

Blinking against the brightness of the light, Hugh
turned back to Ryanne. Unconsciously she had tightened as though shielding herself and he gently reached
out to brush away the hair that had fallen down her back,
obscuring the place he'd been kissing. The movement re-
vealed the puckered remains of a wide, angry scar on her
otherwise perfect body. He saw the line of a surgical incision, but at its center was the unmistakable proof that
the cause of this injury had been no accident.

Hugh had seen scars like this before, but never on a
woman—never on a woman he wanted to love, cherish
and protect. A murderous fury, more potent than anything he'd ever experienced swept through him. Trembling with rage, he cursed viciously and forced Ryanne to
turn to him. Again he brushed away her hair and found
the entry point of the bullet that had ripped into her
body, shattered her shoulder, and exploded out of her
back.

Ryanne fought back tears as she listened to Hugh's
harsh, ragged breathing. He touched her shoulder lightly,
then hurled himself off the bed and began pacing furiously.

He cursed and Ryanne held her breath until he stopped
at the foot of the bed and spoke to her in a cold, flat voice
she never would have recognized as his. "What's his
name, Ryanne?"

"What?" Confused, Ryanne sat up, crossing one arm
over her body, searching with the other hand for something to cover herself with. She found the sheet and

clutched it to her, unconsciously pressing her fist against the scar that had obviously repulsed him.

"I said I want to know his name," Hugh repeated coldly. "I want to know the name of the bastard who shot you!" His voice was as crisp and low as the deadly report of a rifle. He had known all along about the murder Ryanne had witnessed five years ago—in fact, he knew far more than Ryanne suspected he did. But he hadn't known about this. Hugh had assumed that in trying to escape from the murderer she had simply fallen off the warehouse ledge; but this . . . this *defilement* was something he hadn't even imagined.

"Why do you want to know his name?" Ryanne asked softly.

"Because I want him dead! I want the bastard who did this to you to pay, damn it!" Hugh whirled away, stopping his angry tirade. Useless threats of violence weren't going to help Ryanne or take away the horror she'd suffered. But right now, the threats didn't feel useless to Hugh. The full extent of the nightmare Ryanne had lived through had just now hit him in a way that hearing or reading about it never had. Until this moment her blindness and the act of brutality that had caused it had been nothing but an abstraction to him. Now it was real.

Reason slowly seeped back into Hugh's mind and he became aware of Ryanne cowered on the bed, shielding herself from his anger. "I'm sorry, love. I'm sorry."

He moved to her, gathering her into his arms, but Ryanne couldn't melt into his embrace. It touched something deep inside her to know that what she had suffered could affect him so deeply, and yet the very intensity of his emotions had frightened her. For a moment she had shared this room with a stranger, someone cold and hard, someone so unlike the Hugh she knew that it was incomprehensible to her that they could be the same man. The steely passion in his voice told her his threats had not been idle and she realized that the kind, gentle man who had filled her life so completely was capable of killing without a second thought.

Hugh sensed her withdrawal and released her. "We need to talk about it, Ryanne," he told her quietly. "I hadn't known you'd been shot."

"Does it make such a difference?"

"Yes!"

"Why? The bullet didn't kill me. It didn't cause my blindness."

"Yes, it did," he insisted. "The impact of that bullet is what knocked you over the ledge of that warehouse, isn't it? *Isn't it?*"

"So what?" she demanded.

"Oh, Ryanne..." Unable to bear the distance between them, both emotionally and physically, Hugh pulled her into his arms again. He settled back against the headboard with Ryanne's head resting on his chest. "I'm sorry. I don't know how to explain what seeing that scar, what realizing you'd been shot, did to me."

"Try. Please," she insisted softly. She wanted the old Hugh back, not the hardened stranger he'd become for a moment.

Hugh buried his face in her hair. "I've seen violence, Ryanne. In Vietnam you couldn't escape it, so you detached yourself from it in order to survive. I see violence in my work, too, sometimes. But this—" he caressed her shoulder "—this shouldn't have happened to *you*. This kind of...ugliness should never have been allowed to touch you."

"But it did, Hugh. And I survived," she told him softly.

"I know. I guess until now all I've been seeing is the way you live with the aftermath of what happened in that warehouse. I've never let myself imagine what you must have suffered. The pain..." Gently, almost reverently, he traced the surgical incision. "It shattered your shoulder, didn't it?"

"It took some reconstruction, yes," she answered, trying not to remember the hours of excruciatingly painful therapy she'd undergone to regain the use of her arm.

"The blindness, the plastic surgery on your face, this..." He kissed the scar tenderly and Ryanne's eyes filled with tears. "I can't bear the thought of the torment you must have gone through."

Ryanne raised her face to his. "I don't want to think about the past, Hugh. Please..." She found his lips and together they focused completely on the present.

RYANNE AWOKE ABRUPTLY, startled from her deep sleep by a noise she didn't recognize. The room seemed strange to her as well, but it wasn't until she tried to move and felt the stiffness that pervaded every muscle in her body that she realized it wasn't *her* room, it was Hugh's.

The memory of the hours they had spent locked in each other's arms brought a flood of heat to Ryanne's cheeks. She had said things last night, done things that she'd never imagined herself capable of. At the time they had seemed right and natural; facing Hugh in the light of morning was a different story altogether. And, too, Ryanne had to wonder which Hugh would greet her this morning: the gentle, kind one, or the other Hugh she'd been introduced to last night—the one with the voice as cold as steel. It frightened her a little to realize she'd made love with both men. After Hugh had seen her ugly scar and learned the whole story of her brush with death, his lovemaking had become fierce, demanding, and almost overpowering in its intensity.

Instinctively she knew she was alone in the big bed, but she reached out to make certain. As she'd suspected, Hugh was gone. In a way, she was glad, because his absence gave her a chance to compose herself, and yet it also posed a distinct problem. Last night Hugh had taken her clothes off slowly, savoring the removal of each layer, but Ryanne had no idea what had become of it all. Was it scattered around on the floor? Had he tossed the lot into a chair last night, or hung everything in a closet when he got up this morning? Was there even a chair in the room, for that matter? Ryanne had absolutely no concept of what the bedroom was like.

The noise that had awakened her started again and she recognized it as a blender, or possibly an electric mixer. Evidently Hugh was making breakfast for them. Moving toward the sound, Ryanne scooted off the left side of the bed, wrapping the sheet around her. Carefully she reached for the nightstand, found her glasses, then with one arm bent in front of her and the other clutching the sheet, she moved slowly toward the sound.

The blender stopped abruptly, but she kept moving slowly in the same direction, listening to the walls now that the door was no longer helping her. The sheet, too voluminous and unstable to ever catch on as a fashion trend, slipped, causing Ryanne to stumble. She righted herself without crashing into anything, but by that time she had lost her bearings completely. Moving forward gingerly, her shin finally came in contact with something solid and she realized that there was a chair in the room, after all. And there were clothes on it, as well. Dropping the sheet, she investigated and found a shirt. The one Hugh had discarded last night, she guessed. Since her own clothes were nowhere within reach, she slipped into it, welcoming the masculine scent that clung to the soft cotton.

She started off again in search of the door, but found a wall first and moved along it past a louvered closet door and finally came to an opening. She stepped through and knew instantly from the acoustics and the lack of carpeting that she had found a bathroom. Though it was large, she located everything with relative ease, availed herself of the facilities, and splashed cold water on her face to take away the remnants of sleep that still clung to her.

Retracing her footsteps, she made it back to the bedroom and finally found the hall that led to the enormous sunken living room. She could feel the difference in air currents immediately when she stepped through the arched opening, but from there she dared go no further. She could hear Hugh in the kitchen now, but following the noise he was making would be a big mistake. If her mental image of the room was correct, the stairs down to the living room were somewhere in front of her, but if she tried to go down, cross the obstacle course of sofas, chairs, tables and lamps, then go back up, she would probably get totally lost—and break something in the process. Going around the squared-off horseshoe-shaped room was equally implausible, since she had no idea how far it extended toward the entryway to her left.

The thought of calling out to Hugh for assistance was humiliating, but she obviously had no choice.

"Hugh?" The blender started again just as she spoke, drowning out her voice, and she waited. Impatient with her own helplessness, she took a step to the right and unexpectedly came into contact with a tall table. An object—something that sounded ceramic and breakable—

tottered back and forth from the impact and she reached for it instinctively. Her arm connected unfavorably with the shade of a tottering lamp and it crashed to the parquet floor just as Hugh's blender stopped.

"Damn!" Ryanne swore, but resisted the impulse to bend and inspect the damage she'd done. Glass had shattered everywhere and she was barefooted. She waited, furious with herself, as Hugh charged out of the kitchen.

"Ryanne? Are you all right?" He bounded down the stairs and across the room. A tall bank of plants at the edge of the sunken room obscured his view temporarily, and when he reached the landing, he froze. "Don't move, sweetheart. There's glass everywhere."

"I know. I'm so sorry. I'm such a klutz!"

"It was just an accident, Ryanne."

"But it was a *stupid* accident!" she snapped back. Glass crunched as Hugh moved toward her. "Be careful!"

"Don't worry. I'm not *that* chivalrous. I've got on tennis shoes. Are you hurt anywhere?"

"No. Only my pride."

"It'll heal," he assured her, sweeping her into his arms and carrying her toward the kitchen. His gallant gesture startled Ryanne and she threw her arms around his neck, discovering that though he might have had shoes on, a shirt was conspicuously absent. Her hands automatically ran across the smooth, hard lines of his shoulders.

"This must be a record for you—getting to do your Rhett Butler impersonation three times in only two days."

"Wait till you see what I do for an encore," he said suggestively.

"I thought I already had," Ryanne whispered as Hugh's lips closed over hers. A flare of remembered passion ignited their kiss and Hugh lowered her to the floor, then used both arms to pull her tightly against him.

Ryanne's bare legs rubbed against the soft fabric of Hugh's pants and the shirt she wore provided little protection against the smooth hardness of his bare chest. She arched into him as their kiss deepened by mutual consent, and when it ended they were both a little breathless.

"Good morning," he murmured, his voice a little deeper than normal.

Ryanne smiled and snuggled her head against his shoulder so that he couldn't see her blush. "Good morning. I'm sorry about the lamp."

"Don't be. All that broken glass gave me the perfect excuse to get you in my arms again. It saved a lot of awkward maneuvering and planning out a morning-after strategy."

"Does the morning after require a strategy?"

"Definitely. Feeling awkward is inevitable, and I never want you to be uncomfortable with me." He took her arm and guided her to a chair at the table. "Breakfast is almost ready. Why don't you have a seat while I clean up the lamp, then we can eat."

"Fine." Hugh tapped the back of the chair for her and Ryanne sat. "I'd offer to help, but as I just demonstrated, I'm useless in an unfamiliar environment."

There was a long pause that puzzled Ryanne until Hugh reached out and stroked her cheek lovingly. "I'm sorry I left you alone, Ryanne. I thought I could put together a quick breakfast before you woke up. The next time you're here we'll go over the house inch by inch until you know your way around."

"I'd like that," she told him with a smile. She also liked his assumption that there would be a next time.

Hugh gave her a quick kiss, then collected a broom and dustpan from the pantry. The chore took only a few minutes, and before long they were both seated at the table, laughing over the chewy little golf balls that were supposed to have been blueberry muffins. That disaster notwithstanding, it was an excellent breakfast, complete with an omelet and fresh orange juice squeezed from an electric juicer Ryanne had mistaken for a blender.

"You're going to be late for work, aren't you?" Ryanne asked as she sipped her second cup of coffee.

"Only a little. I called Mo and told him I'd meet him at the plant. He can handle things until I get there." Hugh had already explained that MacKenna and Associates were setting up a security system out in Canoga Park. The job had been contracted months ago or Hugh would have changed his schedule in order to stay with Ryanne. This was going to be a rough day for her. "Your appointment is at eleven, isn't it?" he asked.

Ryanne nodded. For days she'd been trying not to think about her impending visit with the country's leading neurologist. "Yes. It's strange...I feel as though I've waited a lifetime to see Dr. Kazlovski, and now that the time has arrived I'd just as soon call and cancel."

"You can't do that, Ryanne. It's important that you find the cause of those headaches."

"If there is a cause. My Aunt Rose used to have severe migraines and no one could ever find out why. Maybe that's why I haven't been too worried about them." She fell silent and toyed with the handle of her coffee cup. Late in the night as she'd lain awake, listening to Hugh's deep, steady breathing, Ryanne had realized something that disturbed her greatly. If she were right, it meant that

Hugh had been lying to her since the day they met. She dreaded confronting the implications of her suspicions.

"Hugh...that first day you came to the house... You knew about me, didn't you? Douglas had told you more than just the fact that I had been a reporter and was blind. He told you everything, didn't he?"

Hugh closed his eyes, cursing himself for ever having agreed to Doug's request that he not tell Ryanne he knew how she'd been blinded. "Yes, I knew. Most of it, anyway. I'm sorry, Ryanne. I shouldn't have pretended not to know."

"Why did you?"

"Doug asked me not to tell you. He wanted someone in L.A. to know your history, but he was afraid you'd be angry with him for telling me. He explained the bare facts and sent me a few newspaper clippings." He reached across the table and took her hand. "This doesn't have anything to do with us, Ryanne, with what happened last night and what's been happening for weeks."

Ryanne wanted desperately to believe that was true, and yet all the time they'd been seeing each other Hugh hadn't tried to take her to bed until she'd practically forced him into it. Had his restraint really come out of a desire to let their friendship solidify before they complicated it, or had Hugh been reluctant to bed her because he didn't want to take advantage of a situation Douglas Sutherland had forced him into?

No, Ryanne thought. That's not the way it was. Her instincts when it came to romance were not well developed, but her instincts about people were acute. Hugh hadn't been pretending with her. He'd met with her that first time as a favor to an old friend, and even if he'd agreed to keep an eye on her after that, there was no need for the elaborate subterfuge of dating. She could understand his reasons for not telling her everything Douglas had passed along to him, as well. At first she'd been a stranger and his loyalties had been to his friend Douglas. And after that first meeting, the subject of her accident had not come up. Somehow she knew that if she hadn't figured out the truth Hugh would have told her eventually.

"Ryanne?" Hugh said tentatively when she remained silent for so long. "Are you angry with me? I wouldn't hurt you for anything in the world. You have to know that."

Ryanne managed a smile. "Yes."

"What made you realize that I knew?"

"You mentioned my plastic surgery last night, but I knew I'd never brought it up. Someone else had to have told you and Judith isn't exactly a chatterbox. That left Douglas Sutherland."

"And you're not angry?"

"No. I know how persuasive Douglas can be—and how overprotective. Somehow I don't think he anticipated that we'd complicate his scheme by becoming a little more than casual acquaintances."

"A *lot* more," Hugh corrected her, bringing her hand to his lips. "And whether he anticipated it or not, I will always be grateful that he brought us together."

"So will I," Ryanne agreed, then grinned impishly. "Why don't you help me pick out a suitable token of appreciation that I can take to him when I go back to Chicago?"

Hugh's hand tightened on Ryanne's and then he released it as though burned by the contact. "Fine. We'll think of something appropriate," he said tightly as he stood. "You'd better get dressed so I can get you home."

He touched her arm and Ryanne stood, puzzled by the sudden chill that had settled between them. "Hugh, did I say something wrong?"

"No, of course not," he reassured her. "I just need to get to work, that's all."

But that wasn't all, and Ryanne knew it. She'd mentioned going back to Chicago, and Hugh had turned as cold as ice. But why? He'd made it clear from the beginning that he didn't believe in long-term relationships. Had something changed his mind, Ryanne wondered, or was she just grasping at straws because letting Hugh go was going to be the hardest thing she'd ever done?

CHAPTER TWELVE

"I'M AFRAID YOU'RE NOT going to think this is good news, Ms. Kirkland," Dr. Kazlovski said as he settled into the chair behind his desk. Ryanne had been at the clinic for what seemed like hours and even after a battery of tests she knew no more now than when she'd entered. Judith was waiting for her in the reception room with Aggie, and Ryanne was anxious to hear what the doctor had to say so that she could leave. She'd spent so much time in hospitals that even after five years the antiseptic smell that pervaded the private clinic made her feel ill.

"You mean you can't find a reason why I'm having headaches?"

"No *physiological* reason," he corrected.

"Then there's no relationship between the headaches and the fall that caused my blindness?"

Kazlovski was silent for a long moment before answering. "I'm not qualified to make that diagnosis, Ms. Kirkland—may I call you Ryanne?"

"Of course." She frowned. "What do you mean you're not qualified? You're the best neurology man in medicine. If you're not qualified, who is?"

"I'm going to ask you to see another doctor, Ryanne. His name is Whitehorn. He's on staff here at the clinic, and I've already spoken with him. He's clearing his calendar so that he can see you today as soon as you and I finish here."

Ryanne's head was spinning. None of this made any sense. What possible tests could Whitehorn run that Kazlovski couldn't? "You're talking in circles, doctor. Would you please tell me what you suspect is wrong with me!"

"Ryanne..." She heard Kazlovski stand and move to the front of the desk where he sat in a chair beside her. "Physically there is nothing wrong with you. Things like this happen sometimes. Your doctor in Chicago sent me all your medical records and I've been able to do a thorough comparison of the X-rays and other tests that were taken right after your accident. Given the state of medical technology that existed five years ago, I probably would have made the same diagnosis as your own physician did. You had massive trauma to your head—there was a blood clot that did eventually dissolve, but I'm sure that was a contributing factor. I can understand—"

"What are you talking about?" Ryanne almost shouted, resisting the impulse to fly to her feet.

"Ryanne, I know this isn't going to be easy to accept—"

"Just say it, damn it! Tell me what's wrong!"

Kazlovski stood. "Nothing is wrong, Ryanne. That's what I'm trying to tell you. There is no physiological reason for your headaches, just as there are no physical indications to explain your blindness."

Ryanne felt as though she'd been hit in the stomach with a two-by-four. It was a moment before she could challenge his ridiculous diagnosis. "I'm blind, doctor," she ground out, throwing one hand up between them. "I can't see my hand in front of my face! I'd say that was a pretty strong *physical indication*!"

"I'm not denying the fact that you're blind," he told her, keeping his voice gentle, regretting the ordeal that was to come. He knew enough about situations like this one to know that accepting her blindness five years earlier had been a piece of cake compared to what accepting the truth was going to be for her now.

"Are you trying to tell me that it's all in my head? That I'm not really blind?" A shudder rippled through Ryanne's body and she suppressed it, trying to think rationally in a world that had suddenly tilted on its axis.

"No, Ryanne, your blindness is real. For some reason your subconscious mind has turned off the switch that allows what your eyes see to register in your brain. That's as real as a detached retina or an atrophied optic nerve. The only difference is that there's no physical damage. It may take a long time to find that switch, but if you can turn it back on you *will* see again."

Ryanne felt too numb to think or move. The full implications were only beginning to sink in. "And the headaches?"

"Headaches can originate from a multitude of sources, but I suspect that yours are only a signal. Almost as though some part of your mind was crying out against the injustice of your blindness. At the same time your subconscious is keeping you from seeing, it's also trying to let you know that you have the capability to restore your sight. Frankly I think that's a very encouraging sign."

"Oh, you do?" she asked, unable to keep the sarcasm from her voice.

"Yes. It may mean that your subconscious is ready to confront the trauma that caused this problem in the first place. As long as you were under the impression that your blindness was irrevocable there was little chance for you to find the source and regain your sight. Perhaps now you can."

Still in a state of shock, Ryanne asked questions by rote, recording the answers in her mind to be taken out and reviewed later. She wanted to know what made him so sure of his diagnosis; she asked how such a mistake could have been made. He lapsed into a technical explanation of the revolutionary improvements in the CAT scan apparatus that provided clear, almost three-dimensional images of the brain, but Ryanne understood little of what he was saying. She wanted to be overjoyed that she might one day see again, but there was one clear, obvious fact that eliminated the desire to rejoice.

Dr. Kazlovski might not know what had caused her subconscious mind to throw the switch that had blinded her, but Ryanne did. It was all so very simple. Five years ago she saw a man commit murder. That same man had tried to kill her, and if she hadn't gone blind, he would have kept on trying until he succeeded. In short, being blind was the only thing that was keeping Ryanne alive.

If her options were darkness and death, Ryanne was quite comfortable with the choice her subconscious had already made for her.

"WHAT IS IT, Judith? What did the doctor say? What's wrong?" Hugh bombarded Judith the instant she opened the door to him. His office had relayed her terse message to the Canoga Park site, and he'd immediately jumped into his car and broken every speed law between the factory and Malibu. He'd tried to reach her from the phone in his car, but the line had been tied up and he was nearly frantic. Seeing Judith's drawn, ashen face didn't help the terrified ache in his heart.

"Please keep your voice down," Judith requested without her usual tartness. "She doesn't know I called you."

Unable to stop himself, Hugh grabbed her shoulders. "What's wrong with her?"

"I don't know!" Judith snapped, wrenching out of his grasp. "She was with the doctor for hours, and when she came out she said there was absolutely nothing wrong with her. When I got her home she shut herself in her room and she's been there ever since. I took a tray in to her a few minutes ago, but she hasn't touched it. She's just sitting there, facing the ocean..." Tears welled in the older woman's eyes and she covered her face with both hands, whispering brokenly, "Something is terribly wrong, Hugh. She's..."

Hugh reached out and pulled her into his arms. He held her while she quickly regained control. "It's all right," he crooned softly, trying to convince himself as much as Judith. "She'll be fine. She has to be."

Judith pulled away from him and dried her eyes. "When she wouldn't talk to me I didn't know what else to do but call you."

"I'm glad you did. I'll go see if I can get us some answers, and if she won't talk to me, either, then we'll get in touch with her doctor."

"I've already done that. He insists that he can't discuss Ryanne's condition without her consent."

"Then I'll just have to get the answers from Ryanne, won't I?" Hugh started down the hall. He knocked softly on her door, calling her name, and when she didn't respond, he turned the knob and stepped inside. "Ryanne?"

She was sitting exactly as Judith had described, in a chair facing the ocean, her eyes fixed and sightless. Her legs were drawn up to her chest with her arms wrapped around them. She looked so forlorn and vulnerable that Hugh's heart broke into a dozen pieces. "Ryanne?"

"Go away, Hugh," she said emotionlessly. Her voice was like something cold and dead.

"I can't go away, Ryanne. Judith is terrified," he told her, closing the distance between them. "So am I," he added softly.

"I told her nothing was wrong."

"Ryanne, if nothing was wrong you wouldn't be sitting here like this." He knelt beside her, steeling himself to ask the question he hadn't wanted to ever have to face. For weeks now he'd been trying not to think about the fact that Ryanne's mother had died of cancer. "Did they find a tumor?" he asked softly.

"I just told you! He didn't find anything!" she shouted. "Nothing! Not one blessed thing! I'm as healthy as a horse. Of course, I'm also crazy as a loon," she added with an ugly, half laugh as she came to her feet. Unable to bear being close to Hugh, she hurried across the room, but there was no place for her to go to escape him and she knew it.

Hugh stood and watched her agitated pacing. He hated seeing her like this, but it was preferable to the emotionless cocoon she'd been wrapped in when he'd entered. "I don't understand, Ryanne."

"Of course you don't," she said bitterly. "It took me a while to comprehend it, too. Dr. Kazlovski told me I need a psychiatrist, not a neurologist."

"Ryanne—"

"I'm not blind, Hugh! There's nothing wrong with my eyes and there never has been! It's called hysterical blindness, and it happens when crazy people like me can't handle reality." In a venomous voice filled with self-loathing, Ryanne repeated everything the doctor had said.

"Then you'll see again someday," Hugh said quickly when she finished. He was enormously relieved to know she wasn't seriously ill, and it was nothing less than miraculous that she might regain her sight. Seeing her so distraught negated his joy, though. She was in shock now, with too many emotions crowding in on her, not the least of which had to be fear, he realized.

"There are no guarantees of that," she answered in a brittle tone. "Dr. Whitehorn explained that the subconscious mind doesn't work that way. Facing the fear that caused my blindness won't necessarily unlock the mechanism that's keeping me from seeing."

"But you said Dr. Kazlovski thinks your headaches were... what? A plea for help? Isn't that a good sign? Something inside you wants to see again, Ryanne."

"Why? So I can watch my own death unfold? That'll be a real pleasure, won't it?"

"Ryanne—" Hugh reached for her but the moment he touched her arm she shrank away.

"Don't. Don't touch me. I don't want to be coddled and comforted. I don't want to hear your platitudes. 'Everything will be all right, Ryanne,'" she mimicked viciously. "Or better yet, 'I won't let anyone hurt you.'"

"You may not want to hear it, Ryanne, but it's very true. I *won't* let anyone hurt you," he told her in a voice that was quiet, but fierce in its conviction.

"That's a lie, Hugh, and you know it," she retorted. "You know as well as I do that if someone wants me dead there's not a power on earth that can keep me alive—not you, not the police, not God, not anybody! If I wake up tomorrow morning and see the sunrise, you can bet your sweet life I won't be alive to see it set!"

Hugh wanted to argue with her, to convince her she was wrong, but he knew she wasn't. There were witness protection programs that sometimes worked—provided the witness was willing to go into hiding and give up friends, family and careers. They also had to be willing to live in constant fear that they would be discovered. Under those circumstances, a normal life was virtually impossible. Certainly it was better than death, but Hugh didn't care for either of those alternatives. If Ryanne did regain her sight and go into a witness protection program he would lose her forever.

The ramifications of the double bind Ryanne was now in hit Hugh like a freight train, and like Ryanne, he had no idea what to wish for. To hope that she would never regain her sight was too cruel for words, and yet to pray for it to return was like sentencing her to death.

"What? No protests? Aren't you going to tell me I'm wrong? Aren't you going to tell me about witness protection programs or something equally encouraging?" she asked sarcastically. Obviously her mind had already traveled the same torturous route as Hugh's.

"No, Ryanne, I'm not."

"Well, tell me something!" she shouted as her fierce anger began to evaporate leaving nothing but cold terror in its wake. "Tell me . . . tell . . ." A wrenching sob shattered her voice and the tears she'd needed to shed finally broke free. "Oh, God, Hugh . . . I'm so scared."

Hugh had her in his arms in an instant, and this time she did not try to pull away. He held her close, stroking her hair and murmuring wordlessly while she cried. He rocked her gently until the storm subsided.

When she was calmer he encouraged her to talk to Judith, who was half out of her mind with worry. He called Ryanne's friend into the room and the two women embraced, holding on to each other as Hugh began the explanation that he wasn't sure she would find reassuring. Ryanne told her about the tests she had taken and the hour she had spent with the psychiatrist.

Judith accepted the results stoically, and when everything had been told, her response was succinct.

"You're a survivor, Ryanne. You'll survive this, too." She glanced at Hugh sharply, giving him a look that charged him with making sure that she did.

He nodded to her, wordlessly accepting the responsibility of keeping Ryanne alive, then he took her back into his arms and held her as the night fell around them.

CHAPTER THIRTEEN

It was 2:00 A.M. in Chicago, and a light, misty rain turned the city streets a shiny black. On the glistening surfaces the street lights were reflected, like diamonds against black velvet. Every so often, a car sped through the intersection, taking advantage of the deserted street, but Arlen Beck paid no attention. He was focused totally, impatiently, on the phone in the booth that sheltered him from the drizzling rain. He checked his watch again and calculated the time difference. In Los Angeles it was two minutes after midnight. If all had gone as planned, Keegan would be calling any second. Beck waited, his heart thundering, ready to grab the receiver, but the phone refused to ring. Five minutes melted into ten; ten melted into twenty.

At two-thirty, Beck began cursing. He swore at the tardy Ace Keegan for keeping him in suspense, and he cursed the rain and the cramped phone booth. Most of all, he cursed Ryanne Kirkland for not having died five years ago as she should have. If not for her stubborn will to live, Beck's life would have been nearly perfect.

He fancied himself an important man in the syndicate, well on his way to the kind of power Del Michelon wielded. He'd started with nothing and now he was on the verge of having it all. At least, he had been until Ryanne Kirkland made an appointment with a hotshot specialist in Los Angeles. As he waited in the phone booth, Beck could almost feel his carefully constructed world tumbling down around his ears.

The later the hour grew, the more that feeling intensified. He simply couldn't afford mistakes. That was why he was out on the street at this absurd hour, miles from his home in the suburbs. After all the planning he'd done, after all the expense he'd put out to keep Keegan in Los Angeles, discreetly watching Ryanne Kirkland for nearly two months, Beck wasn't about to let a little thing like a traceable phone call mess things up. All of Keegan's calls to Beck were supposed to be made from Los Angeles pay phones, and all were received in the same phone booth on Kruger Street in Chicago. Nice, neat, and completely untraceable. Five years ago, Beck had made a grave mistake by not making sure that a busybody reporter was dead. If it became necessary to try to eliminate her again, he was going to be damned sure there would be no need for a third attempt. Del Michelon didn't like inefficiency, and the last thing Arlen Beck wanted was to displease his boss. Others who had done so had, on occasion, paid for their errors with their lives.

At two forty-three the wait finally ended and Beck had the phone's receiver to his ear before the echo of the first aborted ring had faded into the night.

"Keegan?"

"Yeah. It's me."

"Where the hell have you been? What went wrong?"

"Chill out, man," Keegan advised in a negligent voice that infuriated Beck. "Everything's cool. I just ran into a little delay, that's all."

Beck checked his watch unnecessarily. "Yeah, a forty-five-minute delay. What happened? Did you get her records out of the clinic?"

"Nope. That's the delay I meant. It's gonna take a couple of days longer."

A small spike of fear ran down Beck's spine. Michelon was expecting a report first thing tomorrow morning and keeping the boss waiting wasn't a healthy thing to do. "No way, Keegan! I told you I wanted answers tonight, and you promised you could deliver!"

"Yeah, well that was before I knew Simpson was gonna pick tonight to come down with the flu."

"Who the hell is Simpson?"

Keegan sighed audibly. "He's the night watchman at the clinic. For a hefty fee, Mr. Simpson gave me the layout of the joint and agreed to look the other way when I break in."

"Damn you, Keegan—"

"Hey look, man, it's not my fault there's a major bug goin' around. Simpson's sick as a dog—I checked it out for myself. That's why I was late making this call." It was a convenient lie, but Ace Keegan had had a lot of experience making lies sound like the truth. The night watchman really was sick in bed, and Keegan *had* verified it— earlier in the evening. He'd followed the lovely Ms. Kirkland from the clinic to her ritzy Malibu beach house, then he'd gone to arrange a few last minute details with Simpson. He'd found the man in bed, and Ace hadn't spent much time loitering around to offer his sympathies. The last thing he needed was to get bitten by a bug.

Once Keegan had found out there was no way he could get into the clinic tonight, he'd gone to a little bar up in Santa Monica where a couple of local rubes had obligingly lost a few hundred dollars to Ace at the pool table. It didn't bother him in the least that his last game had kept his employer waiting in a damp Chicago phone booth. Nor was he particularly disturbed that Simpson was going to be out of commission for a couple of days. After nearly two months, Hollywood was beginning to feel like home to Ace. He was going to be sorry when this cushy little job was over. Malibu Beach was a great place to get a tan—and the women weren't bad to look at, either.

Beck was fuming. Tomorrow morning, Michelon would expect him to have the results of Kirkland's visit to the doctor, and the syndicate boss wouldn't be happy if Arlen couldn't deliver. A flu virus wouldn't mean a whole lot to Del Michelon. For a moment, Beck considered ordering Keegan to go ahead with the break-in despite the absence of a friendly night watchman, but he knew that wouldn't be a smart move. The risk of getting caught would be multiplied a hundredfold, and if Keegan went to jail they might not find out if Kirkland was going to see or not until it was too late. No, the only option was to wait until Simpson got well and returned to work. Surely a day or two wouldn't make that much difference.

"All right, Keegan. We'll wait—for now," Beck decided. "But I want you to look for another way to get into that clinic, and I want a report on every move Kirkland makes until you get hold of her records. You got that?"

"Yeah, yeah. I got it."

"Good. I'll be waiting at this number for a report tomorrow night. And don't keep me waiting again!" Beck slammed down the phone and realized that his hand was trembling.

"Damn," he muttered, turning up the collar of his jacket as he stepped into the drizzling Chicago rain. Meanwhile, in Los Angeles, Ace Keegan sauntered through the balmy Southern California night back toward the bar he'd reluctantly left just a few minutes ago. It was about one in the morning, but the streets were still buzzing with traffic, and Keegan enjoyed the rhythm of the street.

Yes, indeed, he was going to miss this place. But if it turned out that Beck decided it was necessary to kill Ryanne Kirkland, there was no way Keegan would be able to stay. He'd have to do the job, then head back to Chicago. The thought of reneging on his contract with Beck never occurred to Ace. The old saying about "honor among thieves" applied to hired killers, too. No matter how much he might like to hang around Los Angeles, he wouldn't back out on the job.

But he didn't have to be in any big hurry, either. Not for the first time that day, Ace hoped that Simpson took his time recovering from the flu.

IT WAS WELL after midnight before Hugh could finally persuade Ryanne to take one of the sedatives her doctor had prescribed. The next few days were going to take quite a toll on her and she needed all the rest she could get. Dr. Whitehorn had scheduled daily sessions with her for the next week to help her deal with the intense conflict she was experiencing. He was also going to be searching for that switch in her subconscious Dr. Kazlovski had referred to. Hugh wondered if Ryanne would allow the psychiatrist to poke around in her head until he found it.

Of course, Hugh realized that Ryanne was the only one who could actually flip that switch, and he also knew that even a conscious decision to confront her fear of "Worsted" did not mean her sight would miraculously return. Her subconscious had blinded her and it would be her subconscious that allowed her to see again.

Standing alone on Ryanne's deck with the quiet house behind him, Hugh began to review everything he knew about the attempt on Ryanne's life five years earlier. He wished he had the information Doug had sent him so that he could study it more thoroughly, but the papers were back in his office. Calling upon his memory, his mind floated back to the first conversation he and Doug had had about Ryanne, and almost instantly something he'd forgotten came back to him with terrifying clarity. For weeks now he had been so involved with Ryanne, so consumed with his growing feelings for her that he had completely forgotten the reason Doug Sutherland had contacted him in the first place. It hadn't just been that he'd wanted her security system checked out, or that he'd been playing matchmaker. Doug was convinced that Worsted knew every move Ryanne Kirkland had made in the past five years, and if that were true, the murderer had to have known about her appointment with Dr. Kazlovski. He had to be worried, wondering if perhaps the doctor could restore her sight.... He would make every attempt to learn the results of Ryanne's tests, and eventually he would learn that the woman who could put him in the electric chair might miraculously regain her sight at any moment.

Naturally Hugh was only speculating. He couldn't know for certain that Worsted was aware Ryanne was in Los Angeles, let alone that she had planned to see Dr. Kazlovski. But he didn't dare assume less than the worst, because there was a danger here that no one had yet perceived. Whether or not Ryanne regained her sight might be completely irrelevant. Just knowing that she had the capability could be enough to push Worsted into action. He wouldn't dare wait, because the moment she regained her sight she would be placed under police protection and spirited away into a witness protection program where he might never be able to get at her. He would strike now, while she was blind and vulnerable.

The threat of immediate danger galvanized Hugh into action. With a muffled curse at his own stupidity, he hurried into the house. Turning on the kitchen light, he grabbed for the phone and began making calls.

The first was to Ben Rosenthal, with a terse order to get out to the Burbank hangar and prepare the company jet for an immediate flight. The second roused a groggy Mo Johnson from a sound sleep—possibly the last he would see for days. Without bothering to explain, Hugh told Mo to get to Ryanne's house at once, and before Hugh had even completed dialing his next number, Johnson was half dressed and almost out the door.

Methodically Hugh took the necessary steps to ensure that Ryanne would be protected while he flew to Chicago and back. He had to get to Doug Sutherland and the Chicago police in order to find out everything there was to know about Worsted. Ryanne could tell him the man's real name, of course, but she didn't know where he was or what he had been doing for the past five years. For all he knew, Worsted could have been hit by a crosstown bus or drowned in Lake Michigan. Hugh had to know if the threat to Ryanne was as real as he suspected, and he had to learn all he could about her enemy. Five years ago, Worsted had been a small-time hood, according to Ryanne. Did he have an arm long enough to reach her in Los Angeles?

Ryanne wouldn't be truly safe until Hugh knew exactly what he was up against, and as much as he hated to leave, all the answers were in Chicago.

"Judith?" Hugh knocked softly on the door of her upstairs room. "Judith, wake up."

"What is it?" she asked, opening the door as she wrapped a robe around herself. "Is Ryanne all right?"

"For the time being, yes." Without garnishing the facts, he explained the situation. Judith took it all in calmly, just as he'd expected her to. "My jet is being prepared for takeoff and Mo Johnson will be here any minute with a couple of freelance bodyguards I use from time to time. They're trustworthy, and they're good at what they do. All three of them will stay outside the house—I don't want Ryanne to know what's going on."

Judith nodded. "You're right. She doesn't need this added to everything else. What about her appointment tomorrow at the clinic?"

"Mo will take care of everything. No one will get close to her with him standing guard, I promise. I should be back by tomorrow night. If she should ask about me in the morning, tell her I had to leave early to finish the Canoga Park job, but that I'll drop by later."

Judith returned downstairs with Hugh, making a pot of coffee while they waited impatiently for Mo to arrive. When he got there, Hugh explained the situation to him in a terse, shorthand language that had developed naturally from the years they had worked together.

Once he was satisfied that Mo had the facts he needed, Hugh headed for the airport. The jet was kept fueled and ready for takeoff at all times, and Ben, an experienced pilot, had already filed their flight plan. When Hugh arrived, the jet was on the landing field and within minutes they were in the air.

"HUGH MACKENNA, this is Lieutenant Rube Lilen-thal," Doug Sutherland said. "Rube was the investigat-ing officer on the Vinnie Perigrino murder."

The rotund police officer wiped the raspberry filling of his jelly doughnut off his hand before he extended it to Hugh.

"Sorry about that, MacKenna," he said apologet-ically, referring to the sticky handshake. "Dougie here—" he cocked his head toward Douglas "—got me out of bed a little early. I usually eat breakfast at home, but when he phoned to say an illustrious PI from Hol-lywood was on his way to the station, I figured I'd better dash right over."

Lilenthal's sarcasm was as thick as molasses and the best Hugh could manage was a tight smile. "It's a real thrill to meet you, too, lieutenant."

"Could we cut the crap and get down to business?" Doug interjected, taking a chair opposite Lilenthal's. Hugh's phone call last night had been like a nightmare come true, and today Doug was in no mood to listen to a police officer and a private investigator try to one-up each other. Cops and PIs, everybody knew, were natural ri-vals. Doug had known Ryanne since she was a baby; her father had been Doug's best friend. Her safety was more than a matter of mild concern to him. "Hugh needs to see everything you've got on Arlen Beck."

Lilenthal gave Hugh a thorough once-over, noting the expensive suit he was wearing and the even suntan that virtually screamed California. He'd also arrived in Chi-cago an hour ago via his own personal jet, which in it-self told Lilenthal a lot. MacKenna obviously made a better-than-average living in movieland, and that thought galled the police officer who had spent twenty-four years on the force and could barely pay the rent on his mediocre apartment four blocks from the station house.

Nevertheless, there was something about MacKenna that did command the lieutenant's grudging respect. His tan may have been as pretty as his face, but there was a hard edge around his eyes that suggested he could be as tough as he was civilized if the situation called for it.

Putting his personal bias aside, Lilenthal nodded for Hugh to take a chair, and both men sat. "Doug told me there's a chance we may have an eyewitness to the Perigrino murder, after all," he said, getting down to business.

"There's no way of knowing that for sure," Hugh replied, not happy with the detective's cavalier attitude. He made a supreme effort to keep his tone professional. "There now exists a possibility that Ryanne Kirkland may someday regain her sight, but that possibility alone may place her in a great deal of danger."

"I'd say so, yes," Lilenthal agreed. "As long as she's in California she's out of our jurisdiction, of course. There's not a damned thing we can do to protect her."

"I'm taking responsibility for Ryanne's safety while she's in L.A., lieutenant. What I need from you is information. I have to know what I'm up against. I'd appreciate anything you could tell me about the man you suspect of killing Vinnie Perigrino and attempting to murder Ryanne Kirkland."

Lilenthal nodded and reached for the file under his half-eaten jelly doughnut. He extracted a photograph from the file and tossed it to Hugh. "Arlen Beck, age forty-nine, born and raised on the South Side of Chicago. He started out as a punk, but managed to elevate his status by marrying the daughter of a moderately well-to-do banker who ran a small, legitimate savings-and-loan company uptown. Beck polished up his act just enough to convince his wife's old man to leave him control of the S and L when he died. Seven years ago the father-in-law keeled over from a coronary and suddenly the S and L wasn't so legit anymore. Beck organized a gambling syndicate with some of his old friends from the neighborhood and presto-chango, dirty gambling money went through Beck's S and L washing machine and came out smelling rosy clean."

"Was Vinnie Perigrino one of Beck's bag men?" Hugh asked.

"Yeah. He carried money to Beck. A couple of weeks before he died we busted him on an unrelated drug trafficking charge and he rolled over like a boulder in a landslide. He told us he'd give us Beck if we'd be lenient on the trafficking charge. The district attorney bought it and Perigrino was supposed to set up a time and a place for us to catch Beck in the act of receiving a chunk of the syndicate's cash."

Hugh frowned. "Then why weren't your men in that warehouse when Ryanne was shot?"

It was clear from Lilenthal's expression that he objected to Hugh's accusatory tone, but he answered the question anyway. "We're not quite sure what happened, but we think Perigrino was trying to double-cross us and warn his boss."

"But Beck killed him anyway."

"My guess is that Beck got wind of Perigrino's arrest and the deal he'd made and thought it would be smart to rid himself on one distinct liability. Someone in the D.A.'s office leaked the deal to ace reporter Ryanne Kirkland and she became another of Beck's liabilities."

"So where's Beck now?" Hugh asked.

"Sitting very pretty," Lilenthal said disgustedly. "Two years ago this man—" he extracted another photograph from the file "—Del Michelon, brought Beck's operation under his protective influence. Beck is in the big leagues now."

"Damn," Douglas swore softly. He hadn't known about this.

Hugh looked at his old friend sharply. "You know Michelon?"

"I know about him," Doug confirmed. "He's one of the two most powerful crime bosses in the state of Illinois. If Beck is heavily into Michelon's organization, Ryanne is in real trouble."

"That's right," Lilenthal agreed. "Michelon can't afford to have Beck brought in on a murder rap. Del had nothing to do with Perigrino's death because he wasn't associated with Beck at the time, but he can't afford the possibility that Beck might cop a plea to a lesser charge in exchange for information about Michelon. Believe me, that's a deal the D.A. would snap up in an instant. We want Michelon bad." He paused for a moment. "Of course, it depends on how much Beck knows, and on how much damage he could do the syndicate. But you can bet your life Michelon's not going to sit still and watch us haul Beck in."

"In other words, history is repeating itself," Hugh commented, drawing the correlation between Beck and Perigrino five years earlier, and Michelon and Beck now. But in this situation, the easiest way to minimize losses would be to dispose of Ryanne.

"You grasp the situation perfectly, Mr. MacKenna," Lilenthal told him. "Right now I wouldn't want to be in Ryanne Kirkland's shoes for all the money in Fort Knox."

Hugh stiffened but made no comment. He continued asking questions, garnering every fact he could. Lilenthal was abrasive but cooperative, and Hugh soaked up the information like a sponge.

"You realize, of course, that Beck's not going to come after her himself this time," the cop said as he rose and moved to the door of his office. He flagged down a uniformed officer in the busy squad room and requested a file, then returned to his seat.

"Any ideas on who he might hire?" Doug asked.

"Not really. I'm gonna let you look at our hit file, though, just in case." The young officer rapped once on the door, stepped in and handed Lilenthal a thick file folder, then retreated without a word. "We try to keep this current, but you know how a bureaucracy works. In a perfect world, there would be a photograph, rap sheet and current status report on every known hit man who operates out of Chicago. But this ain't a perfect world. And, of course, nothing's to say that Beck's going to send local heat. He could hire independent muscle in L.A. I imagine you got one or two pretty boys out there who would be willing to take a few minutes away from working on their tans to take the job, right?"

Hugh was already so absorbed in the file that he barely heard Lilenthal's jibe. When he didn't comment, the lieutenant shrugged, picked up the remainder of his jelly doughnut and washed it down with his cold coffee.

The silence lengthened and finally Lilenthal said, "Look, MacKenna, why don't I get you a desk outside so you can peruse that at your leisure. I got work—"

"Are these statistics current?" Hugh interrupted him.

"More or less. Like I said, this is not a perfect world. Why? You find something interesting?"

Hugh looked closer at one particular photograph, then glanced at the list of previous crimes attributed to one Asa "Ace" Keegan. In addition to a basic physical description and a list of previous arrests and convictions, there was also a notation of the man's suspected connection with the Michelon syndicate. By far the most interesting bit of information, though, was a recently added, handwritten memo that stated the alleged hit man had dropped out of sight two months ago—right about the time Ryanne came to Los Angeles.

He handed the papers to Lilenthal, who looked them over dispassionately. "Could be." He shrugged his shoulders and handed the papers back to Hugh.

"Can I get a copy of this to show my men back in L.A.?"

"Technically, no," Lilenthal answered. "However, we do cooperate with law enforcement agencies in other states from time to time. Have you got a friend on the force in L.A.? Someone who might be willing to slip you a copy of a photo that got wired from here to there? After all, it would only be the polite thing for us to let the L.A.P.D. know that they may have a suspected felon in their midst."

"If you can get it to L.A., I can get my hands on it. Send it to Detective Victor Coffin. And while you're at it, why don't you send through a copy of Arlen Beck's photo?"

"I was going to suggest that myself," Lilenthal answered. "If Miss Kirkland should get her sight back unexpectedly, shove that picture in front of her face and get a positive ID, would you? If she fingers him, we'll have him in custody by the time she gets to Chicago."

"What about security?" Douglas asked. "No offense to the department, lieutenant, but members of the force have been known to let things slip from time to time. What steps are you prepared to take to ensure Ryanne's safety if someone tips off Michelon and Beck about an imminent arrest?''

Lilenthal threw Douglas a withering look, then turned the same expression on Hugh. "You get her to Chicago and I guarantee we'll get her to court. Here." He scribbled something on a slip of paper and handed it to Hugh. "This is my home number in case you gotta get hold of me at night. If Ms. Kirkland gets her sight back, I want to be the first person who knows about it. You got that?"

Lilenthal's look was so commanding that it was easy for Hugh to see how he had earned his lieutenant's stripes, but Hugh wasn't one of Lilenthal's officers and he had no intention of pretending that he was. He returned Lilenthal's long look as he stood. "Lieutenant, I appreciate your time and your help. And if Ryanne regains her sight, I guarantee you that you'll be *one of the first* to know. If you learn of anything that might be helpful, you can reach me at this number." He extracted a business card from his jacket and handed it to Lilenthal. "Thanks again for your help."

"Don't mention it," Lilenthal murmured sarcastically, hating that this pretty-boy Californian had just told him who was the boss.

"Do you think there's any chance that Keegan will be the one to go after Ryanne?" Douglas asked a few minutes later as he drove Hugh back to the airport. Hugh noticed that like himself, Doug was treating the threat to Ryanne as fact, not a remote possibility.

"I'd say the chances are roughly equivalent to my being elected Pope by Christmas. More than likely Keegan's disappearance means he'll eventually turn up floating in Lake Michigan."

"So what are you going to do now?"

Hugh shrugged. "Get back to Ryanne as quickly as possible and do what will probably be the hardest thing I've ever had to do in my life."

"What's that?"

"Tell her what we suspect. I can't imagine that this little bit of news will help her cope any better."

With one hand on the wheel, Douglas ran the other through the thin patch of graying hair on top of his head. "I don't know about that, Hugh. Think about it for a minute. From what you've told me, Ryanne's subconscious blinded her to keep her from getting killed. It doesn't take a Rhodes scholar to see the warped logic of that defense mechanism. But once her subconscious realizes that the blindness is no longer keeping her safe, maybe it'll flip that switch you told me about. I mean, at this point, Ryanne could protect herself a whole lot better if she could see, right?"

"That's true," Hugh agreed. "But I don't know if her subconscious is going to see it that way. She just has so much garbage to sort through that I'm afraid she's going to overload. She took the news pretty hard yesterday."

"What else would you expect?" Doug shook his head. "Damn, this is all so eerie. What was it you said earlier about history repeating itself? Truer words were never spoken."

Hugh had the feeling he'd missed part of their conversation. "What? You mean Perigrino and Beck?"

"No. I was referring to Ryanne and her father, Martin Kirkland."

Hugh turned sideways on the seat. "What's Ryanne's father got to do with this? He was killed in a hit-and-run accident when she was a little girl."

Doug's answering smile was grimly ironic. "Is that what she told you?"

"You mean it's not true?"

"Well, yeah...in a manner of speaking. What Ryanne neglected to tell you was that the accident took place two days before her father, Martin Kirkland, was to give testimony before the grand jury that was trying to indict Spence Leroy."

Hugh frowned, trying to remember why that name sounded familiar. "The mobster?"

"The very same."

Gradually the details of the sensational case came back to Hugh. He'd only been a kid at the time, in his senior year of high school, but the trial of Spencer Leroy had been nationwide news. Even a self-absorbed teenager couldn't avoid hearing about it. His current events class had followed the sensational case for weeks, but until this moment, Hugh had forgotten about the reporter who'd gone undercover to get the goods on one of the biggest gangland bosses in the Midwest. Vaguely Hugh recalled that the reporter had been betrayed by a friend who had lured him out of hiding and into a parking garage where he was killed by a car that ran over his body repeatedly just to make certain he was good and dead.

No wonder Ryanne hadn't wanted to discuss her father's death.

"Did Kirkland work for the *Examiner*?" Hugh asked.

"Yeah. And he even won a Pulitzer for the mob story—posthumously," Doug said with disgust. "That wasn't a helluva lot of comfort to Ryanne and her mother at the time. It was all so damned senseless! Martin had already turned over to the police everything his investigation had uncovered and he'd written an entire series of articles we were already in the process of publishing. His testimony would have made Leroy a lot easier to convict, but by the time they killed him, Martin wasn't really vital to the D.A.'s case. They murdered him out of revenge, or maybe as a lesson to others.''

"Didn't they have him under protective custody?" Hugh asked, trying to remember details that had been forgotten long ago.

"Sort of. He took Beverly and Ryanne into hiding, but it was for their benefit more than his own.''

Poor Ryanne, Hugh thought, trying to imagine the fear, uncertainty and ultimately the grief she must have suffered all those years ago. The cause of her blindness was clearer than ever, now. The foundation for it had been laid nearly twenty years ago by her father's death, and when she had been confronted with an uncannily similar situation, her subconscious mind had offered what seemed to be the perfect solution.

The men were silent for the remainder of the drive, each lost in his own thoughts. They reached the airport and Hugh thanked Doug for his help, but the newspaper editor stopped him before he could leave the car.

"Hugh... this isn't just a job to you, is it?" he asked, even though he already knew the answer. "I mean, this has gone a lot farther than you keeping an eye on Ryanne because I asked you to, right?''

"Yes."

"Are you in love with her?"

Hugh took a deep breath and released it slowly. Love wasn't a word he'd allowed himself to use when thinking of Ryanne. She saw their relationship as a pleasant, short-term affair; Hugh saw it as more. To protect himself he'd refused to name the emotion he felt for her, but Doug was forcing him to confront it head-on and Hugh wasn't ready for that.

"I'm not going to let anything happen to her, Doug. I promise you."

"I know that, but you didn't answer my question."

"Ryanne considers what we have is a summer fling," he said tightly.

"Hmm. That doesn't sound much like the Ryanne I know," Doug observed. "How do you feel about it?"

Hugh frowned. He wasn't accustomed to being pressed. "I care about her, Doug. All right? I'll do whatever is necessary to get her out of this mess alive and worry about the future later."

A wry smile crept across Doug's craggy face. "In other words, you love her so much that you can't see straight."

Hugh glanced out the window at a DC-10 that had just taken off. The jet thundered overhead, almost obscuring his quiet answer. "That's about the size of it. You happy now?"

"When I dance with the bride at your wedding, *then* I'll be happy. Right now I'm just very relieved and grateful that she has you to protect her."

"Let's hope it's enough." Hugh opened the door and stepped out. "Thanks again, Doug. I'll keep you posted."

They said a hasty goodbye and Doug sat quietly, watching his young friend hurry across the parking lot toward the small terminal that provided a clearing house for the private planes that came and went out of the busy airport. Hugh's sense of urgency was apparent even in his retreating back, and though the situation was grim, Douglas Sutherland couldn't hold back a small, self-satisfied smile.

"The bigger they are, the harder they fall," he mumbled. "Keep her safe, boy. I love her, too."

CHAPTER FOURTEEN

THE INTERIOR OF Hugh's BMW was as silent as a tomb. Midafternoon traffic on the San Diego Freeway was light, but Ryanne had no way of knowing that. She sat quietly, running over in her mind her session with Dr. Whitehorn—a session that had included Hugh MacKenna. Yesterday when he had dropped by the house after work, he'd made no mention of his trip to Chicago. He had insisted on being allowed to drive Ryanne to her next therapy session, though, and now she knew why. Late yesterday Hugh had made his own appointment with Dr. Whitehorn to discuss how his suspicions regarding Arlen Beck should be presented to her. The psychiatrist had suggested that they tell her together during this afternoon's session. She presumed the doctor had wanted to be around in case she fell apart.

But she hadn't. She was too numb; not surprised, shocked, or even particularly frightened, just . . . numb. Ryanne supposed that given time she would have come to the same realization about Beck that Hugh had, but he had spared her that personal revelation. She wanted to feel grateful not only for his concern for her welfare, but also for the protection she now knew he was providing for her. Unfortunately feeling anything at all was beyond her. She just wanted to be home and safe, but the knowledge that there was nowhere she could truly consider safe made even the desire to be home seem a wasted effort.

The car stopped and when Hugh shut off the engine Ryanne reached for the door handle. Hugh stopped her with his voice. "Just wait, Ryanne. I'll come around and get the door."

She started to protest that such chivalry wasn't necessary, then realized that Hugh wasn't being polite. He didn't want her stepping out of the car alone, making her an easier target. A shudder of apprehension trickled down her spine and she sat patiently, waiting.

He walked beside her as Aggie led the way to the house, and though he didn't speak, Ryanne could feel the coil of alertness that emanated from him. This Hugh was different from the one she was familiar with. His every word and movement now reminded her of the hard, cold stranger she'd been introduced to in Hugh's bedroom three days ago—the one she'd realized was capable of killing if the need arose. As a woman who needed protection, Ryanne appreciated this iron-willed stranger, even as she mourned the loss of the warm, gentle man she'd been so close to falling in love with.

Close to falling in love? Some part of Ryanne's confused, clouded mind mocked the thought. There was nothing close about it. Though she'd refused to admit it, she'd fallen in love with Hugh MacKenna.

Considering my life expectancy now, it's a good thing he doesn't believe in long-term relationships, Ryanne reflected with morbid humor.

Aggie stopped at the front door and before Ryanne or Hugh could reach for the knob, Judith opened it from the inside.

"Thank you, Judith," Ryanne said. She moved into the foyer, well past the door's opening, and while she removed Aggie's harness Judith looked at Hugh as though to say, "How did she take it?"

"Will you two kindly stop exchanging worried glances," Ryanne requested, heading for the living-room sofa. "Your solicitude is so thick I could cut it with a knife."

"Sorry," Hugh said, smiling at the first thing Ryanne had said in three days that sounded like the woman whose indomitable spirit he so cherished.

Judith, too, noticed the return to normalcy and reacted accordingly. "You haven't exactly been a barrel of monkeys yourself." She turned on her heel and left with an explanation that she'd be in the office if anyone needed her.

Ryanne chuckled weakly as she sat. "Now I know everything's going to be all right. Judith's being mean to me again."

"Everything *is* going to be all right, Ryanne," Hugh promised, joining her on the sofa.

She didn't bother responding. "I assume Judith knows about your trip to Chicago yesterday."

"Yes."

"Good."

It tore at Hugh's heart to see Ryanne so quiet and still, when she was normally so animated and bursting with life. He reached for her hand, pressing it between both of his, but Ryanne only gave him a gentle squeeze to thank him for the reassuring gesture before she pulled away. She rested her head against the back of the sofa, slipped off her shoes and placed her feet on the edge of the coffee table. "Who do you have guarding the house? Mo and Ben?"

"Mo is coordinating days and Ben's doing nights."

"Coordinating?" She turned her face toward him.

"I've brought in some extra help. One man can't cover the front and back at the same time." Because she seemed to have a need to know the details, Hugh explained all the precautions he was taking for her protection. The men worked eight-hour shifts, except for Mo and Ben, who worked twelve. "The beach is my biggest concern. One of the men stays near the deck at all times, but he doesn't have much of a view up and down the coast. I have a friend who's loaning me his yacht, though. Tomorrow it will be anchored just far enough off the beach to blend in with the other boats out there and I'll have a couple of men with binoculars scanning the shoreline. If they see anything suspicious they'll report it to Mo."

Ryanne smiled. "How many times has Mo tried to convince you things should be coordinated from the yacht?"

"About a dozen," Hugh answered, chuckling. Ryanne had only met Mo once, but she had pegged the investigator perfectly. Mo had presented Hugh with a number of reasons why he should be the one to pull the cushy duty on the luxurious pleasure craft, but Hugh knew his friend had just been joking. He was certain Ryanne knew it, too.

"This is going to be an expensive operation, isn't it?" she asked. "All those extra men, the surveillance equipment, the yacht . . . I'll have Judith write you out a check before you leave today."

"Ryanne, I don't want your money," Hugh insisted flatly. "This isn't just another job to me, and you're not my client."

"Yes, I am," Ryanne argued. "This is *my* problem— I'm the one who needs protection. I won't let you foot the bill for something that doesn't have anything to do with you."

"Damn it, Ryanne," Hugh swore, coming to his feet. "I care about you. I'm not about to put a price tag on what I feel!"

Ryanne knew she'd wounded Hugh by bringing up the subject of money, but she couldn't let it rest. Whatever their personal relationship, it was still going to cost a fortune to protect her. She refused to let Hugh do this out of some misguided, macho sense of loyalty. Their pleasurable, no-strings-attached affair had come to a crashing halt, and any man with sense would have turned around and walked away from her at the first hint of trouble. Hugh wasn't built that way, though, and Ryanne admired and appreciated his sense of honor. He couldn't turn his back on a defenseless woman in need, but that didn't mean their relationship meant what it once had.

"Hugh, listen to me," she said, keeping her voice soft and even. "I know you haven't looked at all of this in terms of cost—that's not you. But if I didn't have you as a friend, I'd have to find someone else to help me out— at least for the time being—and I'd have to pay for that protection. If you don't want to charge me your own personal fee, fine. I'll accept that gesture with gratitude, but you have to let me pay the salaries of the men working for you as well as any extra expenses you incur."

"Ryanne—"

She leaned forward and cut him off. "Hugh, please! Let me do that much at least! I'm sitting around this house as helpless as a worm writhing on a hook, waiting for a big fish to come along and gobble me up. At least leave me the dignity of knowing I'm doing *something* to help myself!"

Hugh found he couldn't argue with that. He was going to keep Ryanne alive, but he wouldn't strip her of her pride to do it. "All right, Ryanne. I'll talk to Judith later about expenses." He returned to the sofa and took her hand. This time she did not pull away.

"Thank you."

"Ryanne, if you really want to help, there is something else you can do."

"What?"

"I want you, Judith and Aggie to move down the beach to my house. Now before you start protesting, listen to what I have to say. My place sits on a peninsula with nothing around it for a half a mile in either direction. No one could possibly approach it without one of my men being aware of it, whereas here, the houses are close, the beach is almost always crowded.... You'd be much safer there, Ryanne," he concluded, but he could tell from her closed expression that he hadn't been convincing enough.

"I can't do that, Hugh, and you know it. I can't disrupt your life that way."

"It's not a disruption, Ryanne, it's a precaution. I've got a spare bedroom Judith can use and we can set your office up in my study."

"I don't know my way around your place, Hugh. You can't imagine what an upheaval it is to have to learn something new."

"I know it wouldn't be simple, but you could learn. I want you to move in with me."

"For how long?" she asked brusquely, tugging her hand out of his firm grasp. "A week, a month? A year?"

For forever, he thought, unbidden, but didn't dare say it out loud. Ryanne had enough to handle without adding to it a declaration of love she probably didn't even want. "For as long as it takes," he said finally.

Ryanne shook her head, stood, and meandered around the room. "Hugh, do you realize how absurd this is?

What if we're wrong about Worste—Beck." She forced herself to say the name she had avoided for so long. "What if he and this Michelon person don't know about my visit to the doctor? What if they never learn the results of the tests? I'm living in an armed prison camp, and for what? The flimsy chance that *maybe* Beck or someone hired by him will make an attempt on my life." She turned to him, her voice plaintive and soft. "I'm walking a tightrope wearing a blindfold, Hugh. I'm so confused and frightened and just plain damned angry with myself and the world that I don't know what to do or which way to turn. Until I figure that out, I'll take precautions and live with the guards and the boat and all the rest of it, but I have to keep some sense of order and routine in my life or I'll go nuts. Can you understand that?"

Sighing, Hugh moved to Ryanne and gathered her into his arms. "Of course I understand." His hands cupped her face and he pressed an undemanding kiss to her lips. "I'll pack a few things and move up here tonight."

"Hugh, no—"

"Yes." He cut her off forcefully. "I'm not leaving you alone. I may come and go during the day, but at night I *will* be with you. If that means giving you a bill for my services as well as my men's, so be it, but you're not getting rid of me."

Ryanne knew it was pointless to argue, particularly when the knowledge that he would be nearby made her feel much safer and far less empty. With a nod and a half smile, she told him, "I'll help Judith make up the bed in the downstairs guest room."

Hugh opened his mouth to tell her he had no intention of sleeping in any bed other than hers, then stopped himself. Ryanne was in no shape to be pushed; he had to

let her define the parameters of their relationship for the
moment. If she couldn't handle intimacy with him—
whether it was making love or just holding her close and
safe in his arms—he wouldn't force the issue when she
was so vulnerable.

"There's no point in bothering Judith," he told her,
pulling her close again. "I never did quite get the hang of
hospital corners, but I can make a bed myself. Just point
me toward the linen closet."

"In a minute," Ryanne murmured, pressing her face
against Hugh's shoulder so that he wouldn't see her disappointment and hurt. She had hoped she was wrong
about Hugh's motives for protecting her, that despite the
turmoil she had brought into his life he still craved the
intimacy they had briefly shared. But she hadn't been
wrong. Hugh didn't want her anymore, or he would have
argued about their sleeping arrangements the way he'd
argued about everything else.

She was a client now, nothing more. She was a responsibility, a job to do thoroughly and efficiently. The
friendship they'd forged wasn't strong enough to with-
stand the kind of pressure Ryanne's predicament placed
it under, and she knew that once Hugh was satisfied and
the danger to her had passed, he would be gone from her
life forever.

The thought of losing him brought a sob to her throat,
but she choked it back, sliding her arms beneath his
jacket to pull him closer. The movement brought her in
contact with the gun holstered beneath his arm and her
blood turned to ice because it reminded her that if Hugh
wasn't very good at his profession he wouldn't be the one
to leave her. She would be leaving him....

RYANNE HAD NEVER known a week could creep by so slowly. She was in a state of suspended animation. It was as though time had simply stopped and left her hanging in midair while the rest of the world went blithely about its business. A feeling of impending violence infused every waking hour and even haunted her sleep. She began having nightmares that left her drained and drenched with sweat, exhausted, yet too terrified to return to sleep.

More than once she had started to call out to Hugh; she'd wanted to beg him to take her into his arms until the trembling passed, but she had resisted that urge. It had become a matter of honor to make it through the night alone, and there was very little else that made her feel honorable these days. Despite Dr. Whitehorn's continued reassurance that what her subconscious mind had done to her didn't decrease her worth as a person, Ryanne couldn't shake the feeling that she was a coward of the highest order. She berated herself for having taken the easy way out of a bad situation, and nothing the psychiatrist said decreased her feelings of guilt. She thought about her father, of how he had died for something he believed in, and she couldn't escape the knowledge that she had betrayed Martin Kirkland and everything he'd stood for.

She talked about her father at length in her sessions with Dr. Whitehorn, of course. The parallels in their situations had always been obvious to her, and now she knew her father's death had contributed greatly to her blindness. Whitehorn said it had likely been the foundation of her subconscious's solution to her conundrum. Knowing that didn't help much, though. As far as Ryanne was concerned, the only thing that would redeem her now was regaining her sight and bringing Arlen Beck to justice.

Unfortunately her subconscious refused to come to the same conclusion. Even the knowledge that being blind was no longer a sure way to keep her alive didn't flip the elusive switch that lurked somewhere in the dark recesses of her mind.

Dr. Whitehorn had two theories about that particular stumbling block, and Ryanne felt both were probably correct. The first was that there was no real proof yet that she was in danger. Her subconscious was still operating on the theory that as long as she was blind, she was safe. Until it was proved otherwise, she would probably remain sightless. The second theory made sense as well; even if the danger was real, her subconscious had no reason to change the status quo as long as Ryanne had Hugh MacKenna protecting her. Her trust in him, the feeling of security and safety she achieved when she was with him made any action on the part of her subconscious unnecessary.

It was a catch-22 situation. If she sent Hugh and his guards away, she stood a better chance of regaining her sight—as well as a better chance of dying.

Ryanne found neither choice palatable. The thought of being without Hugh was as terrifying as the knowledge that Arlen Beck wanted her dead. Hugh was her rock, the only foundation she had in a world of treacherous, shifting quicksand. His presence made her feel safer, but more than that, he reminded her that there was life and hope and happiness beyond the walls of the self-inflicted prison now caging her in. For a few short weeks and one passionate night, Hugh had filled her life with joy. Inch by inch, he had wedged open a door Ryanne had kept sealed; and even if she emerged from this nightmare alive, that door would swing shut with Hugh on one side and Ryanne, alone, on the other.

"Ryanne?" Hugh poked his head into the office where she had been sitting motionless in front of her typewriter for almost an hour. All week long, she'd been making an effort to work on her screenplay, but Hugh knew she had accomplished next to nothing. Considering everything she was trying to cope with, it amazed him that she even bothered.

"Yes, Hugh?" She swiveled toward him.

"It's getting late," he reminded her gently. "Are you going to stay in here all night?"

Ryanne shrugged. "One dark room looks pretty much like any other." She ducked her head the moment the words were out of her mouth. "Sorry. That was supposed to be a joke, but it didn't come out that way, did it?"

"It's all right, Ryanne. No one expects you to be the life of the party."

"That's fortunate." She managed a smile. "Is Judith still on the phone with Webb?"

Hugh leaned against the door frame and shook his head. "No. She went upstairs about a half an hour ago. When I made my rounds checking all the doors and windows, she was in her room, curled up with a good book."

"It was nice of your father to call her. I don't think Judith expected it," Ryanne told him. Webb's phone call had surprised everyone, especially Judith. Webb had been in for a surprise, too, when he had discovered that his son had taken up residence at Ryanne's. Hugh had explained the situation to him and Webb had insisted on talking to Ryanne. They had spoken for several minutes and Ryanne had been immensely grateful that her new friend had resisted the urge to offer meaningless platitudes of encouragement and reassurance. Just knowing that he cared helped more than anything.

After her brief conversation with Webb, Ryanne had handed the phone over to Judith, then left her alone to talk in private. This ordeal was taking its toll on Judith as well, Ryanne knew, and she was grateful that her friend had someone to talk to. She only hoped that Judith would take advantage of the sympathetic, supportive ear Webb would be only too happy to lend her.

Hugh moved to Ryanne's desk and sat on the edge. "Frankly when Dad arrived I don't think he expected to be quite so...taken with your secretary. I certainly wouldn't have guessed it, that's for sure. Dad hasn't been a monk since he and Mother divorced, but he hasn't gone out of his way to develop a social life, either. He's kept his world centered almost totally around his business."

"Then you wouldn't mind it if a little romance blossomed between them?"

"Dad deserves only the best, and as far as I'm concerned Judith Tremain fits very nicely into that category. She's a wonderful woman."

Ryanne smiled, pleased that Hugh realized how special her friend was. "She doesn't let many people close enough to see that."

"So I noticed. Ryanne..." There was a slight, uncomfortable pause as Hugh sought a gentle way of telling Ryanne he had some special precautions he wanted to take tomorrow when she visited the doctor. Ryanne sensed his hesitation and the sudden tension in him, though.

"You didn't come in here just to chat, did you, Hugh?" she asked.

"Actually, no," he replied, grateful that the ice was broken. All week long he'd tried hard to be supportive of Ryanne when she needed support, and to stay out of her way when she didn't. There was a strain in their relationship that had never been there before, however, and no matter how often Hugh told himself that it was simply a result of the incredible pressures on Ryanne, he knew it went deeper than that. Until Ryanne's world had come crashing down, they had never had trouble talking. Now everything they said seemed stilted, as though words had to be censored or sifted through a filter before being spoken aloud. Maybe it was because he was no longer her lover; instead, he had become her protector—or her jailer, it sometimes seemed. And it could have a lot to do with requests like the one he was about to make.

"I wanted to discuss the clothes you're going to wear to the clinic tomorrow," he told her.

Ryanne frowned. Hugh had never expressed an interest in her wardrobe before. "Why? Are you afraid I'll mismatch the colors again?" she asked, remembering the day before yesterday when she'd accidentally donned her lime-green camp shirt instead of the lilac one that matched her cotton trousers.

Hugh laughed lightly, remembering the incident. "No, that's not it. I just want to pick out a jacket—"

"A jacket? Hugh, tomorrow is the third of July and the weatherman is predicting a temperature of one hundred. I don't think a jacket is really necessary."

"It is if you're wearing a bulletproof vest," he told her softly. Ryanne's face turned chalk-white and Hugh cursed himself for having caused the resurgence of panic in her already haunted blue eyes. He would have given anything to spare her this, but it was necessary. Tomorrow was Friday, and he had a gnawing feeling in his gut that all hell was going to break loose. He knew better than to ignore his own premonitions.

Ryanne tried vainly to keep her voice calm. "Have you heard something? Has one of the men seen—"

"No, Ryanne, nothing like that," he reassured her quickly. He saw no reason to tell her that Mo had been fairly certain he'd spotted a car following them to the clinic earlier in the day—probably the same one that had been seen cruising the neighborhood the day before. They had no proof, just suspicions, and Hugh couldn't bring himself to enlighten Ryanne without evidence. "Nothing has changed. I just want to take this extra precaution."

Ryanne nodded, understanding his concern. Here at the house she was well guarded, with Hugh inside and the others outside, not to mention the boat that sat just offshore during the day. Breaking in would be nearly impossible, so it would be logical for someone to go after her while she was out of the house—en route to the clinic, for example, or while she was there. If her therapy sessions hadn't been so important, she was sure Hugh would have insisted she remain in the house at all times.

Hugh moved toward the door, and Ryanne stood. Aggie, who'd been napping under the desk, raised her head sleepily. Ryanne heard the jingle of her choke chain and ordered the dog to stay, then accompanied Hugh down the hall. "I've never worn a suit of armor before. This should be an adventure," she commented dryly.

In Ryanne's bedroom, Hugh closed the door and opened the closet to search for a lightweight jacket that would camouflage the dark bulletproof vest he'd had one of his men deliver. "The vest is as hot as the dickens and weighs about a ton, but it'll make you feel more secure."

Ryanne laughed shortly. "Wanna bet?"

"Hey." Hugh stepped out of the closet and moved to her, pulling her against his chest. She wrapped her arms around him immediately, and held on fiercely, as though she could lose herself in his warmth and strength. "We're going to make it through this, Ryanne. I promise."

She nodded, her face pressed against his throat. "I know."

"No, you don't know," he murmured sadly. "You want to believe it, but you can't quite."

"When it's all over I'll be happy to hear you say I told you so," she said teasingly, desperate to lighten their dark mood. She needed to escape the grimness of the reality that even if she regained her sight and was able to testify, it might be years before Beck came to trial. Until he was convicted, Ryanne would never be safe; the most she had to look forward to was the same uncertainty and fear.

Hugh seemed to sense her thoughts and her need to escape them. "I never gloat, although I have been known to preen from time to time."

Ryanne chuckled. "That I'd like to see."

Hugh's voice became serious as he cupped her face tenderly between his hands. "You will someday, love. You will."

She was so beautiful with her face tilted up to his that Hugh couldn't resist. A week of wanting her but forcing himself to keep that desire under control had taken its toll on him, and without even thinking, he removed her glasses. As he lowered his face to hers, Ryanne sensed his intent and closed her eyes, accepting the whisper-soft pressure of the kisses he placed on each delicate eyelid.

From out of nowhere, Ryanne remembered the story of Sleeping Beauty, who had been awakened from a hundred-years' slumber by the kiss of a handsome prince. With all her heart, she prayed for that same magic to touch her now. She felt Hugh's breath warm her useless eyes, and for a fleeting moment she was filled with the

certainty that when she opened them she would see
Hugh's face, a face she knew only with her heart. He
drew back, and Ryanne reached deep inside for the
courage to raise her eyes to his.

All that greeted her was blackness.

A sob of anguish forced its way out and she arched,
offering Hugh her lips. His mouth closed over hers and
the desperation of their separate fears and needs merged
into one consuming flame. Roughly Hugh pulled Ryanne
to him, sealing their bodies as his mouth ravaged hers.
His tongue plunged deep in symbolic union, and Ryanne
eagerly clasped the back of his head, urging him on,
begging for more. With a muffled groan, Hugh filled his
hand with the weight of one of her breasts, his thumb
teasing the crest to hardness.

Ryanne's breath caught in her throat and stayed there
for a long moment before finally shuddering outward.
Need so great it was almost a physical pain sliced through
her with every stroke of Hugh's thumb across her breast.
A sob of desperation welled but came out as only a
breathy moan, and Ryanne felt a rush of liquid heat settle between her thighs.

Longing overwhelmed her and she reached with frantic, clumsy fingers for the buttons of Hugh's shirt. They
refused to yield to her and she abandoned her quest and
began tugging the tail of his shirt from his pants. She
needed to touch him, needed to feel him touching her
without the restricting barrier of clothes between them.
His shirt came free, and Ryanne's hands dived beneath
it, wildly savoring the hardness of his back and firmly
muscled chest.

Hugh's hunger matched Ryanne's and when she
touched him it was more than he could bear. He swept
her into his arms and carried her to the bed without

breaking their soul-shattering kiss. As though she were a priceless treasure, he lowered her to the bed and covered her body with his, pressing her into the mattress. He undid the buttons of her shirt with trembling fingers, and drew the fabric aside, trailing kisses down her neck and shoulders until he came to the lacy fabric of her bra.

With murmured sighs and whispers, Ryanne urged him on. She arched when his lips began caressing her breasts through the thin scrap of material, and the liquid ache intensified a hundredfold. Hugh was taking pleasure and giving it, but Ryanne wanted more. She wanted completion, and she wanted the sweet oblivion that could be found only when Hugh's body was joined to hers. She groped for the closure of his trousers, but when Hugh pulled away from her to discard them, Ryanne cried out at the loss of his warmth and weight pressing into her. She reached for him blindly and Hugh returned immediately. He dispatched her clothes quickly and their fevered need took control. He entered her swiftly, surely, in a frenzy of passion that engulfed them both. Separate needs, separate fears, merged into one brilliant moment of perfect oblivion in which the world consisted of nothing but intense pleasure and two souls became only one.

For that short time, Ryanne and Hugh existed only for each other, but when the moment had passed, the feeling of separateness that came as they returned to the real world was more than Ryanne could bear. The beauty of their union and the desolation of its lonely aftermath wrenched a storm of tears from her. Without really understanding why, she began to cry as though her heart would break.

Ryanne wept almost soundlessly, her head buried at Hugh's throat, and he held her tightly as his reason began to return. He felt Ryanne sobbing pitifully against him and self-loathing started seeping into every crevice of his mind. He had taken Ryanne in a fevered heat of animal passion, without care or consideration. And worse, he had taken advantage of her incredible vulnerability. Her need had been as great as his, but he had selfishly used her with no thought of what was best for Ryanne. Now she was weeping as though she had been stripped of what little pride this nightmarish week had left her. Hating himself, Hugh waited until her tears began to subside before he pulled away.

"I'm sorry, Ryanne. I'm so sorry," he whispered against her temple, then released her and moved to the edge of the bed.

"Sorry?" Ryanne murmured, stunned. Hugh was sorry he'd made love to her. She had thrown herself at him, abandoning any vestige of pride even though he'd made it clear he no longer wanted her. She had deliberately inflamed him and Hugh had given in because he'd felt sorry for her. Now he was just sorry, period.

After a long, hard week, this was another humiliation. Ryanne wondered what she'd done to deserve it. Trying to salvage what little pride she had left, she sat up and wrapped the lightweight bedspread around her as she slid to the edge of the bed opposite Hugh. "No, I'm the one who should be sorry." She laughed mirthlessly. "I seem to have a habit of forcing you into things."

Hugh twisted toward her. "Forcing me? Ryanne, how can you think that?"

"Why else would you be sorry you'd made love with me?" she demanded, wiping the tears that refused to stop falling. "I threw myself at you and you took pity on me—"

"Took pity on you?" Hugh was across the bed in an instant, grabbing Ryanne by the shoulders to turn her

toward him. "What just happened here had nothing to do with pity, Ryanne. I want you. God, I've never stopped wanting you! I've lain awake thinking of you alone in this room, and I swear, some nights I've thought I might go out of my mind with that wanting."

"Then why did you stay away?" Ryanne demanded brokenly.

"Because I thought you didn't want this . . . want me. You're the one who put me in the guest bedroom, remember?"

Ryanne raised her face to Hugh's. "I remember you didn't give me any argument."

"My God . . ." Hugh would have laughed at their folly if he hadn't been so moved by Ryanne's tears. He dried them with his lips and asked gently, "Did you think that because I agreed to separate sleeping arrangements I didn't want you anymore?"

Ryanne nodded. "No sane man would want a woman with my kind of problems."

He would if he loved you as much as I do, Hugh was on the verge of saying, but he stopped just in time. Ryanne wasn't asking for a commitment or an avowal of love, and he refused to complicate her already complicated life with one more item to worry about. Just as he had no intention of allowing anything to happen to her, he was equally adamant about not letting her go, but this wasn't the time to tell her that.

"I want you, Ryanne. Whether it's sane or not, it's a fact."

"Then why did you apologize for having made love to me?"

"Because I thought I had taken advantage of you."

Ryanne smiled at that. "I don't remember offering any resistance—in fact, I was the one who started the ball rolling."

"And we finished it together," he said, putting his arms around her and pulling her close.

"I don't want it to be finished, Hugh," she whispered, her face pressed against his throat. "Will you stay with me tonight?"

"Only if you promise to fall asleep in my arms," he told her softly, lowering her to the bed as his lips closed over hers.

CHAPTER FIFTEEN

THEY SPENT the long night making love and talking, then making love again. Their passion unlocked a floodgate of emotions in Ryanne, and as she lay nestled in Hugh's arms, drawing from his deep well of strength, she told him things she'd expressed only to Dr. Whitehorn—and a few she'd never dared say to anyone. She explained the deep, mortal shame she felt for having been unable to cope with her fear of Arlen Beck, and her sense of having betrayed everything she'd ever believed in or believed herself to be.

As she talked, Hugh realized that discovering she was hysterically blind had almost totally shattered Ryanne's entire ego structure. She no longer trusted her own judgment about anything, and she saw herself as a coward and a weakling. Her new lack of faith in herself made Hugh want to cry out because it was so unjustified, and he tried to tell her that the way she'd confronted her problem this week only proved that her strength of purpose and character had not deserted her. But nothing he said convinced her. Ryanne was going to have to come to that conclusion on her own, Hugh finally realized, and for now, all he could do to help was hold her close and assure her that she had not diminished in his eyes or anyone else's.

They talked into the night, long after Judith had turned out her lights upstairs. Ryanne had taken Aggie outside, then placed her on the bedchain beside her and Hugh.

Hugh brought up the subject of Ryanne's father, admitting that Doug had told him how Martin Kirkland had died, and Ryanne was grateful that he knew the story. It saved her from recounting the details that were still horrifyingly painful to her. She talked instead about her childhood and how devastated she'd been when her beloved father had been brutally murdered. She talked about her mother's death, too—the wastefulness of it, and the resentment she still couldn't quite overcome.

"For a long time after she died," Ryanne told Hugh, "I swore I'd never let myself fall in love. It just didn't make sense that anyone could give up on life like that."

"Do you still feel that way, Ryanne?" Hugh asked, wondering if he'd found an explanation for Ryanne's apparent reticence to become more deeply involved with him.

She shook her head. "No. Once I got older, I realized that the problem had stemmed from my mother's insecurities, not the institution of marriage. Without her husband, she didn't have the will to go on. I was there, needing her more than ever, but that just wasn't enough for her."

Hugh let a handful of Ryanne's silky hair slide through his fingers. "Were you and your mother close before your father died?"

Ryanne thought for a moment. "No, I don't think so—not the way some mothers and daughters are close. I loved her, but Daddy was the one I went to when I had a problem, and he was the one who sat by my bedside reading me stories when I was sick. He would stay with me until Mother would come in and insist he let me get some sleep."

Ryanne frowned at the memory. "Even when I wasn't sick she was like that. Every time Daddy started to spend time with me, Mother would always interrupt. Daddy would come home from work, put me on his lap and ask me what I'd done that day; and just as I'd start to tell him, Mother would send me on an errand or make me go do my homework. Looking back on it, I really think she was jealous of me."

"They say all mothers and daughters feel some degree of rivalry, Ryanne. That doesn't mean she didn't love you," Hugh said gently.

"She didn't love me enough to believe that I was a good reason to fight for her life. Frankly I think she was relieved when they diagnosed her cancer. She really did want to die, Hugh." Ryanne turned toward him, laying her head on his shoulder and draping one arm across his chest.

"Right after Daddy was killed she sent me to stay with Aunt Rose and Uncle Charley for a while. Mother stayed at our house alone..." Her voice drifted off as she dredged up a painful memory. Hugh's lips pressing against her temple gave her the courage to continue. "I came home from school one day and there was this incredible tension in the house. Everyone was behaving almost exactly as they had just before they told me Daddy had been killed. I was already scared to death, and so miserably lonely that I could barely function, so their attitude really terrified me. Aunt Rose bustled me off to my room, pretending that nothing was wrong, but later that night when I crept back downstairs to eavesdrop on her and Uncle Charley, I learned that mother was in the hospital. She'd tried to kill herself by taking an overdose of sedatives."

Hugh tightened his arms around her, stroking her back comfortingly, but he made no comment. Ryanne didn't need platitudes now, she simply needed to talk. He held her close and listened.

"No one ever told me directly what happened, and I never told anyone I knew because I felt so guilty. I figured it had to be my fault that she wanted to die."

"You know now that's not true, don't you?"

Ryanne nodded. "Yes. I stopped blaming myself a long time ago."

"Good." He brushed his lips across her forehead. "After your mother got out of the hospital, did she take you back home with her?"

"No, she came to stay with Aunt Rose and Uncle Charley, too. Aunt Rose was Dad's sister, but Mother didn't have any family of her own. I suspect they pressured her into coming to live with them because they were afraid that if someone didn't keep an eye on her she'd try to kill herself again. Uncle Charley took care of selling our house, Aunt Rose took care of me, and Mother just stayed in her room grieving, willing herself to die.... And she did."

"Ryanne, have you considered that maybe your mother's death was just as important a factor in your blindness as your father's death?" Hugh asked quietly.

Ryanne frowned. "No, I hadn't."

"Watching her waste away and die only strengthened your incredible will to survive. You father's death may have laid the groundwork for your subconscious's solution to a situation similar to his, but the unfairness of your mother's death may be what made you determined to live at any cost."

Ryanne considered the theory, making a mental note to discuss it with Dr. Whitehorn tomorrow. So far, her therapy had concentrated only on the attempt on her life and her father's death. Maybe it was time to move on to her relationship with her mother; perhaps that's where they'd find the key to restoring her sight.

They talked on, and as Hugh listened to Ryanne's outpouring of thoughts and fears, Hugh ached with so much love that he thought his heart might burst. What would it take, he wondered, to make her realize that she had a strength that was unbreakable? Like the willow, she could bend with the worst of storms and still remain standing when the tempest had passed.

"In all this soul-searching, Ryanne, have you taken any time to dream?" Hugh asked. It was nearing dawn and they both needed sleep, but neither was capable of letting go of the quiet night.

Ryanne pulled away from him and raised herself on one elbow. "Dream?" She said the word as though it was one she'd never heard before.

"Yes, dream," Hugh reiterated, winding a lock of her hair around his hand to draw her close again. "You once told me there were certain dreams that were luxuries you couldn't afford because of your blindness. But you can dream now, Ryanne, because someday soon your sight will return. If you woke up tomorrow morning and could see, and the threat posed by Beck miraculously went away, what would you do? What would you want?"

Hugh was right. Ryanne hadn't allowed herself to dream beautiful dreams of the future and she was afraid to do so now because shattered dreams were unbearably painful. But because it was late, because she was wrapped safely in Hugh's arms, Ryanne overcame her fear of disappointment and let an imaginary light illuminate what her heart wanted most.

"I would want..." *to see your face, to know you were mine forever, to share your life, bear our children and know that the darkness could never touch me again because you are my light....* The words were there in thoughts that burned brightly at the center of everything Ryanne was or hoped to be. But it was a futile dream, and saying it aloud would only make it hurt that much more when it didn't come true. Her future was too uncertain and she was too unworthy of such happiness.

Rather than give voice to her heart's deepest desire, then, she chose a simpler dream, one more realistic and less painful.

"I would want my old life back," she told him. Years of believing she'd never fulfill that lost dream added conviction to her words. "I'd get down on bended knees in front of Douglas Sutherland and beg for my old job. I would reestablish my old contacts and make new ones, and go back to fighting for all the things my father believed in. The things he taught me to believe in." Ryanne's eyes pooled with tears because she realized this dream was real, too. "I want to redeem myself and make Daddy proud of me...."

Her voice broke and the tears began to flow freely. Hugh sipped them, murmuring, "He would be, Ryanne. Never doubt it. He would be *so* proud of you."

Hugh held her tightly while she cried, and he prayed that her tears would be cleansing. Ruefully he wished that he could shed a few himself. Maybe tears would ease the terrible ache around his heart. He was the one who'd opened the door on Ryanne's deepest desire, secretly wishing that she would make him a part of her dreams. Now, he would have to live with the knowledge that when Ryanne imagined her future she saw no place for him in it. He couldn't bring himself to accept it yet, but somewhere in the deep recesses of his mind he realized that someday he'd have to let Ryanne go. Until then, though, he would hold her, keep her safe, and cling to the selfish knowledge that as long as she needed his protection he would be allowed to stay at her side.

"Hugh?"

"What?" He shook himself mentally and returned to the present when he realized Ryanne had been talking to him. "What did you say?"

Ryanne smiled into Hugh's shoulder. "Did you finally fall asleep on me?"

"I must have drifted off for a minute," he lied. "What did you ask me?"

"I asked what you want from life," she said, sliding her fingers through the soft blanket of hair on his chest. "You've achieved so much, but you must have dreams, too."

A painful stab of sorrow pierced Hugh's heart. "No, Ryanne…no dreams." His voice sounded hollow and far away. "I have everything I want right now."

CHAPTER SIXTEEN

"EXCUSE ME, Mr. Michelon, but Mr. Beck is here to see you. I told him you were at breakfast, but he insisted you would want to speak with him."

"Show Mr. Beck to the library, Gray," Del Michelon ordered the butler, who bowed deferentially and left as silently as he'd entered.

Michelon pushed back from the table, placed his napkin beside his half-eaten breakfast and glanced at his wife. "I'm sorry, dear. This will only take a moment."

He rose and ambled to the room that served as his study. His instinct was to keep Beck waiting, make him sweat, but Del was too concerned about the outcome of Ryanne Kirkland's medical tests to play that game. The day of her appointment had come and gone four days ago, and still the man Beck had sent to Los Angeles had not been able to obtain conclusive evidence as to whether or not she would regain her sight. Michelon didn't like to be kept waiting, nor did he like inefficiency. And most of all, he didn't like Arlen Beck, who'd put him in this uncomfortable position in the first place.

"Well, Arlen, I presume you have some news for me—finally," he said unceremoniously as he entered the massive room decorated in oak and leather.

Beck watched as Michelon assumed the chair behind a huge desk that Beck had always thought of as his employer's throne of power. Not that he'd been privileged to enter this inner sanctum very often. Michelon kept his personal life and his "business" interests well separated, maintaining the image of a genteel man of wealth and breeding that fooled very few. Del Michelon was a gangster, and the only people who didn't know it were the ones who didn't *want* to know it.

"Yes, sir. Keegan was finally able to break into the clinic late last night. The night watchman he'd bribed to look the other way while he gained entry didn't return to work until yesterday."

"Was Mr. Keegan successful?"

"Yes. He made the break-in look like a drug theft and vandalized Dr. Kazlovski's office as well as several others. It will take days to reconstruct their files and realize Kirkland's is missing."

Michelon nodded his approval. "Excellent. What exactly did the file say? I understand from what you told me yesterday that Ms. Kirkland has been surrounded by a cordon of bodyguards on what have become daily visits to the clinic. Were we correct in our assumption that she may regain her sight?"

Beck nodded and gave Michelon the details Ace Keegan had related to him on the phone just hours ago. Most of it had been medical mumbo jumbo to both men, but the final notation had made the situation clear: *Diagnosis: conversion reaction-hysterical blindness. Prognosis: favorable if patient consents to intensive therapy. Referral: Whitehorn.*

"So her sight could return at any time," Michelon concluded, leaning back in the soft leather chair.

"That's right. Should I tell Keegan to go ahead before they discover her file is missing and increase security around her?"

Michelon eyed the troublesome banker disdainfully. "Is there any other alternative?"

"No, sir."

"Then see that it's taken care of. Today."

"Yes, sir." Beck rose. "Ryanne Kirkland is as good as dead."

THE WEATHERMAN'S ESTIMATE of the temperature for the third of July had been way off. One-hundred would have been a blessing, and Mo Johnson didn't feel the least bit blessed. Standing just outside the bank of doors that led to the clinic, he kept an alert eye on the street and tried to ignore the sweat that poured down his torso. Without his jacket he might have had a chance of being comfortable, but the .32 Smith and Wesson nestled in his shoulder holster would have raised more than one curious eyebrow, so he suffered in silence. He glanced at his watch and noted with relief that Ryanne's session would soon be over and they could leave.

Like Hugh, Mo had a feeling that today was going to be the day. Tomorrow was Saturday, the fourth, the start of a three-day holiday, which meant that Ryanne wouldn't be back to the clinic until Tuesday. It only made sense that if an attempt on her life was going to be made, it would go down today. The best time would be in the few moments Ryanne was traveling between the clinic doors and the car, which meant Mo's scrutiny was focused not only on the street, but also on the two- and three-story buildings across the street.

So far, though, nothing had struck him as out of the ordinary. The only car parked on the street was Hugh's. Everyone else had heeded the No Parking signs. Thanks to Vic Coffin, Hugh's friend on the police force, a patrol car circled the block every few minutes and the uniforms always gave Mo a jaunty wave and ignored the illegally parked BMW.

A car squealed around the corner of Santa Monica and Beverly, and Mo straightened reflexively, his hand sliding to the gun. The car came to a squealing stop behind the black BMW and Mo relaxed. Detective Vic Coffin started toward him as Mo resumed his slow scan of the neighborhood.

"That kind of driving is bad for the tires, Vic." Mo shot him a quick grin.

"Yeah, but it's great for my macho image." Coffin was short but athletically built, and he made up for his small stature by projecting a tough-guy personality that most people believed was just a cover-up for an even tougher guy that lurked underneath.

"What brings you down here? You change your mind about giving us a little more police protection?" No actual threat had been made against Ryanne and the L.A.P.D.'s involvement was strictly unofficial.

Coffin shook his head. "No, but I ran across a report today that I thought you guys might want to know about. Could be nothing, but I've got a gut instinct that says different."

"There's a lot of that going around today," Mo said dryly. "What have you got?"

Vic cocked his head toward the building behind them. "This place was broken into last night." Mo's full attention was suddenly riveted on the police detective. "The investigating officers said it was a routine drug theft, but I don't buy it. The drugs were taken out of the downstairs clinic area, then the perpetrator went up to the second-floor office wing and trashed three offices."

"Including Kazlovski's?"

"Naturally. According to the report it'll take them days to get their files back together."

"Damn!" Mo swore. "The drug theft was just a cover-up to get Ryanne's file."

"That's what I figure. Which means your bad guy in Chicago knows all there is to know about Ms. Kirkland."

"And he's gotta go after her." Mo clapped the detective on the shoulder. "Thanks, Vic. I gotta run upstairs and let Hugh know about this. Can you cover the door for me?"

"You think it's going to go down today?"

"I'm positive."

Coffin pointed toward the door as he started to his unmarked police car. "You go back up Hugh and I'll get a couple of uniforms over here. Bring the girl down in the elevator and we'll be waiting!"

"Done!" Mo called back as the glass door closed behind him.

FROM HIS VANTAGE POINT in the corner next to the water fountain, Hugh had a clear view of the only two doors that led to the rabbit warren of offices where Ryanne had entered nearly fifty minutes ago. The door opposite him, to his left, opened into a comfortable waiting room and reception desk guarded by a pleasant young woman whose appearance reflected the clinic's upscale clientele. The door to the right, far down the L-shaped hallway, was the physician's unlabeled entrance.

Every time a patient or staff member rounded one of the corners that snaked out of his sight, Hugh tensed fractionally. He gave each person that passed him a nod or a friendly smile as he assessed them, looking for the telltale bulge of a weapon, but so far no one had looked suspicious.

A pretty young woman he had seen enter the reception room about thirty minutes earlier stepped through the patient's door on his left and flashed him a smile. With the aid of twin metal crutches, she hobbled toward the water fountain beside him.

"Still waiting, huh?" she asked as she began the laborious process of shifting her crutches and balancing her weight so that she could bend to the fountain.

"Here. Allow me," Hugh offered, returning her friendly smile as he stepped over to the fountain. He held down the button that activated a cold geyser, and the girl mumbled her thanks as she bent. Hugh repositioned himself so that he was facing the left branch of the hall, but the right was still visible in his peripheral line of sight.

Far down the right hall, a man in a white lab coat rounded the corner and moved purposefully toward the physician's entrance. He barely spared a glance at the man and woman facing the water fountain before moving on to the door, but that slight moment of hesitation was all it took for Hugh to recognize Ace Keegan.

Instinctively Hugh reached for his gun, then remembered the girl in front of him. If he called to Keegan there was no telling what the hit man's reaction might be, and if he opened fire the girl would very likely be hurt. Forcing himself to remain frozen, he waited until Keegan disappeared through the physician's entrance, then he dashed toward the reception room, leaving the startled young woman behind.

By the time he got to the door, his gun was drawn and his mind was working furiously, mapping out the twists and turns of the inner corridors that led from the physician's entrance to Dr. Whitehorn's office. He passed the receptionist's desk with a terse command to call the police, then turned down the hallway that would put him on a collision course with the man who had been sent to kill Ryanne Kirkland.

"IT WAS A GOOD SESSION, Ryanne," Dr. Whitehorn said as he helped her into the jacket that covered the bullet-proof vest that had been one of their topics of conversation today. "I'll see you at the same time next Tuesday and we'll discuss making your visits every other day rather than every day, depending on how well you do this weekend."

Ryanne gave him a reassuring smile as she picked up Aggie's harness. "I don't think I'm going to fall apart, doctor, if that's what you're worried about. Though I can't say I'm looking forward to *Independence* Day tomorrow."

Whitehorn took her free hand. "It is an incongruous holiday, considering what you're going through."

"It's as good as any, I suppose." She shrugged. "I don't care for the implications of Memorial Day, and Thanksgiving would be totally inappropriate, don't you agree?"

The doctor squeezed her hand, amazed at how well she was coping with the extraordinary stress of her situation. "If you need anything at all, Ryanne, please don't hesitate to call my answering service. They'll contact me immediately and I'll get right back to you."

"Thank you."

He dropped her hand and opened the door. "Take care."

"I will, doctor. Thanks again." She gestured with her right hand. "Aggie, out. Hup-hup."

The retriever moved Ryanne into the doorway, then paused for directions. "Good girl! Left, le—"

"Ryanne, no! Get back!"

It happened so fast Ryanne had no time to comprehend what was going on. She heard Hugh's voice, but the thundering report of two bullets fired in swift succession transported her back five years into a darkened warehouse. The sense of déjà vu, of the inescapability of the hit, obscured the pain she knew she should be feeling as the two bullets slammed into her back and knocked her forward, into the door frame. Her legs tangled with Aggie's harness and she fell to the floor in a heap, conscious of more shots being fired, of the distant sound of running feet, and finally, of Hugh's voice close by, murmuring her name over and over again.

"Ryanne? Damn it, Ryanne, talk to me!" Hugh begged, tearing at her jacket to inspect the vest that had saved her life.

"Hugh! Are you all right?" Terrified, Ryanne reached for him blindly, desperate to know he was unharmed.

"I'm fine, love." Fiercely he pulled her into his arms, rocking her back and forth until she could regain the wind that had been knocked from her lungs.

From seemingly out of nowhere, Mo Johnson appeared at the door, but Hugh didn't pause to question why his associate had abandoned his post downstairs. "It was Keegan!" Hugh told him, his voice once again filled with the same cold, hard edge Ryanne had heard the night he'd discovered the scars on her shoulder. "He went down the back hall. Go!"

"Coffin's downstairs calling for back up!" Mo shouted as he started off in pursuit of the gunman.

"Are you sure she's not hurt?" Dr. Whitehorn asked, bending over the couple on the floor, doing his best to remain calm and professional. He'd never considered psychiatry a dangerous profession until just a moment ago.

"I'm fine." Ryanne finally found her wits and eased out of Hugh's embrace, fighting the instinct to remain safe in his arms. She had to find the strength to cope with this on her own. "Aggie? Where's Aggie?"

"Right here, love. She's fine." The dog, startled by the shots, had hunkered down by her fallen mistress, and Ryanne reached out to her, crooning words of reassurance. Hugh helped her to her feet and into a chair as the hall outside came alive with the sound of curious, excited voices.

Taking charge, forcing the horrible image of Ryanne's brush with death from his mind, Hugh instructed the doctor to tell everyone that the police were on the way, then to close the door.

"You didn't get him, did you?" Ryanne asked.

"No," Hugh answered, keeping her hand in his. "We came around opposite ends of the corridor at about the same time, and you were standing between us. By the time I could get off a shot, he was already moving out the way he came in." Hugh glanced toward the door at the psychiatrist who was still as white as a ghost. "You look as though you could use a shrink, Dr. Whitehorn."

The pun cut through some of the tension in the room and they all laughed. Neither Hugh nor the doctor were surprised when Ryanne's laughter quickly turned to tears.

Hugh went to his knees, holding her while she sobbed, and Dr. Whitehorn patted her shoulder comfortingly. "Let it all out, Ryanne, that's it. This is only natural. Your body has to rid itself of all that fear-induced adrenaline, and crying is one of the best ways to release that tension."

Hugh couldn't have given a medical description of what Ryanne was going through, but he knew that what she needed now was reassurance that she had survived. He held her close, stroking her hair, until the storm had passed, but his mind was already at work on what had to be done next.

"Hugh?"

He glanced at the door as Mo and Vic Coffin came into the office, closing the door on the mayhem in the hall. Hugh caught a glimpse of a uniformed officer holding back a curious crowd. "Did you get him?"

Mo shook his head. "Sorry. He had a car waiting at one of the emergency exits downstairs. I got the license number, but I'll lay you even money the car is either stolen or rented."

"I've already got an APB out on Keegan and the car," Coffin added. "Is Miss Kirkland all right?"

"I'm fine," Ryanne told him, wiping her face with the tissue Dr. Whitehorn handed her. Hugh introduced her to the police detective, and they murmured strained how-do-you-dos.

"How did you get here so fast, Coffin?" Hugh finally thought to ask.

Vic explained about the burglary report that had crossed his desk. He also apologized for not having made it to the clinic in time to avert the near disaster. "Now that this has become an official police matter, we'll be taking you into protective custody, Miss Kirkland," he informed her. "I've got—"

"No." Hugh stood and squared off against his friend.

"Look, Hugh, you can't take her back to the house in Malibu."

"I have no intention of taking her there, and I'm not turning her over to you, either." He looked at Johnson.

"Mo, get on the phone to Ben and tell him to get the jet ready and file a flight plan for Toronto."

Mo's eyebrows went up in surprise. "Toronto?"

"Just do it, okay? I'll explain later. And after you talk to Ben, I want you to head for Ryanne's place and pick up Judith. Have her throw a few of Ryanne's things and her own into a suitcase, then take her straight to the jet."

Confused, Ryanne reached out and found Hugh's arm. "What are you planning?"

"Please trust me, Ryanne. We've got to move quickly."

Hugh's precautions had already saved her life once today, so she fell silent and listened as he issued orders that only he seemed to understand. Mo was already on the phone as Hugh turned back to Coffin. "Vic, can you get a policewoman over here?"

"Yeah, sure, but—"

"And get the coroner down here, too."

"The coroner! Hugh—" Coffin stopped as he finally caught on to the investigator's intent. "Oh, I get it."

"Well, I don't!" Ryanne snapped, disturbed by his mention of the coroner. It was a grisly reminder that she'd come too close to needing one. "Hugh, please—"

He knelt beside her again. "Ryanne, unless Keegan got a good enough look at you to realize you were wearing that vest, he thinks you're dead. Or at the very least, that you're critically wounded. If we can convince him that he succeeded in killing you, then you'll be in the clear. Beck will have no reason to send someone else after you."

Like Coffin, Ryanne finally saw where Hugh was leading. "You're going to treat this area like a murder scene and have me switch places with a policewoman," she guessed, trying to ignore the cold shiver that ran down her spine.

"That's right." He looked at Coffin again. "Can we do it?"

"Piece of cake." The detective grinned as he moved to the phone Mo had just finished with, and started making a few calls of his own.

Ryanne sat quietly, listening intently as the charade began to unfold. Hugh moved her from the chair onto a sofa behind the door so that no one would see her when the office door was opened to admit a steady stream of policemen. Dr. Whitehorn joined her on the sofa, quietly encouraging her to talk about what she was feeling, but mostly Ryanne felt numb and there were only so many ways to express that kind of blank emptiness. With half an ear she listened to Whitehorn's attempts to reassure her, but her real comfort came from the sound of Hugh's commanding, controlled voice. Just knowing he was nearby made her feel safer.

It took almost an hour to set the stage for Ryanne's departure. Mo was already on his way to Malibu. He'd taken Aggie with him, and Ryanne had exchanged clothing with a policewoman who was about her size. The uniform fit a little snugly across her breasts, but a police-issue flak jacket similar to the vest that had saved her life effectively covered that flaw. Hugh tucked her long hair up into the officer's hat as a coroner's stretcher was brought in.

"This is spooky," the policewoman muttered to no one in particular as she slipped onto the stretcher and let the two attendants pull a sheet up over her head. "Somebody be sure to remind the coroner I don't need an autopsy, okay?" she mumbled from beneath the sheet, then went perfectly still as the door opened and she was carried out.

Coffin followed the stretcher into the hall, making sure the officers out there had the crowd cleared away. "Okay. Let's do it."

Hugh took Ryanne's hand and slipped it through the crook of his arm. "You ready?"

She nodded. "This is where five years of trying not to look blind comes in, right?"

"You just try to look as though you belong in that uniform and I'll do the rest," Hugh advised her, pressing a quick kiss to her lips, startling Ryanne. "I've never kissed a cop before," he explained with a reassuring smile in his voice.

"If we can hang on to the uniform for a while, I'll let you do more than kiss a cop."

"I like the sound of that," Hugh murmured seductively, hoping that their banter was achieving its purpose of putting Ryanne a little more at ease.

Apparently it was working, because she smiled her effervescent smile at him for the first time all day. "And I like the idea of falling asleep in your arms again tonight."

"That's a promise." Reluctantly he returned to business. "All right, let's go. Vic has cleared the hall and stairwell down to one of the side exits where his car is waiting at the door. No one will look twice at a detective and a uniformed officer escorting an eyewitness down to headquarters for questioning."

"What about the press?" Ryanne asked as Hugh moved into the hall. In the melee of the preceding hour she'd heard someone say that every news team in the city was downstairs.

"They'll all be focused on the body being loaded into the van, and the coroner is going to make a brief statement that should keep everyone occupied until we're out of the area."

Hugh and Coffin had covered all the bases, it seemed. Ryanne fell silent and concentrated on playing her role. When they reached the outer door, Hugh quietly gave her instructions so that it appeared she was escorting him to the car rather than vice versa. He opened the door and slipped into the back seat. Ryanne followed him as Coffin moved purposefully to the driver's seat and pulled away.

"Turn toward me and look down as though you dropped something, Ryanne," Hugh ordered sharply as the unmarked car passed a crowd of onlookers at the edge of the police blockade. When they were clear, Coffin picked up speed and Hugh told Ryanne she could relax.

"Next stop, Toronto?" Vic asked, grinning triumphantly in the rearview mirror.

"That's right," Hugh confirmed, returning the smile.

Like Mo, Ryanne didn't understand why Hugh would want to take her to Canada. She started to ask him to explain, but Hugh sensed her question and silenced her with a kiss.

"Trust me, Ryanne," he whispered, for her ears only.

She nodded and relaxed into the circle of Hugh's arms.

CHAPTER SEVENTEEN

WITH HER FEET PROPPED on the *Mary Ann*'s transom, Ryanne leaned back in the padded fishing chair and let the warm Gulf breeze wrap itself around her. Behind her, up on the flying bridge, Judith and Webb were engaged in a good-natured argument. Hugh was inside the main cabin radioing Mo and Ben, who were miles away back in Bay St. Louis, making sure they hadn't been followed after they rerouted from Toronto to the Gulf of Mexico.

For the first time in what seemed like years rather than just barely a week, Ryanne relaxed. She'd had her first good night's sleep since her ordeal of fear began, and though she knew this sense of peace couldn't last, she felt truly safe. Content to enjoy the respite, she let her mind float with the even rhythm of the boat.

Unavoidably her thoughts skidded back to the traumatic events of the previous day, but she refused to dwell there for long. She preferred to think about how kind and supportive Webb had been when his son and a decidedly tense entourage had arrived unexpectedly at his house the previous night. By the tone of his voice, Ryanne had known that the poor man was exhausted. He had just returned home after a long day with a boisterous fishing charter, yet he welcomed Ryanne and the others heartily.

Hugh had explained the situation and Webb understood immediately what his son intended to do. He had ushered Ryanne and Judith off to bed in his room, and while they slept, the men spent most of the night making sure Webb's forty-foot cabin cruiser, the *Mary Ann*, was ready to get under way before dawn. The five boats in his fleet had all been booked for the day, but he'd done some creative shuffling and combined two small parties into one larger one so that the *Mary Ann* was free for what Webb insisted on calling a family outing.

And now they were in the Gulf, with nothing around them but miles of ocean in every direction. Except for Douglas Sutherland, no one knew where Ryanne was, and the man who wanted her dead thought he had succeeded in eliminating the threat she posed to him. Ryanne recalled the morbid joke she'd made about Independence Day only yesterday. Ironically, today she did feel like celebrating her brief glimpse of freedom. Smiling faintly at the sun that warmed her, she slid lower in the chair and floated with the gentle rocking of the boat.

Hugh stepped out of the air-conditioned cabin and froze at the sight of Ryanne. Reclining in one of the two swivel chairs that were bolted securely to the deck, she looked like a sleek, sensuous cat sleeping in the sun. Her hair cascaded down the back of the chair, and the sundress she'd worn the day she met him was drawn up to her thighs so that the sun could worship her long, shapely legs.

The bunched-up dress exposed far less than a bathing suit, or even a pair of shorts would have, and yet the way the dress billowed and fluttered with the breeze was far more enticing. A stab of desire so strong it was painful sliced through Hugh and he moved across the wooden deck toward her.

"Hugh?" she questioned, cocking her head to one side, presenting him with an even better view of her lovely profile.

"Right here."

"Is everything all right back at the port?"

"Just fine. Mo says to tell you he found an excellent veterinarian who had facilities to board Aggie. She settled in okay, but she misses you terribly."

Ryanne sighed. Poor Aggie. It would have been inhumane to bring the animal aboard the boat, but Aggie wouldn't realize that this was for her own good. She would be miserable without Ryanne, but there had been no other choice.

Hugh stepped behind her chair, gathering her silky hair in one hand while the other gently cupped her chin. His husky voice erased all thoughts of the golden retriever from Ryanne's mind. "You are the perfect picture of hedonistic sensuality," he murmured, dipping his lips to hers for an upside-down kiss that was slow and lazy and incredibly arousing.

"Umm..." Ryanne's hand drifted to the back of Hugh's head and she gave herself over completely to his tender ministrations. "You do that very well, sir," she mumbled when he started nibbling a slow trail along her jaw and down her throat.

"That's because I'm...inspired," he replied between kisses. A sudden gust of wind shifted Ryanne's dress higher up on her thigh and she snatched at it to cover herself more modestly, but Hugh stayed her hand. "No, no, no," he chided. "I like that just where it is." With teasing strokes, he caressed the long line of her thigh. He moved to her side and rested one hip on the chair's arm so that he could press Ryanne back with a drugging kiss. She gasped against his mouth when his hand slipped to

the inside of her thigh and slowly worked its way upward. Despite the delightfully liquid sensations he was
creating, she tore her mouth away from his to protest
weakly.

"Hugh, no.... Judith and your father..."

"Are up on the bridge and can't possibly see us. However, if it's propriety you're worried about—" Without
warning, he grabbed both her hands, pulled her unceremoniously to her feet, and dragged her across the deck to
one of the long cushioned seats that lined the outer
bulkhead of the main cabin.

"Wait a minute! I was working on my tan!" Ryanne
protested halfheartedly as Hugh plopped her down on his
lap in a spot that not only was shaded from the sun, but
also eliminated any possibility that they could be seen
from the deck above.

"Isn't that just too bad." He silenced her with a kiss
that was not demanding, but was far from casual.
Ryanne's arms snaked around his neck, sealing their
bodies together, and all thought of play vanished. The
kiss went on interminably, fueling itself on each sigh of
pleasure, and when it finally ended, Ryanne and Hugh
were both gasping for air.

"Well...that was certainly...masterful," Ryanne
teased when she could finally draw a breath.

"No, that was certainly frustrating," Hugh corrected.
"Do you think we'd be missed if we disappeared into one
of the cabins below for the rest of the day?"

"Why? Are you thinking of claiming your reward for
saving my life yesterday?"

Ryanne felt Hugh's entire body tense as though she'd
struck him. "I'm sorry."

"I don't want to think about that, Ryanne," he said
harshly, tightening his arms around her protectively.

"Seeing you standing in that hall with your back to Ace Keegan's gun was a scene from my worst nightmare."

"Mine, too."

"I thought I'd lost you," he whispered fiercely. "They won't ever get that close to you again, I swear."

His words acknowledged what they both knew to be the truth: this ordeal was far from over. Ryanne nestled her head snugly against Hugh's shoulder. "How long, do you think?"

Hugh didn't bother to ask her to clarify. He knew she was asking how many days of tranquillity they had before someone figured out she wasn't dead. In Chicago, Doug Sutherland was going through the motions of preparing a funeral service, but that wouldn't fool anyone for very long. The national media had been quick to pick up the news that mystery novelist Ryan Kirk, aka Ryanne Kirkland, had been slain in a Los Angeles medical center by an unknown assailant.

With network news teams battering at the door, eventually someone would leak the news that Ryanne's death had been greatly exaggerated. There were too many people on the L.A. police force who knew the truth, from Vic Coffin down to the policewoman who'd impersonated Ryanne on the stretcher.

"Two or three days at the most," he answered finally. The thought of varnishing the truth had never occurred to him. Ryanne had proven a dozen times over this week that she was strong enough to handle virtually anything. "And, presuming anyone is looking for us, another day or two to figure out we're down here and not in Toronto. But by then we'll have moved on."

Ryanne straightened and eased off Hugh's lap, sitting beside him but still remaining in the circle of his arms.

"To where? Hugh, you can't keep shuffling me around like a deck of cards."

"I'll do whatever is necessary to keep you safe, Ryanne."

With a sweep of her hand, Ryanne gestured to the ocean. "This is wonderful, Hugh. I feel safe for the first time in days, but I can only run away for just so long, and then it has to stop."

Impatient with his own lack of solutions, Hugh released Ryanne and began pacing the deck. "Damn it, what else can we do? I am not going to let that bastard get at you again!"

Ryanne heard the anguish in his voice. If ever she had any doubt that Hugh cared for her, it would have been erased by what she heard in his voice. Though she hated to broach the subject that had been on her mind for several days, she knew she had to. For both their sakes. "Then maybe we should start thinking about ways to make me disappear permanently."

Hugh scowled. "What do you mean?"

"I mean, create a new identity for me—phony birth certificate, work history, credit cards under a new name, the whole works. My own personal witness protection program. Ryanne Kirkland has to vanish."

"That's not a solution, Ryanne! You can't go into hiding alone."

"What other choice do I have, Hugh? I can't live like this, and I can't ask you or Judith to live like this, either."

"Let us be the judges of that, okay?"

"Hugh—"

"No. We're not going to discuss this anymore," he told her with finality. The thought of losing her, of exiling her to an unfamiliar city where she would be alone and vulnerable was more than Hugh could stand. If it came

236 WHEN I SEE YOUR FACE

down to that necessity, he would do what had to be done, but he wouldn't send her off alone. He would create a new identity for the two of them and they would start a new life together.

That meant living in the shadows, always being afraid of discovery. No matter how hard he would try to make Ryanne feel safe, she would always have a cloud of fear haunting her, and Hugh refused to accept that kind of life for Ryanne. She was a creature of light and beauty, and somehow he would find a way to keep her out of the shadows.

He returned to the lounge, gathered her into his arms and softened his voice to a lover's caress. "We'll talk about it later. You're safe here for the time being, so let's just enjoy that."

Ryanne nodded and put thoughts of the future out of her head. Like Hugh, she preferred to focus on the moment. She flashed him the smile that never failed to take his breath away. "You broke your promise to me, you know."

Hugh frowned despite the quickening of his pulse. "What promise?"

Ryanne brought her hands to his chest and splayed her fingers, savoring the firmness of his body. "You promised me I'd fall asleep in your arms last night, remember? Having Judith snoring next to me wasn't quite the same thing."

Hugh chuckled at the pout that bowed her lips. "Don't worry, love. I've taken care of that little problem. Because of Mo and Ben we were short on beds at Dad's place last night. I am happy to report that no such problem exists today. The cabin known as the master suite is all ours. Dad will occupy the captain's cabin just off the main salon, and Judith has a cabin all her own right across from him.''

''What did Webb say about those arrangements?''

''Oh, he approved, but he did say he thought I should make an honest woman out of you. He even offered to perform a wedding ceremony we could make legal later.'' The words were spoken lightly, but Hugh held his breath, watching Ryanne's face intently, trying to judge her reaction.

Ryanne's heart turned over in her chest, but she was careful not to let her face reflect the intense emotion Hugh's casual comment aroused. Something warm and tender curled inside her at the thought of belonging to this man, of spending the rest of her life being touched by his passion and cocooned in his indomitable strength. For just a moment she caught a glimpse of a life that included Hugh and children and an overpowering serenity and joy that was almost too beautiful to bear.

But Hugh was only joking. He had no idea how close he'd come to her heart's greatest, most unattainable desire. They had an agreement that said no strings, no commitments. She knew Hugh cared about her, but that wasn't the same thing as loving someone enough to want the kind of life Ryanne was foolishly envisioning. If she betrayed her emotions now, Hugh would only feel sorry for her. He wouldn't reject her immediately, of course— he was too kind to pull the rug from under her in the middle of this nightmare—but he would begin to pull away from her. Pity would replace the warm, wonderful emotions that surged between them now, and Ryanne didn't think she could live with that.

Somehow she managed an impish smile meant to show Hugh how foolish his father's suggestion had been. ''Did you quickly disavow him of any such notions?''

"No," he said a little stiffly, unable to mask his hurt. Ryanne still considered their relationship a passing fancy. The danger that had disrupted their lives clouded and confused the issue, but in Ryanne's mind nothing else had changed. If this ordeal miraculously ended tomorrow, she would pick up the pieces of her life and go on without him. Hugh had the desperate, sinking feeling that keeping Ryanne alive was going to be easier than convincing her he wasn't going to spend the rest of his life without her.

"Hugh? What is it? What's wrong?" Ryanne asked. The change in his mood was dark and drastic.

For a moment, Hugh debated telling her exactly what was wrong, but his conscience stopped him. He couldn't add to the incredible weight of the burdens she already bore. Making a supreme effort, he lightened his tone and relaxed. "Nothing's wrong, sweetheart, but I think I'd better go up to the bridge and see what Dad has in mind for lunch. If we stay here like this much longer, food is going to be the last thing on my mind."

Ryanne accepted his glib lie and shooed him off on his errand, proclaiming she was starved. In her heart, though, she knew she hadn't been mistaken about his sudden change in mood. Something she had said bothered him deeply. Or perhaps he was just regretting having mentioned his father's remark. Had he read the thoughts Ryanne had tried to keep hidden from him? Had he seen in her sightless eyes that she loved him more than either of them wanted her to?

Acting on Captain MacKenna's orders, she and Hugh prepared lunch, managing to work well together despite the cramped quarters and the impediment of Ryanne's blindness. She had spent most of the morning exploring the intricate ins and outs of the boat so that she could move through the restricted space with relative confidence, but the continuous rocking motion of the drifting vessel occasionally made her lose her bearings. Fortunately there were no breakables sitting around and all the furniture was nailed solidly onto the deck. Ryanne's shins were the only things that suffered because of her lack of coordination.

After lunch, Webb offered to teach Ryanne the finer points of deep-sea fishing. He brought out the gear and harnessed Ryanne into one of the swivel chairs. A huge rod and reel were then attached to the harness, and the fishing began. Webb and Hugh both gave her endless instructions on what to do in case she got lucky, but their good advice went straight out of her head when her rod whipped forward and something very large began running out the line.

Because of the hours she'd spent with her guide dog, Ryanne's arms were strong, and she gamely fought the fish, reeling in, then adjusting her position to accommodate the devious twists and turns the fish made. In the end, though, the fish's strength won out over her own.

"It's gone!" she wailed. She turned the reel, but the slack line confirmed that her prey had escaped. The brief struggle had been great fun, though, and she turned her flushed face toward Hugh. "It was a marlin, you said? How big was it?"

"Oh, at least twenty feet," he told her, barely able to hide the smile in his voice.

"No, I'd say more like twenty-five. Maybe even twenty-eight," Webb corrected.

"Oh, for crying out loud, you two," Judith complained from the top of the ladder that led to the flying bridge. "You show me a marlin that big and I'll show you a fish that was spawned off the shore of Three Mile Island."

Ryanne, who knew very well the men had been teasing her, swiveled her chair around toward Judith. "How big was it really, Judith?"

"Nine, maybe ten feet at the most."

Ryanne harrumphed. "Well, I see who I can trust around here."

"It's not their fault, Ryanne," Judith allowed generously. "Men wouldn't know how to tell the truth about the size of a fish if their lives depended on it."

Webb took exception to the slur, and a lively battle ensued. Ryanne and Hugh laughed at their bickering, and when the good-natured storm passed, they returned to the task at hand. Ryanne tried to convince Judith to come down and take her turn with the rod and reel, but Judith preferred to remain at the controls of the boat. She trolled slowly through the Gulf, complaining all the while about how the others were passing the time. After all, she pointed out, what were they going to do with a huge game fish even if they caught it? A dead fish would hardly make a suitable companion for the next two or three days they'd be aboard the boat. Judith's grumbling notwithstanding, they kept at it.

"I had no idea Judith could handle a boat," Ryanne commented to no one in particular as Hugh checked once again to make sure her harness was secure.

"Oh, sure," Webb replied matter-of-factly. "Judith is an old salt from way back. Her late husband was an avid fisherman. They kept a thirty-two-foot cabin cruiser up on Lake Michigan and they came down to Florida every other year for deep-sea fishing."

Ryanne turned toward Webb, stunned. She'd known Judith for years, yet her friend had never imparted that information to her. Webb MacKenna, on the other hand, had known Judith for barely two weeks and obviously knew her life story. Ryanne didn't know whether to be amused or insulted. "That's amazing."

Not realizing the source of Ryanne's befuddlement, Webb told her, "Yep, your Mrs. Tremain is quite a woman. She's spent most of the day telling me how I can double my fleet's profits during the off-season."

"Really?" Hugh looked at his father with barely concealed amusement. "Is that what you two have been arguing about all day?"

"Of course. I can't let her think she knows everything, can I? A woman's got to be kept in her place."

"And where, *exactly*, is that?" Ryanne asked, bristling at the sexist remark.

"*Any*where she wants to be," Webb answered.

They all laughed and returned to the serious business of fishing. Ryanne's marlin apparently was too smart to be hooked a second time, though, and it appeared that he had warned all his friends that these were dangerous waters. Shortly before sundown they abandoned their efforts, and while Hugh and his father fixed supper, Judith affixed braille markings to a deck of playing cards she'd found. After they had eaten, Webb brought out a set of poker chips and over the next few hours, Judith proceeded to take them all to the cleaners.

"It's a damned good thing we're not playing for cash," Webb grumbled as he tossed one of his last three chips into the kitty while Judith shoveled out cards like a Vegas hustler. "That woman would own the *Mary Ann* by now—and the rest of my fleet, too."

Ryanne smiled at him as she read the raised dots on the cards. "By the way, Webb, I've been meaning to ask you how this lovely boat got her name. Who is the *Mary Ann* named after? A long lost sweetheart?''

"Well, actually—" Webb began, but Hugh cut him off hurriedly.

"You don't want to know, Ryanne. It's a very boring story.''

Hugh's reticence told Ryanne that the story wasn't boring at all. Embarrassing, maybe, but hardly boring. She was barely able to suppress a giggle of anticipation. "Oh, I wouldn't be bored, I'm sure. Would you, Judith?''

"Not a bit," Judith answered evenly, deliberately laying the cards down and staring at Hugh. "I'd give anything to know what's got Hugh squirming."

Webb chuckled. "Like he said, it's no big deal. You see—"

"Dad..." Hugh sent him a quiet warning, which his father proceeded to ignore.

"You see, I didn't name her, Hugh did. He was down here with me on his summer vacation when I got the boat, and he insisted on calling her the *Mary Ann*.''

"Aha!" Ryanne leaned toward Hugh and pounced. "As I asked earlier, who was Mary Ann? Some teenage femme fatale?''

"No, she was one of the cazamas n gilginlm," he said swiftly, putting his hand over his mouth to blur the words.

"What?''

"She was one of the castaways on *Gilligan's Island*!" he practically shouted. "There, are you happy now?''

Even the hand Ryanne clapped over her mouth couldn't muffle her shriek of laughter. Judith and Wcbb joined in and the raucous laughter went on and on, rolling through the cabin, feeding on itself like an infectious disease until everyone but Hugh was wiping away tears and fighting the hiccups.

"I'm glad you find this so amusing," Hugh said irritably, staring at them as though they'd lost their collective minds. His disgruntlement only fueled the dying mirth and they started up again.

Slapping his thighs in disgust, Hugh threw in his poker hand and stalked to the galley where he snatched a beer from the refrigerator. "Can I get anyone anything while I'm here? MacKenna Charters is having a special on hemlock today. I recommend it highly."

Ryanne shrieked again, enjoying the best laugh she'd had in longer than she could remember, and Hugh decided he'd had enough. "Okay, that's it!" he said to no one in particular as he started for the door. "If anyone wants me for something other than a good laugh, I'll be outside—alone."

Without Hugh to heckle them, Judith and Webb brought their hilarity under control quickly. Ryanne took a little longer, but she eventually got herself down to tiny giggles spaced intermittently between gasps for air. "Do you think I should go after him?"

"Only if you're ready to humble yourself and soothe his wounded ego," Judith warned her.

"I could probably handle that. Webb, did Hugh really have a crush on the girl on *Gilligan's Island*?"

Webb lowered his voice confidentially. "My son would never speak to me again if I told you that he actually wrote her a fan letter and kept her autographed picture pinned up in his room all that summer."

"Well, I wouldn't tell me that, then, if I were you," Ryanne advised him, rising.

"Never crossed my mind. I wouldn't dream of embarrassing the boy like that."

Ryanne laughed and made her way slowly to the cabin door, leaving Judith and Webb behind to play a ruthless game of blackjack. She stepped into the night air and let the subtle sounds of the wind and the ocean wash over her.

"Hugh?" she called softly.

"I'm here in the chair, Ryanne. Wallowing in my humiliation."

"Oh, you poor thing," Ryanne cooed as she moved to him. "Did we hurt your feelings?"

"I am devastated," he told her in a tragic tone that would have been exaggerated even in Shakespeare's time. "I have been cut to the quick, wounded to the very marrow of my existence, flayed open by—"

"A simple yes or no would have sufficed," she cut him off dryly. "Is there anything I can do to make it up to you?"

"As a matter of fact—" he reached out and pulled her onto his lap "—there is. A kiss from a gorgeous redhead has been known to do wonders for a man's flagging ego."

Ryanne snuggled closer. "I thought you went for pigtailed brunettes," she said teasingly, bringing her face close to his but withholding the suggested remedy.

Hugh lowered his voice until it was nothing more than a husky, seductive whisper. "Hey, I'm flexible."

In answer, Ryanne wiggled her bottom seductively against him. "I think I'd have to argue about that, Mr. MacKenna."

Hugh moved his lips a little closer to Ryanne's and ran his hand down the long line of her leg, then back up again, pushing up her dress on the return trip. "Believe me, Ryanne, that's a purely involuntary reaction. I was sitting out here in the scented night air, remembering past delights, and this unslakable passion consumed me."

Ryanne gasped when his roving hand moved higher and her breathing became sharp and erratic.

"I saw that beloved face," he continued sensuously. "I could almost feel those beautiful breasts beneath my hands..." Matching words to deed, Hugh unfastened the ornamental buttons on the bodice of her dress and lowered his head to the slope of her breasts, fanning her skin with kisses and soft words. "Even on this dark, moonless night, I could imagine moonlight illuminating that tiny waist and gently flaring hips—" He peeled back the bodice and closed his lips over the crest that had already hardened and blossomed beneath his touch. Ryanne's breath caught in her throat and she clasped her hands to his head, twining her fingers in his hair, pressing him closer.

Hugh's own breathing became labored as well, but he continued with his erotic story, slowly working his way back up Ryanne's throat until his lips were at her ear. "And then the phantom moonlight faded, my vision disappeared, and I was left alone...aching...and I called out . . . Mary Ann! Mary Ann, come back!"

Hugh chuckled devilishly at his own joke and Ryanne instantly snapped out of the wonderful lethargy he had induced. "You snake!" she hissed, playfully slamming her clenched fist against his shoulder. "I'll make you think, 'Mary Ann, come back!'" she mimicked wickedly, grabbing a handful of hair at the back of his head and dragging his mouth to hers. As a retaliatory measure she teased him by undulating her hips and stroking and tempting his tongue with her own, in the same rhythm her body was moving to.

Hugh responded immediately, giving back measure for measure the pleasure Ryanne was giving him. Starved for the taste and feel of each other, their kiss deepened and their bodies strained to get closer, until finally Ryanne pulled her lips away from Hugh's.

"Do you think we would be missed if we disappeared into our cabin for the rest of the night?" she asked, paraphrasing the tempting suggestion Hugh had made earlier today.

"I couldn't care less." He kissed her tenderly. "I am going to make love with you tonight, Ryanne, and God help anyone who tries to stop me."

CHAPTER EIGHTEEN

WRAPPED IN HUGH'S arms, Ryanne closed her eyes and willed sleep to come, but her mind was racing too quickly to allow that peaceful oblivion. She stirred restlessly, remembering the words Hugh had whispered over and over again during their lovemaking.

"I love you, Ryanne...I love you...I love you..." He had chanted the words tenderly as he had taken possession of her body but with each passionate thrust that pushed Ryanne to the edge of sanity, the words had become fierce and intense. Still, they had been uttered so quietly that they had barely registered at the time. Now, though, she could hear nothing else.

Restless and confused, Ryanne slowly eased out of Hugh's embrace. He stirred as she left him and Ryanne froze until he settled back, his breathing returning to a deep, even cadence. Quietly, so as not to disturb him, she found her robe hanging on the back of the door and she shrugged into it. Walking carefully, she made her way to the deck and sat in the swivel chair with her feet on the transom. The breeze was cool but still comforting, and she let it wrap around her while she tried to make some sense of what she was feeling.

"I love you, Ryanne...I love you..."

The words wouldn't go away, and Ryanne didn't want them to. Selfishly she wanted to believe they weren't just meaningless phrases spoken in the heat of passion, only to be forgotten in the morning. She had fallen in love with Hugh, and it wasn't the kind of love that could be ignored or forgotten. It was the kind that made a woman want to entwine her life with that of a man she knew would love, cherish and protect her.

But Ryanne knew she didn't have the right to hope that Hugh felt that kind of love, too, that he might want to share a future with her. She didn't have a future. Whether or not she regained her sight, she was going to have to go into hiding. She would have to live with the constant fear of discovery and the ever-present sense of danger. Love couldn't flourish in that kind of environment.

Though it was painful, Ryanne forced herself to face the terrible injustice she had done Hugh. She'd always prided herself on her independence, and yet this past week she had depended on him totally. She had used his strength when her own had failed. Worst of all, she had let the man she loved risk his life to save hers.

But no more. She couldn't go on drawing her courage from Hugh; she couldn't continue to put his life in jeopardy. She would never be able to live with herself if something happened to him while he was trying to protect her. Ryanne had to face her grim future and allow Hugh to get on with his life.

Today, Hugh had refused to talk about helping her disappear, but tomorrow Ryanne knew she had to make him talk about it. And if he wouldn't help with the necessary arrangements, then she would find someone who would. The sooner she was out of his life, the better.

The thought of losing Hugh was almost more than Ryanne could bear, and yet she knew her decision was the right one. The fear she had managed to keep at bay for most of the day crowded in on her, and she wrestled with it, trying to imagine how the incredible mired mess her life had become could possibly turn out all right. She lost all track of time, but when a gust of wind grabbed her robe she came back to the present. The *Mary Ann* was riding waves that were no longer gentle, and the air had the taste of an approaching storm. Ryanne knew that the sea anchor—a sievelike affair that slowed the boat's motion and kept its bow turned into the waves—would prevent them from capsizing if a storm did arise, but in that eventuality the last place she wanted to be was the deck.

Shivering slightly from a sudden chill in the wind, Ryanne slid her feet to the deck and stood. The rocking of the boat seemed far more violent than it had when she'd been sitting, and she grabbed on to the arm of the chair to steady herself. It gave way beneath her weight, swiveling out of reach, and the trust she had placed in its solidity was her undoing. The *Mary Ann* slid abruptly up to the crest of a large wave and Ryanne flailed wildly as she tumbled backward onto the transom. Her hip collided with the narrow ledge, and her cry of pain quickly turned into a short-lived shriek of panic as the momentum of her fall carried her over the edge.

She landed with a sickening thud on the iron grating of a swim platform that was partially submerged. A backlash of water hit her in the face, and she struggled for breath and for a handhold that would keep her from sliding into the black ocean. Again the boat swayed with the waves, though, and Ryanne was tossed mercilessly into the sea.

What had happened in an instant felt like a lifetime to Ryanne. She struggled to the surface, gasping for air and reaching frantically in every direction, searching for the platform. A wave that took on monstrous proportions in her terrified mind grabbed her, swept her up and dropped her again, and Ryanne realized that if she didn't force herself to remain calm she would drown in a matter of minutes.

Keeping her head tilted back as she began treading water, she took several deep, calming breaths of air, then began calling for help. Each time she opened her mouth, saltwater slapped her face, but she continued screaming, shouting for help, calling Hugh's name or Judith's or Webb's until her throat was raw from the effort.

Trapped in the world of her own blindness, surrounded by an even blacker sea, Ryanne shoved aside thoughts of sharks and other creatures of the deep whose domain she had unwillingly invaded. Instead she focused all her powers of concentration on listening for some sign of the *Mary Ann*—water lapping against its hull, or a faint echo of her weakening shouts. All she heard, though, was the eerie silence of the sea.

Time passed, but she couldn't have guessed how much. Bobbing like a cork, she forced herself to face the grim reality that she was probably going to die. She was strong and healthy, and if she conserved her strength, she could last for several more hours—possibly even until dawn— but by then she would be miles away from the boat. She could picture Hugh awakening in the morning, finding her gone and searching the ship to no avail. She imagined the search they would initiate. They would notify the Coast Guard and other boats would be brought in, but by then she would have grown too tired to maintain the struggle of keeping her head above water. Tomorrow night the evening news would report that renowned mystery writer, Ryan Kirk, aka Ryanne Kirkland, had died for the second time in one week.

The thought of Dan Rather trying to explain that one to twenty million viewers struck Ryanne as immensely funny. Her spontaneous, hysterical laughter was silenced by a mouthful of water, and she sputtered and choked, trying vainly to conquer the laughter that was more symptomatic of terror than amusement.

Alone and frightened, all sense of time deserted Ryanne. Hours passed and each minute was filled with nothing but thoughts of remaining afloat...staying alive. She found a rhythm in the waves and flowed with them, rather than against them, sometimes treading water, sometimes floating on her back to conserve energy. A sense of unreality overcame her. Images from the past began playing in her head like an old movie, and she became completely disconnected from what was happening to her. She saw vivid pictures of her mother and father, her Aunt Rose and Uncle Charley. She saw distant relatives and high-school acquaintances she hadn't thought of in years. A kaleidoscope of colorful scenes danced before her eyes. Some logical part of her mind suggested that she was becoming delirious from exhaustion and sensory deprivation, but when she saw lights blinking wildly in the distance, she knew she must have gone mad.

Too tired to mourn the loss of her sanity, Ryanne moved instinctively. A voice spoke to her—her father's voice—telling her to swim, and she obeyed without question. One stroke followed another, then she rested a moment, but her father's soft, quiet tones soon told her to move, and she did. Every muscle in her body cried out in pain, but she continued toward the mirage that flickered and winked at her. Saltwater stung her eyes and she closed them, pausing to rest, treading water, being lifted by the waves, then plummeted into the troughs....

The wind that stirred the water set up a ferocious roar, and Ryanne waited for the lights to reappear. She opened her eyes, expecting them to return, but they did not; her treacherous mind had taken the mirage away as easily as it had created it.

Frustrated by the disappearance that had stolen her sense of purpose, Ryanne screamed at the wind. She screamed in rage and frustration and fear until there was nothing left of her voice. Her screams turned to voiceless sobs that robbed her of what little strength she had left. The blackness of her blind existence was slowly absorbed into the void of unconsciousness, and though she fought briefly with the last ounce of her incredible will to survive, the effort was wasted.

Her last clear thought as she slipped into death was that the storm must have missed her, because the stars were twinkling overhead like a million brilliant diamonds.

"DAMN IT, cut the engine! Listen!" Hugh shouted above the roar of the *Mary Ann*'s powerful motor. Webb pulled back on the throttle and everything was silent. Manning the powerful searchlight on the bridge, Judith skimmed the beacon across the surface in a slow moving arc. They all listened. They all prayed.

"There!" Hugh shouted again, pointing to starboard. "Do you hear it?"

"I don't hear anything!" Judith hollered, unable to keep from her voice the desperate fear that had gripped her the moment Hugh had awakened her with the news that Ryanne was nowhere on the boat. For nearly an hour now they had watched and waited, trolling the water slowly in the desperate hope that they might possibly be headed toward Ryanne rather than away from her. No one had dared voice the possibility that she was already dead.

Adjusting the searchlight to the direction Hugh indicated, Judith narrowed the scope of her search, praying Hugh wasn't just hearing something he wanted to hear. But there it was again, a hoarse cry that could have been the wind; somehow they all knew it wasn't.

"She's out there!" Judith yelled.

"But where, damn it? Where!" Hugh shouted in frustration, never taking his eyes off the narrow beam of Judith's light.

"*There*! Go back! Take the light back!" Webb commanded and Judith complied. Thirty yards away a patch of scarlet spread out on the water like a trail of blood.

The boat sprang to life and Judith kept the light fixed on the object until they were close enough to see Ryanne, face down, floating still and lifeless, her robe fanned around her like a crimson cloud.

"*Nooooo!*" Hugh's agonized cry reverberated in the dark long after he sliced into the water. With strong, sure strokes, he reached her in seconds, shoved her face out of the water, and turned her in his arms like a limp rag doll. Webb brought the boat alongside them, and moments later Ryanne was sprawled on deck with Hugh feverishly repeating resuscitation techniques.

Fighting back tears, he poured his life's breath into her lungs, then flipped her over and straddled her hips, pressing against her back with hard, even strokes.

"Breathe, Ryanne, breathe," he commanded, his voice broken by the tears he couldn't hold back. They ran down his face, mingling with the saltwater that spilled in rivulets from his hair. "Please, baby, breathe... breathe... breathe... God, please... let her breathe... breathe," he chanted, never breaking the rhythm of his strokes. Frantic, he switched techniques, rolling her over again to give mouth-to-mouth while Webb applied repeated pressure to her rib cage until, finally, Ryanne coughed and began fighting her own battle. Choking and sputtering, she expelled the seawater from her lungs and stomach while Hugh held her from behind until she finally drew a ragged breath and sagged against him, spent but alive.

"Thank God," Judith whispered.

"Amen. Here, son." Webb extracted two blankets from one of the lockers and handed one to Hugh, who wrapped Ryanne snugly and helped her onto a bench. Kneeling in front of her, he rubbed her vigorously with the blanket, talking to her softly until the shock of her ordeal could pass.

Numb with exhaustion and relief, Ryanne sat motionless, trying to absorb the wonder of being alive. Every light on the boat seemed to be shining right in her eyes, and she blinked against the slicing pain. Strong, gentle hands pushed her sopping hair back and dried her face, and a deep voice filled with emotion spoke softly to her as the numbness gradually went away. The lights pierced the fuzziness of her mind, and her entire being suddenly focused on the voice—Hugh's voice. And hands... Hugh's hands. Slowly, forgetting the pain, Ryanne raised her eyes to a masculine torso with corded, rippling muscles, covered with a dark matt of fine, damp hair. It was a beautiful body, strong and perfectly proportioned, exactly as she'd always imagined it. But she wasn't imagining this.

Terrified that she was living a dream that might be cruelly snatched away from her, Ryanne reached out and touched the smooth skin of Hugh's shoulder, matching the sight of it to the feel she had already memorized. Her hand looked small and delicate against the broad planes of his chest. Gingerly she moved upward, touching him, following the movement with her eyes, across his shoulders, up his throat, until finally his jaw was cupped in her palm. It was a strong jaw, she realized distractedly... and his lips were full. She brushed them with her thumb before moving upward past his long, not-quite-perfect nose, to his deep-set eyes, which were filled with a mixture of puzzlement, relief and unmistakable love.

"Ryanne? Are you all right?" Hugh questioned her softly, growing worried. Her eyes met his in that mysterious way she had of making him believe she was looking straight at him, and the look on her face was almost rapturous. Her agile fingers flitted to the deep cleft between his brows that he knew gave him a look of perpetual arrogance. "Ryanne? Say something, love. Are you—"

"You are so... beautiful..." she whispered, her eyes filling with tears. "I never imagined..."

"Oh, dear God," Hugh murmured as he realized what had happened. A smile started somewhere deep in his heart and battered its way outward until it reached his lips and lit up his eyes. "Can you see me?" he asked in a voice that broke with emotion.

Ryanne nodded, smiled, too, and impatiently wiped the tears that blurred the most important sight she would ever see. "I see you." Her voice was hoarse and ragged, but strong enough to carry the depth of her joy. *"I can see you!"* she croaked as Hugh gathered her into his arms, lifted her up and swung her around in a jubilant circle. Her tears turned to a sob of happiness when Hugh kissed her long and deep, holding her as though he would never let go. And then Judith was there, hugging her and laughing, and then Webb had her in his arms. Ryanne returned his hearty embrace, then pulled back to satisfy her curiosity. As she had suspected, his strong, sun-weathered face was an older, more mature version of his son's. She looked back and forth between the two men, smiling through renewed tears, then went into Hugh's arms again.

"How did you find me? How did you even know I was gone?" she asked hoarsely, unable to take her eyes off the handsome face her heart had imagined a million times.

"You were supposed to spend the night in my arms, remember?" he reminded her, becoming vividly aware that Ryanne's silk robe was plastered to her body like a second skin, and the only thing he was wearing was a pair of sodden jeans. "When I woke up and you weren't beside me or on deck, we started searching."

He didn't describe the horrible panic he had felt as he'd awakened the others. They'd torn the ship apart hoping against hope that what they all suspected couldn't be true. "When we realized you'd gone overboard, Dad calculated the drift of the boat as opposed to that of a single object being swept along by the current."

"In other words," Judith chimed in, "he spit into the wind and took a damned good guess."

"That's about the size of it," Webb agreed, wrapping a fresh blanket around Ryanne's shoulders.

She smiled at him from the circle of Hugh's arms. "I'm glad you're a good guesser. Thank you." She blinked against the brightness of the searchlight that was focused on the deck, but the pain that darted behind her eyes was a welcome one. She thought back to the last memories she had of her ordeal in the ocean. "I suppose my subconscious realized that the only thing that would save me was being able to see again. When I saw the lights in the distance, I thought I'd gone crazy. I swam toward them, but they disappeared."

"You probably got turned around and were just look-ing away from the boat," Judith suggested.

"If we hadn't heard you scream we might have passed you by," Webb told her.

Ryanne rubbed her raw throat. "I was so angry that the lights had vanished, and I was so tired I could hardly move. And then I saw the stars . . . and after that, noth-ing—" she looked at Hugh, unable to resist the over-whelming impulse to touch his face again "—until I saw you."

Their eyes met and held as emotions too powerful for words passed between them. They froze in that tableau, savoring the sight of each other even above the feel of their bodies pressing so close together.

Judith watched the tender emotions that played across both their faces and sent up another prayer of thanks-giving that Ryanne was safe and that she had Hugh's arms to lean on. No one deserved the love of a strong, courageous, giving man more than Ryanne. A sob welled in her throat and she choked it back with a no-nonsense bark of exasperation.

"Oh, for crying out loud, you two. Stop mooning around like a couple of moonstruck calves and get be-low. Ryanne, you take a shower and get into some dry clothes, and Hugh—"

"I'll take care of her, Judith," Hugh said with a laugh. "Why don't you make us some coffee and open a can of soup. Ryanne's going to need something to eat."

Ryanne groaned at the thought of food on top of all the seawater she had swallowed, but a hot shower and dry clothes sounded like heaven. Weak and light-headed, she let Hugh guide her inside.

Judith watched them go, her jaw set stubbornly against the tears that just wouldn't seem to go away. Webb moved to her, instinctively understanding what she was feeling. "That girl's like a daughter to you, isn't she?" he asked quietly.

The dam holding back her emotions gave way, and Judith nodded mutely, going into Webb's arms without question. He rocked her gently while the horror of the last hours was cleansed away by her tears.

"There, there, Judy honey. It's all right now. It's all right," he crooned until the sobs subsided. Her arms were wrapped around him and he pressed a kiss to her forehead, enjoying the way their bodies fit together in all the right places. He felt almost bereft when she finally pulled away.

"Better now?" he asked, smiling despite the sharp ache that had unexpectedly centered itself in his loins.

"I'm fine," she replied brusquely, as though to deny the vulnerability she had just shown.

"You know, you don't have to pretend with me," he told her a trifle sadly. "I figured out a long time ago that there was a very loving, giving woman under that crusty exterior."

"Of course you did." She said it as though she'd never thought otherwise.

"Then you don't have any reason to pull away from me, do you?"

Judith lifted her chin proudly. "No, I guess I don't." She closed the scant distance between them, put her arms around him again, and pressed a long, slow, stunning kiss to Webb's mouth—a kiss he returned with equal intensity until they were both a little breathless.

They broke apart as suddenly as they had come together, and while Webb was trying to gather his addled senses, Judith smiled at him sweetly. "Webb?"

"Uh...what?" he asked, unable to take his eyes off her.

"If you ever call me 'Judy honey' again, I'll break both your legs," she promised, then disappeared into the cabin with a saucy little sashay that left Webb alone on deck, roaring with laughter.

CHAPTER NINETEEN

RYANNE STEPPED OUT of the shower and dried off, barely able to believe that she could actually see the steam that clouded the room and condensed on the mirror above the lavatory. She wrapped the damp white towel around her, tucking in the edges just above her breasts, then reached for the extra one Hugh had left. Unfolding it slowly, she studied the floral print, savoring the riot of colors that assaulted her senses. Soon she would be seeing real flowers again, not just smelling them and trying to remember their beauty as she had for the past five years. For now, though, the roses stamped onto the terry cloth would do just fine. She could see now, and that was what mattered.

Smiling at her sentimentality, she bent over and wrapped the towel turban fashion around her head. When she straightened she saw her own vague outline in the steamy mirror and her heart began throbbing in her ears. Transported back in time, she remembered the months her face had been swathed in bandages. She recalled the pain of operation after operation, and she remembered her doctor's voice, calm and reassuring, praising his own handiwork.

If she wiped the steam from the mirror she would finally be able to see the face he had created, but something held her back. This night had already been a roller coaster of overwhelming emotions, and she didn't think she was ready to deal with her new face just yet. Instead she unwrapped her makeshift turban, towel dried her hair vigorously, then began brushing out the tangles. She extracted a blow dryer from the large cosmetic bag placed on the small vanity, plugged it in, then began drying her hair. The hot air dried the steam from the mirror much more quickly than it did her hair, but Ryanne kept her face carefully averted from the glass.

Her heartbeat accelerated with every second she avoided the inevitable, and she fervently wished Hugh hadn't spirited her straight into the shower when he'd brought her into the tiny bathroom off the bedroom they shared. It would have been a comfort to have his moral support when she saw her new face for the first time. But Ryanne had been swathed in a blanket from head to foot when she'd passed this mirror the first time, and now Hugh was down the hall showering in the other—tiny— stall. He couldn't help her confront this.

Exasperated with her own lack of courage, Ryanne finally stopped fussing with her hair. Mustering all her courage, she put the dryer down, turned and looked in the mirror. What she saw had her heart thundering all over again.

Intellectually Ryanne had known that she wouldn't recognize her surgically altered face, but seeing another woman's features where her own should have been was completely confusing and a little frightening. For a moment, she felt disconnected from her body, and she studied the mirror impassively.

It was a beautiful face. There was no denying that. It had a symmetry that was almost too perfect. The sharp angles she had lived with until her accident were all gone. Someone else's pert nose had taken the place of her own longer, upturned one. The square jaw she'd inherited from her father was gone now, too. It was a lovely face, but it wasn't hers.

A sudden, deep emptiness came over her as all sense of identity was swept away. *Where is Ryanne?* she wondered, reaching out to the mirror, tracing the unfamiliar lines. *Is that really me?*

"Ryanne?" Hugh rapped twice on the door before poking his head inside. "Are you feeling better?"

The door was to her left, and Ryanne could see him in the mirror, sharing space with her own strange reflection. Her bleak, puzzled stare alarmed him and he stepped inside. "What's wrong?"

Ryanne looked at herself again, gesturing vaguely at the mirror. "I don't know that woman," she said plaintively.

"Oh, sweetheart..." Until that moment it hadn't dawned on Hugh that Ryanne had never seen her new face, but he realized instantly how traumatic the sight of it had to be for her. Without hesitation he moved behind her and pulled her securely against his chest. Her eyes met his in the mirror and he smiled. It was the most beautiful smile Ryanne had ever seen. "I know that woman, Ryanne. I know her very, very well."

She gestured to her reflection again. "But that isn't... *me*."

"Oh, but it is, love. Because everything that makes Ryanne Kirkland magnificent is right *here*." Instead of pointing at the mirror, Hugh placed one hand over Ryanne's heart as he pressed a kiss to her temple. "Your face is beautiful, but what makes it so very special is that warm, wonderful smile that comes straight from your soul and makes a man go weak in the knees. Your spirit and your courage are *inside*, Ryanne. They shine in your eyes, and without them that surgically perfect face would be nothing but a pretty shell.''

A mist of tears clouded Ryanne's vision. Hugh was exaggerating what he thought were her special qualities, and yet he was right. That face in the mirror didn't change who and what she was. ''Thank you,'' she whispered.

''For what? It's the truth.''

She touched his hand, which was still nestled between her breasts. She was fascinated by the sight of it next to her body. ''Thank you for being here...for always knowing just the right thing to say... for saving my life. Again.''

''Don't thank me for that, Ryanne,'' he told her gravely, his arm tightening around her waist. ''Saving you was just self-preservation. I don't know what I'd do if I lost you.''

Ryanne met his gaze in the mirror and wondered if the intense, possessive look in his eyes was the same one that had been there when they had made love. She remembered the heat of his passion and the pleasure they had shared, but she also recalled the words he had repeated over and over—the words that Ryanne's heart had wanted to hear, but couldn't accept.

''Hugh—''

''Hush.'' He silenced what he knew instinctively was meant to be a protest. He'd come too close to losing her to pull away now. Turning her in his arms, he murmured softly, ''Let me love you, Ryanne.'' His mouth closed gently over hers and pried her lips.

A part of Ryanne accepted Hugh's kiss eagerly. For an instant, she allowed herself the pleasure of arching, opening to him and taking everything he was offering her. But there was an even stronger part of her that protested her surrender. Hugh wasn't asking her to make love with him, he was telling her he loved her and asking her to love him—to acknowledge his love, accept it...and return it.

More than anything in the world, Ryanne wanted to do just that, but she couldn't. Everything had changed the moment her sight had returned; there was no longer any question of what her future held. She had to go back to Chicago and identify the man who had tried to kill her. The path her life would take after that was painfully predictable. To protect his star witness, the district attorney would put her in a witness protection program. Ryanne would be given a new identity. She would go into hiding and leave every remnant of her old life behind, knowing that with the incredible backlog in the judicial system and the delaying tactics of Beck's lawyers, it could take years to bring him to trial. And all that time, he would be turning heaven and earth trying to find Ryanne so that she would never be able to testify against him. It was a bleak, frightening future, and Ryanne knew that if she accepted Hugh's love she would automatically make him a part of it.

Hating herself because what she had to do would hurt both of them, she pushed at Hugh's shoulders until he broke the kiss and released her. "I can't, Hugh. I'm sorry, but I can't." Her voice faltered under the weight of her confused emotions and she twisted away from him, hurrying into the cabin next door.

"Ryanne?" He chased after her, grabbing her arm and turning her to him before she could reach the outer door. Her eyes were liquid with unshed tears, yet he could see that she had locked the most valuable part of herself— her heart—away from him. He didn't bother pretending that he misunderstood her rejection, and he couldn't hide his own heart any longer. "I love you, Ryanne."

The agony of hearing the words and not being able to return them tore Ryanne's heart in half. Every intense emotion she'd experienced these past few days crashed in on her—the fear, the frustration, the terror, the brief glimpses of joy and love and passion, the shattering experience of almost drowning, the relief over the return of her vision—everything was right there on the surface, exposed like a fresh, bleeding wound. "Don't, Hugh. Please," she begged.

"Don't what?" he demanded, unable to believe this was happening. The tortured expression that filled Ryanne's eyes sliced a searing dagger into his heart. "Don't tell you I love you? Or just don't love you, period?"

"Don't love me."

"Well, I'm sorry, but it's a little too late for that!" Hugh heard his hateful tone and stopped. He'd never said I love you to any woman before. Until Ryanne, he'd never even imagined saying it. But even with that lack of experience he knew that this wasn't the way to go about it.

Desperately trying to convince himself that Ryanne was just overwrought from her ordeal in the ocean, he gentled his voice and placed his hands lightly on her arms. "Ryanne, I love you. I'm not going to let you slip away from me—not now, not ever. I know you have to be frightened about what's ahead of you, but we'll see it through together, whatever it takes."

He meant it. Ryanne could hear it in his voice and see it in his warm, amber eyes. Hugh loved her and would do anything for her, but she wondered if he really understood that loving her meant giving up everything: his career, his company, his home, his life-style—and possibly even his life. He was offering to make an unbelievable sacrifice for her and Ryanne loved him far too much to allow him to do it. Mustering all her courage, she tried to blank all emotion from her face.

"I am really so sorry, Hugh. I didn't mean for this to happen. I thought you understood that what we had was only temporary."

Hugh stiffened as though she'd slapped him. "You're telling me you don't love me, is that it?"

Ryanne had to turn away to answer. If he saw her eyes he would know she was lying. "That's right."

"I don't believe that, Ryanne!" Hugh almost shouted, grabbing her arm to whirl her toward him. "When you looked at me before, up on deck, what I saw in your eyes was love!"

"That was gratitude!" She jerked her arm from his grasp. "That was the wonder of being alive and being able to see again! I was grateful to you for saving me, and I'm grateful to you for everything you've done to protect me."

"But you don't love me?"

"No!" She shouted the word because it was the only way she could force the lie out.

Hugh backed away, unable to believe how much it hurt. "Well, I guess that puts me in my place, doesn't it? Good old Hugh was great for a roll in the hay or a little protection from the bad guys, but that's all. What we had was great as long as it was light and meaningless! Too bad one of us had to go and spoil it by falling in love, right?"

"It wasn't meaningless, Hugh . . . not to me." Ryanne clenched her fists to hold in the pain. "But you were the one who made the rules, remember?"

"Ah, yes, the rules. Well, I got hoisted on my own petard with that one, didn't I? Tell me, Ryanne, just what is it about loving me that you find so unthinkable?"

She looked at his face, so new to her and yet so dear. In his deep, expressive voice, Ryanne had heard dozens of emotions and had imagined them all playing across the face she'd only been told was handsome. She'd visualized his teasing humor, his intense passion, his warm, seductive smile, and had mourned her inability to see them. Now her sight had returned, and all she could see were dark eyes filled with pain that she was putting there. The knowledge that she was doing it for his own good didn't help any. "Oh, Hugh... Loving you is not unthinkable. And having you love me is a beautiful gift I don't deserve—and can't accept."

"Damn it, Ryanne, why not?" he asked harshly, grabbing her arms, but she pulled away sharply.

"Because I don't believe in happily ever after, Hugh! And you don't, either. You told me so yourself. I don't believe in vine-covered cottages with pretty white picket fences! I don't want you to love me because I refuse to start thinking about knitting baby booties and hearing the pitter-patter of tiny MacKenna feet around the house—a boy who looks like you and a girl who looks like me! I don't want that, Hugh!"

"Then what the hell do you want?"

"I told you that the night before we left L.A.! I want my life back!" she answered, trying to find some conviction in the words so that she could convince both of them she was telling the truth. "I can see again, which means eventually I can have back the life I lost in that warehouse five years ago. I can have my career and my freedom. I have to go to Chicago and identify the man who tried to kill me, and then I'll go into hiding until the trial is over. And when it's done, I'm going to take back everything Arlen Beck stole from me. I'm going to try to forget that these past five years ever happened and get on with my life!''

Ryanne wanted to cry out as she watched Hugh's face close against her, becoming cold and hard and emotionless. Whatever love he might have felt for her died in that instant; she had killed it.

"And there's no place for me in that life," he stated flatly, not bothering to phrase it as a question. He'd known the truth two nights ago, but he hadn't wanted to believe it. Now he had no choice.

"No."

Hugh's answering laugh was harsh and cynical. "I guess there's no way I can argue with that, is there? 'So long, Hugh, it's been swell.'" He turned and started for the door, then stopped, keeping his back to her. "I'll have Dad plot a course back to port, and I'll see that you get to Chicago safely so that you can get your life back as soon as possible." He stalked out, never looking back.

"Oh, God," Ryanne whispered, wrapping her arms around herself. She sank onto the edge of the bed she had shared with Hugh a lifetime ago, rocking back and forth, waiting for the pain to go away.

But it didn't.

CHAPTER TWENTY

AT SUNRISE Ryanne was standing on the *Mary Ann*'s deck, wishing she could find some joy in being able to see the dawn for the first time in five years. The exhilaration she should have been experiencing escaped her, though. Hugh was on the bridge, guiding the boat back toward Bay St. Louis just as he had promised. They hadn't spoken since he'd left the cabin just a few hours ago, but she knew he intended to fulfill what he saw as his responsibility to get her to Chicago. After that, he would be gone from her life forever.

"You want to talk about it?" Judith asked as she came on deck and handed Ryanne a mug of coffee.

"Talk about what?"

Judith laughed shortly and sat in one of the fishing chairs. She looked tired, as though she hadn't slept all night, either. "Ryanne, honey, this is a very small boat. If you think your quarrel with Hugh was private, think again."

Too tired and dispirited to even blush, Ryanne sat in the chair that had betrayed her the previous night and sent her tumbling into the ocean. Her movements were stiff, as though she believed she could lessen her heartache if she kept her body under the same rigid control as her emotions. "What did you hear?"

"Enough to know that some pretty ugly things were said."

"Mostly by me." Ryanne finished the thought for her.

Judith shrugged. "I did hear you tell Hugh you didn't love him. You know, Ryanne, I think that's the first time I ever caught you in an out-and-out lie."

"It's the truth," she said lifelessly.

"Honey, I don't believe that for an instant, and if Hugh's smart, he won't either, once he's had a chance to think about it."

The thought of going through another scene like the one she'd barely survived was more than Ryanne could take. She looked at Judith fiercely. "He has to believe it."

The older woman turned and looked out to sea. "Well, who knows. Maybe he will buy it. Falling in love with you took him completely by surprise and you did trounce his heart pretty hard. It may take a while for him to get far enough past the pain and humiliation to realize that you're only trying to protect him."

Ryanne looked at Judith in amazement. "How did you know that?"

She laughed lightly. "Honey, I know you like a book. You think you're saving him from having to go through whatever ordeal you've got to face, right?"

"Yes."

"Ryanne..." Judith's voice demanded that the other woman look at her. "Don't you think that should be his choice?"

"No, I don't. He's put himself in enough danger because of me. I couldn't live with myself if something happened to him. And I can't let him sacrifice everything he's achieved in his life out of some misguided sense of loyalty or pity."

"Pity?" Judith scoffed. "Where did that come from? Hugh hasn't felt a drop of pity for you since the day you met."

"Don't you understand? I'm a damsel in distress. Hugh thinks he has to play knight errant and save me from the fire-breathing dragons."

"Oh, for crying out loud. You don't really believe that, do you? Ryanne, there were no dragons breathing down your neck until you found out the truth about your blindness. Hugh was in love with you long before that."

Ryanne covered her face with her hands and shook her head. "Judith, please . . . I did what I had to do. Just accept it and don't interfere. I've hurt Hugh enough already—I don't want to make it any worse than it already is."

Fighting her disgust, Judith stood and looked down at her young friend. "Honey, I've got news for you. It's not possible for a man to hurt any more than Hugh did last night when he realized you'd gone overboard. He thought he'd lost you then, and he's convinced he's lost you now. It's the same pain he'd have felt if you'd died, only you've managed to take away whatever illusion of comfort he might have gained from thinking that you loved him."

With that parting salvo, Judith retreated into the cabin, leaving Ryanne alone to wrestle with the decision she'd made. She knew how much she'd hurt him—it had all been right there in his eyes—but she couldn't change her mind. Eventually Hugh would forget about her and the pain would go away. And more importantly, because he wasn't sharing Ryanne's danger, he would live to see that day. Ryanne knew that she would go to her grave loving Hugh. What she didn't know was when that might be. . . .

The sun was a little more established in the sky by the time they arrived in Bay St. Louis. The bright light hurt Ryanne's sensitive eyes and Judith loaned her a pair of sunglasses. Neither woman commented on the effective way they also masked the dark circles that were the result of stress, exhaustion and too much crying.

Despite the deep, aching sorrow Ryanne felt about the way things had worked out with Hugh, there was something exciting about returning to the real world and being able to see all the things she had only remembered or imagined these past years. She watched the bustling port avidly, enjoying the color and movement. Even the aged gray wood of the pier looked beautiful to her as they docked.

She caught sight of Hugh as he tossed a line to a man waiting on the dock, and she marveled at the strength and symmetry of his body. He had a lithe, catlike grace that was beautiful to watch. Following his every movement she stored the sight of him in her memory. Once they reached Chicago, memories were all she would have left.

The man on the pier tied off the *Mary Ann*'s bow as Hugh moved toward the stern to secure that line as well. He moved surefootedly along the narrow ledge beside the main cabin, grabbed hold of the ladder that led up to the bridge and swung down to the deck in one graceful, athletic motion. The movement put him face-to-face with Ryanne, but she could have been a stranger for all the notice he gave her.

No, not a stranger, Ryanne reflected, fighting the urge to cry. Hugh would have smiled at a stranger, but there was no smile on his face when he looked at her; just a cold, hard glare that bespoke utter contempt. He brushed past her without a word, finished securing the boat, then returned to Ryanne and snatched up the small suitcase at her feet.

"Let's go," he said brusquely, grabbing her arm none too gently and propelling her onto the deck. He handed the suitcase to the man who had tied off the boat, and Ryanne realized he had to be Mo Johnson.

"Where's Ben?" Hugh asked sharply, scanning the busy dock area.

Ryanne watched the puzzlement that played over Mo's face. He was a big, beefy man, but she could tell there wasn't an ounce of fat on his massive body. Despite his size, though, he had a kind, expressive face that at the moment was filled with questions. Ryanne knew that Hugh had radioed his men early this morning that the *Mary Ann* was coming in, but she assumed that no explanation had been provided.

"Ben's making a call," Mo answered, making a gesture that indicated he needed to speak with Hugh alone. Ryanne almost smiled at his pantomime efforts that were obviously meant to keep her from knowing that something was up.

"You're wasting your time, Mo," she advised him, taking off her dark glasses so that she could look him square in the eye. "If you have something to say, you can say it in front of me."

Mo's mouth dropped open as he looked at her and realized what had happened. A wide grin split his face. "You can see."

Ryanne nodded. "Yes."

"That's great!" His smile faded as he realized it wasn't quite that simple. "Or is it?"

Ryanne's subdued smile reassured him. "Yes, Mo. It's great."

"Could we cut the celebration short?" Hugh asked impatiently. "Just tell me what's going on."

Mo cast an uncomfortable glance at Ryanne before answering. "After you radioed this morning, Ben and I heard on the news that Asa Keegan was arrested at the airport in L.A. last night. Ben's calling Vic Coffin now to get some details."

"Is there a problem, Hugh?" Webb asked as he and Judith joined them on the dock.

Hugh repeated Mo's news, then looked back at his friend. Though he suspected he knew the answer, he asked, "What else?"

Mo sighed. "The broadcast we heard said that he was being charged with the *attempted* murder of Ryanne Kirkland."

"You mean the media knows I'm alive," Ryanne interpreted.

"Yep."

"And if the media knows, then Arlen Beck and Del Michelon know," Hugh completed the thought on everyone's mind. Taking hold of Ryanne's arm, he began dragging her down the dock unceremoniously. "Come on. We'll go back to Dad's place while I make some calls. Mo, you go find Ben and meet us at Dad's."

Ryanne fought the urge to wrench her arm out of Hugh's painful grasp and tell him she didn't appreciate being treated like a piece of rotted meat that needed to be disposed of as quickly as possible. She held her tongue, though, and allowed him to pull her along, with Judith and Webb in their wake. Mo hurried off to the harbormaster's office to look for Ben, and fifteen minutes later they were all ensconced in Webb's attractive little beach cottage that sat just around the point from the harbor.

From the chair on which Hugh had all but tossed her with an admonition to sit down and stay out of the way, Ryanne watched as he made phone calls and issued orders like a drill sergeant. He ignored her assiduously and talked about her as though she weren't present. Had he not been doing it all for her sake, Ryanne would have exploded after the first five minutes. She saw the confused looks Mo and Ben exchanged as they tried to figure out what had put their boss in this foul mood, but when their speculative looks moved to her, Ryanne glanced away. She felt too much guilt already; she couldn't let anyone add to it.

She was relieved when the two men finally left for the small airport about thirty miles away where Hugh's jet was awaiting them. It spared her the constant reminder that she was responsible for the harsh tone Hugh was using with them.

From the conversations she heard, Ryanne knew that Ben hadn't been able to reach Vic Coffin in Los Angeles, and Hugh hadn't had any better luck. He was reluctant to speak to anyone but Vic, so he switched his attentions to reaching Rube Lilenthal in Chicago. Ryanne remembered the police lieutenant from the times he had questioned her while she was swathed in bandages, lying near death in the hospital. Even his name brought on a flood of painful memories. Quietly she slipped out of the cozy living room and into the kitchen, where Judith and Webb were quietly drinking coffee, trying to stay out of Hugh's way.

"What's the latest?" Judith asked as Ryanne poured herself a cup of coffee and joined them.

"Mo and Ben just left to get the jet ready for takeoff." She looked at Webb. "I think Hugh expects you to drive us to the airport to meet them."

"No problem." It had already been agreed that for the time being Judith would remain behind with Webb for her own protection. Hugh didn't want to take the chance that Beck might think he could get to Ryanne through her friend.

"Judith, after we're gone, will you look in on that vet who has Aggie? Make sure she's all right?"

"Of course. Do you want me to keep her with me?"

"I'll leave that up to you. I know Webb will want to get back to his business, and if you intend to go out on the *Mary Ann* with him, it would probably be best to leave her where she is. As soon as I know what's going to happen in Chicago, I'll send for her." She smiled wanly. "I wonder how Aggie will like being just a pet rather than a working guide dog?"

Judith made a scoffing sound. "She'll love it, trust me. She'll be fat and lazier than ever inside of a month."

Judith's feigned animosity for Aggie reminded Ryanne of all the lighthearted skirmishes that had filled her life these past few years. She was going to miss Judith's caustic wit and unflagging friendship. It hit her like a lead weight that this might be the last time she would see Judith in a very long time, and a lump of painful emotion formed in her throat. She reached for Judith's hand as her eyes misted with tears. "I could never have asked for a friend—"

"Nope." Judith stood quickly and moved to the coffeepot. "Not yet," she said, trying to mask the sudden quiver in her voice.

"All right." Ryanne looked at Webb. She knew she had to thank him for everything he'd done, but there was a questioning sadness in his eyes that stopped her. If Judith had heard the argument she'd had with Hugh, so had Webb, she realized. It was hard to believe that he didn't hate her for the pain she was causing his son, and yet she saw no recriminations in his sad gaze.

He reached out and took her hand. "You'll always be welcome here. You know that, don't you?"

Tears brimmed in Ryanne's eyes and her jaw quivered. "I didn't mean to hurt him, Webb."

He patted her hand tenderly. "I know you didn't, Ryanne. I think someday when Hugh's wounded pride stops smarting, he'll realize it, too."

Ryanne looked from Webb to Judith, then back, wondering if her friend had told Webb why she had denied her love for Hugh, or if Webb had just figured it out on his own. "I hope not. For his sake."

"All right, let's go," Hugh ordered tersely as he came in from the other room. "Dad, would you mind driving us to the airstrip?"

"Glad to."

Ryanne took a deep breath and turned to Hugh. "What did Lilenthal have to say?"

Hugh didn't bother looking at her when he answered. "He'll have a tight security force waiting for us at the station house at three this afternoon."

"Why not at the airport?" Webb asked.

"Because I didn't tell him where we are now or where we'd be arriving. Ben's laying in a flight plan to take us into one of the small suburban airports outside Chicago. It'll be a lot safer if we rent a car and drive in, just in case Michelon has someone in the police force on his payroll."

"That's an encouraging thought," Judith snapped.

Hugh shrugged indifferently. "Those are just the facts of life." He stabbed a cold glance at Ryanne. "Get your things so we can go," he ordered, then turned on his heel and stalked out.

"Hugh!" Webb took exception to his son's hateful tone and started to upbraid him, but Ryanne put out a hand, stopping him.

"Please, don't. I couldn't stand it if you two had words because of me."

Out of deference to Ryanne, Webb restrained his temper, but the ride to the airport was decidedly tense. No one spoke until they reached the small terminal where Mo was waiting. Hugh said a hasty goodbye to his father and left Mo with Ryanne while she said her tearful goodbyes to Judith and Webb.

It was hard for Ryanne to look at her old friend. She hadn't changed at all in five years, and Ryanne wondered if the next five would be as good to her. She glanced at Webb and the look they exchanged told her that Judith's future was secure. Fighting back tears, she reached for Webb's hand.

"You take care of her."

"Don't worry, Ryanne. I will. You take care of yourself." He gave her a big bear hug, then stepped away quickly, leaving Ryanne alone with Judith, who had abandoned all pretense of emotional stability. Tears streamed unashamedly down her face, and when she held out her arms, Ryanne went into them.

"I love you, Judith," she whispered.

Judith patted her back comfortingly. "If I'd ever had a daughter, Ryanne, I couldn't have loved her any more than I love you."

Ryanne pulled away, taking Judith's hands and squeezing them together. "Thank you...for everything. I'll be in touch."

They embraced again clumsily, then Ryanne tore herself away and let Mo lead her onto the plane.

She boarded, keenly aware of how different the plush interior looked compared to the way she'd visualized it on her first flight. She belted herself into a comfortable leather chair by a window and tried to relax. Thoughts of what lay ahead crowded her mind, but she pushed them away, focusing instead on the wonder of being able to see the ground slide quickly by as they took off. She watched the patchwork of the landscape below them as they flew north. Hugh was in the cockpit with Ben, and he left the copilot's station only once.

Without acknowledging Ryanne's presence, he moved through the main cabin, disappeared into a room near the back of the plane and emerged a few minutes later. He had changed out of his jeans and sweatshirt into a lightweight, pale blue suit. Ryanne realized that he probably kept several changes of clothes on the aircraft, since he hadn't had time to pack anything before they'd left Los Angeles, yet he'd had a change of clothes with him on the *Mary Ann.* Obviously they had come from his wardrobe on the plane.

On his way back to the cockpit, he stopped for a moment to inform Mo they would be arriving in about forty minutes, but still he refused to look at Ryanne. She sat frozen like a statue until he had gone, then quietly turned toward the window so that Mo wouldn't see the tears that steamed down her face.

By the time they reached their destination on the outskirts of Chicago, Ryanne had conquered her tears, but the trip to the main precinct house was a test of her already thin control. Sandwiched between Hugh and Ben in the back seat of the rental car, with Mo at the wheel, Ryanne thought she might go crazy. Each time Hugh leaned forward to speak to Mo, the gun strapped beneath his arm brushed against her, reminding her of the danger she was walking into. Far worse than that, though, was the coldness that radiated from Hugh each time their eyes met. Logically Ryanne knew that he was only protecting himself from the pain she had caused him, yet she caught him looking at her several times with something so akin to hatred that she thought she might actually die from the agony that was congealed around her heart.

With Ben consulting a city map, they made their way into Chicago. Gradually Ryanne began to recognize the familiar sights of her hometown and took over the job of navigator.

"Take a right at the next corner," she instructed Mo. "The station house is just a couple of blocks up."

It had been more than twenty-five years since Hugh had lived in Chicago, so his memory was certainly not to be trusted, but he did remember the neighborhood from his trip to the station with Doug. Ryanne's directions were accurate, so he let her guide Mo while he kept his attention focused on the busy street and sidewalks.

Part of his mind was alert to the potential danger of their situation, yet he knew he wasn't as alert as he should be, not with Ryanne so close beside him. He could smell her distinctly feminine scent that he knew so well, could hear the growing animation in her voice. He could tell that despite the circumstances of her return home, she was excited about being able to see the places she had only visualized for so long. This was where her life was— the life she had so clearly wanted to return to, the life that didn't include him.

Choking back the pain of her rejection, keeping the barriers he'd erected in place, he focused on getting her to Lilenthal in one piece. After that she would no longer be his responsibility. He could go home, pick up the pieces of his own life and forget he'd ever heard the name Ryanne Kirkland.

Their arrival at the police station had been timed almost perfectly. It was nine minutes after three, yet the cordon of police protection Lilenthal had promised was nowhere to be seen. Hugh cursed violently at the negligent lieutenant.

"You want me to drive around the block?" Mo asked.

"No, just park right in front and we'll get her up the steps fast. Get ready to move, Ryanne," Hugh ordered without looking at her.

The car rolled to a stop and in an instant Hugh had the door open and was pulling Ryanne out. Before she even had time to realize what was happening, she was sandwiched between Hugh and Ben, with Mo bringing up the rear. They spirited her across the sidewalk and up the steps into the main lobby. The front desk was a madhouse, and Hugh bypassed the beleaguered desk sergeant altogether, pulling Ryanne toward a flight of stairs.

Ryanne's depth perception was still out of kilter, and she misjudged the height of the steps. She stumbled, and Hugh barely gave her the chance to regain her balance before he virtually dragged her toward the squad room and finally Ryanne decided she'd taken all she could.

"Damn it, let go of me! We're in the station. We're safe. You can cut the strong-arm tactics!" She wrenched out of his grasp, but Hugh recaptured her quickly and pulled her close.

"When Rube Lilenthal surrounds you with half a dozen hand-picked bodyguards, *then* you'll be safe. And you'll be *his* responsibility, not mine. Until then, you stay with me and you stay close, you got that?"

"I got it!" Ryanne snapped back, letting anger override the desire to crumple into tears.

Furious at Ryanne, Lilenthal and the world in general, Hugh stormed through the swinging double doors into the busy squad room. He moved toward the lieutenant's office just as Lilenthal came lumbering out in the midst of a phalanx of plainclothes cops.

"Damn it, Lilenthal, where the hell were you?" Hugh demanded, not bothering to wait until the officer was free before assaulting him. "You were supposed to have your men outside at three!"

"Calm down, MacKenna—"

"I'll calm down when you prove you can provide Ryanne with the protection you promised!"

As the other officers dispersed, Lilenthal looked at the three men surrounding Ryanne. "I'd say Ms. Kirkland already has about three times as much protection as she needs."

"Will you all stop talking about me as though I'm invisible!" Ryanne demanded, angry at the whole lot of them.

"Sorry, ma'am," Lilenthal apologized. "I was real glad to hear you got your sight back."

Ryanne started to thank him, but Hugh was in no mood for niceties. "What did you mean about—"

Lilenthal pointed toward his office. "Miss Kirkland, if you and your suntanned friends would step into my office, I'll explain what's been happening around here today."

"Thank you, lieutenant." Ryanne emphatically snapped her arm from Hugh's grasp and stalked into the office with Hugh and the others right behind her. Lilenthal settled in behind his desk; Ryanne, in a chair opposite him. Mo and Ben remained at the door like sentries while Hugh took a position right behind Ryanne.

He glared at the lieutenant. "Well?"

Lilenthal ignored the well-dressed Californian, extracted a photograph from a file on his desk, and handed it to Ryanne. "Miss Kirkland, is this the man who tried to kill you? The one you saw murder Vincent Perigrino?"

Ryanne's hand trembled as she reached for the photograph. It had obviously been taken without the suspect's knowledge or permission, while he was eating dinner in a restaurant. The picture was grainy and the pose not particularly flattering, but Ryanne would have recognized him anywhere. She fought back her instinctive fear and tried to keep her voice steady. "Yes. Is that Arlen Beck?"

"It is. I'll have someone take a formal statement from you in a minute, but first—" Lilenthal handed her a second photograph "—is this the man who made an attempt on your life two days ago in Los Angeles?"

Ryanne accepted the photo, but all she could do was shrug helplessly. "I don't know. My sight hadn't returned—"

"That's him," Hugh stated flatly. "Asa Keegan. But I told you on the phone this morning that he'd been captured."

"Yes, you did," Lilenthal agreed. "And right after I talked to you, that detective friend of yours, Vic Coffin, called me to request that we pick up Arlen Beck. It seems Keegan folded like a house of cards when they questioned him. He knew there was an eyewitness—you—" he indicated Hugh "—but he didn't know that you and the L.A.P.D. knew his identity and even had that photo I wired to Coffin. Once they had him in custody he decided he wasn't going to take the fall alone."

Ryanne leaned forward in her chair. "You mean he confessed to conspiracy to commit murder and named Beck as his coconspirator?"

"That's right. L.A. put out a warrant for Beck's arrest and I sent a couple of men to pick him up."

"Then you've got him in custody?" Hugh asked. "Lieutenant, that still doesn't eliminate the threat to Ryanne. Beck's lawyers will have him out on bail—"

"No, they won't, Mr. MacKenna, because we don't have him—exactly."

"What do you mean, *exactly*?" Ryanne demanded. Like Hugh, she was growing impatient with the lieutenant's cavalier attitude.

"Well, you see, the coroner's having a little trouble finding all the . . . pieces."

Ryanne paled. "Pieces?"

Lilenthal gave her an ironic smile. "Arlen Beck was killed this morning by a fire bomb under the seat of his car."

"Oh, my God," Ryanne murmured, absorbing only the gruesome fact, not its implications.

"Michelon?" Hugh asked.

"Undoubtedly." Lilenthal leaned back in his chair. "Of course, we'll probably never be able to prove it. Just one more unsolved, mob-related killing."

"What makes you certain Beck was in the car?"

"Two of his neighbors saw him get in just seconds before it exploded. They were positive it was Beck."

"But why? Why would Michelon want to kill one of his own men?" Ryanne asked, then realized what must have happened. She answered her own question. "Of course. Once Keegan had fingered Beck, my testimony on the Perigrino murder became irrelevant. Michelon was afraid that if you brought Beck in on conspiracy, he might plea-bargain for a lesser charge in exchange for information about Michelon's syndicate."

"That's the way I figure it." Lilenthal nodded in appreciation of her grasp of the situation. It was obvious she hadn't lost her reporter's instincts.

Hugh still saw a few flaws in the story, though. "How did Michelon know that Keegan had been picked up in L.A.? I mean, you don't listen to the seven o'clock news and find someone who can whip up a fire bomb on ten minutes' notice."

Lilenthal laughed. "Keegan told him. Well, not directly, of course. The idiot used his phone call last night to contact a lawyer here in Chicago who is well-known for handling Michelon's legal problems. The lawyer advised Keegan to find an attorney in L.A., then undoubtedly turned around and called Michelon. That gave Michelon most of the night to figure out the most expedient way of dealing with a messy problem. And if I know Del Michelon as well as I think I do, he probably had the fire bomb as a contingency plan, anyway. My guess is that Keegan is so low level that Michelon doesn't see him as a threat."

"In other words, it's over," Hugh interpreted.

"So far as Miss Kirkland is concerned, yes. She's got nothing on Michelon." He looked at Ryanne. "We need a statement from you so that we can officially close the books on the Perigrino murder, and after that, I'd say you're free to go. The D.A.'s not happy about losing a chance to get Del Michelon, but I imagine you're ecstatic, right?"

Without waiting for an answer, Lilenthal rose and started for the door. "If you'll just hang on a minute I'll set up a stenographer and an officer in an interrogation room so we can get your official statement. Oh, and

MacKenna—Coffin says he needs you back in L.A. as soon as you can get there."

Lilenthal left and the room became as silent as a tomb. Ryanne was still in a state of shock. *It's over.* The words echoed in her head, but they were just barely sinking in. A broad, happy smile lit up her face and she rose, turning to Hugh. "It's over!"

Hugh watched her smile bloom—the smile that had captured his heart the first moment he saw her...the smile that would haunt his dreams for as long as he lived. A tight fist of pain squeezed his heart, but he refused to let the wall he'd built crumble now. "Congratulations, Ryanne," he said coldly. He watched her beautiful smile fade, but he refused to regret that he'd erased it. "I guess that means you'll be getting your life back a little sooner than you expected."

He was looking at her with so much venom that Ryanne was struck speechless. She was free now, with no shadows haunting her life. She was free to tell Hugh that she had lied to him, that she loved him desperately; but his forbidding expression made the words clog in her throat. The decision she'd made the previous night for his own good now seemed like a horrible mistake.

"We need to talk, Hugh, please—"

"Please what? Please don't make a scene? Don't worry, Ryanne, I won't. I had enough of that last night." Neither Ryanne nor Hugh noticed when Mo and Ben slipped quietly out the door; Hugh was too consumed with pain, and Ryanne was too preoccupied with finding a way to bridge the incredible chasm she had created between them.

"You really hate me now, don't you?" she asked softly, unable to believe she had gone from one horrible nightmare straight into another.

Hugh gave a short, ugly laugh. "I expect I'll get over that in a few years."

"Oh, God... Hugh, listen to me, I—"

"Okay, Miss Kirkland. Detective Clinton is waiting for you." Oblivious to the tension in his office, Lilenthal took hold of Ryanne's arm. "If you'll come with me, we'll get this over with so you can go."

"Lieutenant, please wait," Ryanne begged, pulling away from him, unable to tear her eyes from Hugh's forbidding face. "Can I have just a minute—"

"I'm sorry but we're kinda busy today," Lilenthal told her brusquely. "Let's get your statement out of the way, and then you can thank the diligent Mr. MacKenna in any way you see fit."

"No thanks are necessary, *Ms. Kirkland*," Hugh said with biting sarcasm. "Just doing my job. I'll send my bill to your L.A. address with a notice to forward it to your *permanent* address here in Chicago."

It was such a cold, blatant slap in the face that Ryanne had to bite her lip to keep from crying out. It was a moment before she could speak. "Hugh, we have to talk. I'll be back as soon as I give my statement."

Lilenthal started out and Ryanne followed. Giving a simple statement was a small price to pay for her deliverance from the dark future she had anticipated, and yet she couldn't help cursing the lieutenant, Detective Clinton, and the entire Chicago police force because they were keeping her from clearing up this agonizing mess with Hugh. But she went into the small interrogation room as directed, officially identified Arlen Beck as the man who'd tried to kill her five years ago and answered endless questions. She finally emerged over an hour later, physically exhausted and emotionally drained, with no thought on her mind except seeing Hugh.

"Miss Kirkland?"

Ryanne was so busy surveying the busy squad room that she barely noticed the fresh-faced policeman who addressed her. "Yes?" she answered distractedly.

"Lieutenant Lilenthal said I should take you home—or wherever you want to go."

"Thank you, but I have someone waiting for me. Hugh MacKenna is—"

"'Scuse me, ma'am, but he's gone."

"Gone?" Ryanne turned to the officer, finally giving him her undivided attention. "Gone where?"

The officer shrugged. "He and the other gentlemen left right after you went into the interrogation room."

Ryanne closed her eyes to fight back a sudden rush of tears. She could barely muster enough strength to ask, "Did he . . . leave any message for me?"

"No, ma'am," the officer replied, wishing he could do something to ease the obvious distress of his lovely assignment. "He just said something about having a plane to catch, and left."

The news was one emotional blow more than Ryanne could bear. Her ability to think and reason left her just as suddenly as Hugh had, and the pain of his desertion crashed down on her. With a wrenching sob, she crumpled under the weight of the pain, oblivious to the sympathetic officer who grabbed her in time to keep her from hitting the floor.

CHAPTER TWENTY-ONE

HUGH STOOD on his deck staring at the horizon, wondering how long it would be before he could watch a beautiful sunset without trying to imagine how he would describe the clouds and the colors to Ryanne—for that matter, before he stopped looking at everything that same way. It had only been a week since he'd left her in that Chicago police station, but already Hugh had realized it was pointless to wonder how long it would be before he forgot her completely and the pain of losing her went away. Right now he couldn't believe it would ever happen, but he kept hoping that at least memories of the little things like the sunsets they'd shared would eventually fade.

The persistent ringing of his doorbell drew Hugh's attention, but he seriously considered ignoring it. The moment he'd returned to Los Angeles the previous week the media had pounced on him like a pack of hungry wolves, and the only way he'd been able to avoid them was to take off for the small cabin he owned in the mountains near Lake Tahoe. With no phones and no television there, he'd been able to escape the press, but not himself, and certainly not Ryanne.

Since she'd never been to his cabin, Hugh had thought it might be easier to think there, but memories of her had followed him, haunted him, until he'd finally given up the effort to outrun the pain. He'd returned to Los Angeles only a few hours ago, hoping that returning to work would be better therapy for his aching heart.

Whoever was at his door refused to give up, and finally Hugh relented and went to answer it. Mo Johnson was standing there, and Hugh stepped back to admit him.

Mo gave Hugh a quick once-over, noting the dark circles under his eyes and the growth of a week-old, untended beard. He noted, too, the faded jeans and cropped football jersey that had seen better days. "Are you trying to set a new fashion trend, or is this a costume for undercover work on skid row?"

Hugh shut the door and ignored the jibe. "How did you know I was home?"

"I saw the Jeep in the driveway."

"With detecting skills like that, I may have to give you a raise." He moved to the bar. "You want a drink?"

Mo pointed to the glass already in Hugh's hand. "What are you having?"

"Soda water. I tried staying drunk for a few days, but it didn't help."

"That seems obvious."

"There you go detecting again."

"Just give me a beer," Mo instructed and Hugh complied.

"How are things at the office?" Hugh started out to the deck again and Mo followed.

"Not great. We're being sued."

Hugh barely raised an eyebrow. "By whom?"

"Miller. He's unhappy that we brought in a subcontractor to finish the job in Canoga Park while we were...busy elsewhere."

Hugh heard the slight hesitation and almost smiled. "You mean while we were protecting Ryanne. It's okay to say her name, Mo. I've just about stopped flinching every time I hear it."

Hugh was at the edge of the deck, facing the sunset, and Mo joined him. He leaned against the rail and gave his friend a sidelong look. "She's back in L.A., you know."

Hugh schooled his face to show no emotion. He'd just bragged that hearing about her didn't make him flinch and he refused to make a liar out of himself so soon. "No, I didn't know, but I guess it's not surprising. She's got that screenplay to finish."

"I don't think so. The report of her death apparently shook up the producer and director pretty bad. *Entertainment Hollywood* is reporting that they grieved for about ten minutes, then hired another writer. No one seems to know if Ryanne is going to let it pass or sue."

"She won't sue," Hugh said flatly. "She's too anxious to get back to Chicago. By now I'm sure Doug Sutherland has offered her back her old job."

"Maybe." Mo fell silent for a moment before dropping the next bombshell. "She called the office asking for you every day you were gone."

Hugh gave a half laugh. "She probably wanted to complain about the bill I sent her."

"Don't you think you should at least call her to make sure?"

"No."

"You're being pretty thickheaded about this, aren't you?" He held up one hand to stop Hugh's reply. "Look, I don't know what happened to change things between the two of you, but—"

Hugh turned to Mo impatiently. "I told her I loved her, and she handed my heart back to me on a platter."

Mo nodded sadly. "That's kinda what I thought. I always figured that when you fell, you'd fall hard. But I thought Ryanne had fallen pretty hard, too. It doesn't make sense."

Hugh stiffened, remembering Ryanne's flat rejection of him. "She wanted to go back to her old life."

"That's understandable. After all, she's been pretty restricted for the past few years, being blind and all. Maybe if you gave her some time—"

Hugh turned to his friend. "Look, Mo, she made it perfectly clear that there was no room in her life for me. How much am I expected to take from her?"

Mo shrugged. "As much as she's worth."

Hugh turned back to the ocean without a word, but Mo refused to be dismissed. "Tell me, Hugh. This declaration of love you made to her—was that before or after she spent a couple of hours in the ocean wondering if she was going to die before or after the sharks got her?"

Mo wouldn't have thought it was possible for his friend to get any more tense, but Hugh did. "After."

"And after she got her sight back, too—which was all after she'd been shot in the back by a hired hit man."

"Look, is this leading anywhere?" Hugh demanded harshly.

Mo raised his hands as though to ward off Hugh's belligerence. "No, no. I was just getting ready to applaud your timing. Most guys declare their love over an elegant candlelight dinner. I gotta hand it to you, Hugh. You've got style. Ryanne had just gone through some of the most traumatic experiences any human could. That's good timing, buddy. I imagine she was really emotionally equipped for your confession."

"Believe me, Mo, she wasn't at all confused about her feelings for me. I know she'd been through a lot, and or top of it all, she was still terrified about whether or not she was going to escape from Beck. But I told her I would see her through it, no matter what happened, even if she had to go into hiding.''

"Oh, great!" Mo declared expansively. "I'm sure she really needed to feel responsible for your life as well as her own!''

"That's not the way it happened!"

"Are you sure?"

"Hell! I'm not sure of anything!" Hugh shouted, fighting the urge to hurl the glass in his hand onto the rocks below him.

Mo placed his hand on his friends shoulder and softened his voice. "Talk to her, Hugh. She couldn't possibly say anything that would make you hurt worse than you do now. And who knows—you might feel better." He moved his hand and started toward the house. "I'll let myself out. Will you be in the office tomorrow?"

Hugh nodded without turning. "Yeah."

"Okay. See you there."

Mo left and Hugh stared at the colorful horizon. Had Ryanne really called him every day? he wondered. He hadn't yet checked the message service that handled his home number, and suddenly it became important that he did so. He hurried inside and dialed his service. The woman on the switchboard sounded overjoyed to hear from him and began reading the dozens of messages that had stacked up while he'd been gone, but he cut her off, asking for only the ones from Ryanne Kirkland.

There were ten of them, and they all said the same thing. *Please call as soon as you return. Ryanne.* Simple and to the point, but without a hint of why she wanted to speak to him.

Taking the cordless phone with him, Hugh returned to the deck, dialed four digits of her number, then hung up. If he was going to put himself through the torture of speaking to her, it might as well be in person, he decided. It was hard to admit he'd have grabbed any excuse to see her again.

He tossed the phone into a chair and started for the stairs that led to the beach, then stopped abruptly. Ryanne was there below him, standing on the rocks, staring up at the house—and at him. He froze, waiting, his heart beating so hard he thought it might burst out of his chest.

Finally, Ryanne thought, praying that the gaunt, forbidding man staring down at her wasn't just a figment of her imagination. He looked different with a beard, but it was Hugh, she was certain. Her agonizing week of waiting was finally over.

After he'd left her in Chicago, Ryanne had collapsed from emotional and physical exhaustion. Lieutenant Lilenthal had wanted to call an ambulance, but Ryanne had insisted that he notify Doug Sutherland instead. Doug had taken her back to her condominium and stood guard, keeping the media at bay, while Ryanne slept for nearly thirty hours straight. When she'd awakened, her only desire had been to talk to Hugh, but by then he had disappeared, and his loyal staff at MacKenna and Associates had refused to tell her where he could be reached.

Ryanne had spent the next few days in a sickening state of suspended animation that was remarkably similar to the frightening hours she'd spent alone and adrift in the ocean. Being without Hugh, knowing how much she'd hurt him, and not knowing if he would ever forgive her had nearly driven her insane. Meanwhile she was besieged by reporters, all clamoring for details of her brush with death and the miraculous return of her sight. When Judith brought Aggie home, they all returned to the beach house to wait . . . and wait . . . and wait.

She called Hugh's home and office every day, and she spent a lot of time on the beach, walking up to this house, which she knew in her heart had to be Hugh's. Until she saw him standing there on the deck, though, she hadn't been certain. Now she was. Hugh was home, and one way or another for good or ill, this torture was going to end.

Picking her way carefully across the rocks, her heart thundering in her chest, Ryanne continued climbing until she was standing on the deck with Hugh. The distance between them was only a dozen feet, but four yards had never seemed more uncrossable.

"Hello, Hugh."

"Ryanne."

Despite the forbidding scowl on his face, Ryanne managed a small smile. She'd been through a week of hell, waiting for him to return home, and she wasn't about to be frightened off now that she finally had his attention. It terrified her to think that she might have hurt him so badly that he would never forgive her, but she owed him the truth. After that, it would be up to him to decide what to do with it.

"I almost didn't recognize you—" she touched her own jaw "—with the beard and all."

"How did you know I would be here?" he asked, turning back to the sunset so that he wouldn't have to look at her magnificent face. The desire to gather her into his arms despite whatever protests she might make was overpowering, so he gripped the rail until his knuckles turned white from the strain.

Ryanne followed him to the seaward edge of the deck, but kept her distance. "I didn't know. I've been walking

296 WHEN I SEE YOUR FACE

up here every day since I got back last Tuesday. I wasn't even positive this was your house. I'm finding that nothing I see looks the way I had visualized it."

"That must be hard for you," he said without turning to her.

Not as hard as this, she wanted to say, but didn't. "I'm coping. Judith is a big help, but she won't be with me much longer. She's taken a new job, you know."

"No, I didn't know. But I suppose it makes sense. Not many reporters have private secretaries, do they?"

"No, they don't." Ryanne fought to keep her voice even despite Hugh's bitter tone. She didn't have the right to wish that he would make this easier for her. She wanted to just blurt out what she came to say, but those words wouldn't come, so she kept up her inane chatter to fill what would otherwise have been intolerable silence. "I guess you haven't talked to your dad."

"Should I have?"

"I suppose not. But you see, Judith's going to work for him as his new business manager."

That bit of news forced Hugh to look at her. "I didn't know he needed one."

Ryanne smiled. "Neither did he until Judith convinced him he did." There had also been some mention of marriage, but Judith had refused to speculate on whether anything would come of it, and Ryanne felt that Hugh should hear that particular development from his father, not from her.

Hugh nodded and looked away from Ryanne again. "I hope it works out. They'll make a good team."

"Yes."

A long silence stretched between them. Hugh wanted to demand that Ryanne say what she had come to say and then leave. But she'd be gone forever, and as tortur ous as being with her like this was, being without her was going to be even worse. "Mo was just here," he told her, making conversation to fill the uncomfortable silence. "He told me Ted Braxton signed someone else to finish your screenplay."

"That's right."

"Are you going to sue?"

Ryanne shrugged. "I don't know. I haven't really been able to think about the future yet."

"Didn't Doug offer you your old job back?"

"As a matter of fact, he did."

Hugh laughed humorlessly. "And you didn't snap it up?"

"No." Ryanne looked out at the sunset. "The *Chicago Daily Examiner* isn't the only newspaper in the country. And I still have several Cameron Lawe books under contract. I thought I might write one a year and still be able to work in journalism . . . maybe even here in L.A."

Hugh's breath hissed as though she'd struck him and he turned to her with his eyes narrowed sharply. Living without Ryanne was going to be hard enough, but having her in the same city might very well be impossible. The temptation to see her would always be there, tantalizing him. "Why in hell would you want to stay here?" he demanded harshly.

Ryanne turned then and poured all her heart into one simple phrase. "To be near you."

The look Hugh saw in her brilliant blue eyes nearly took his breath away. He saw warmth there, and a touch of fear, but most of all, he saw love. Or, at least, what he wanted to believe was love. "Damn it, Ryanne, what are you trying to do to me?"

Ryanne reached up and touched his face as tears pooled in her eyes. "I'm trying to tell you what I wanted to say a week ago in Chicago—what I *couldn't* say that night on the boat. I love you."

Hugh would have sold his soul to believe it, but her abrupt change of heart didn't make sense. "Look, Ryanne, if you think you owe me something—"

Ryanne's heart sank. She'd told him how she felt and he didn't believe her—or he didn't want her. Ryanne wasn't sure which was worse. "I do owe you something, Hugh—"

"No, you don't! If you want to thank me for protecting you, fine! Paying your bill will be thanks enough. But don't feed me your pity, lady, because I don't want it!"

"Pity?" Ryanne could hardly believe what she was hearing. "You pigheaded oaf! I don't pity you, I love you!"

"Since when?"

"Since...since..." Confused and upset, she tried to remember when she'd first realized she loved Hugh, but it seemed that she'd loved him forever. "Since...I don't know when! June first, maybe. Possibly the second, but certainly no later than the third!"

The tight fist of pain in Hugh's gut began to uncoil as laughter bubbled in his chest. Ryanne loved him, and nothing else mattered. "June third, huh?" he asked, chuckling at Ryanne's belligerent pose.

"About then, yes," she answered, her own smile growing. It was going to be all right. The pain was slowly disappearing from Hugh's wonderful golden eyes.

"So you're telling me that you lied to me on the boat," he said softly.

"Yes."

"But why, Ryanne? Why?" Hugh wanted to draw her into his arms, but he couldn't, not just yet. He had to understand first.

Ryanne's eyes filled with tears. "*Because* I love you."

Suddenly it all became clear. She had lied to protect him, to keep him from sharing the dangerous, uncertain future she had been expecting. She had loved him enough to give him up. Overcome with emotion, Hugh could bear the distance between them no longer. He reached for her and she went to him.

"Damn you, Ryanne. Damn you," he murmured, his arms locked around her, his face buried in her silky hair. "You were trying to protect me, but you had no right to make that decision."

"Yes, I did!" Ryanne insisted. "It was the only way I could be certain you'd never be hurt. I couldn't let you go on risking your life for me!"

Hugh grabbed Ryanne's shoulders and held her away from him, fighting the urge to shake her. "Don't you realize I have no life without you?"

Ryanne's jaw quivered as she tried to hold back tears of joy. "Does that mean you might eventually forgive me for lying to you?"

"Eventually," he said grudgingly, though he held nothing back in the look he gave her.

"Do you think you might someday... marry me?"

"Even if I have to carry you kicking and screaming to the altar." He drew her toward him again, intent on sealing their strangely worded proposal with a kiss, but Ryanne pulled away. Taking hold of Hugh's hand, she led him into the house, through the living room, into the bedroom.

There she released his hand, and Hugh watched, puzzled, as she moved through the room, opening the drapes to let in the fading sunset, turning on every lamp until the room was ablaze.

When she had finished, she knelt on the bed, and held her arms out, her eyes brimming with tears and love. "Share the *light* with me?"

Hugh thought his heart might burst. He moved to her, taking her into his arms as he murmured, "Oh, yes. The light, the dark, the twilight, the dawn, and everything in between."

"Forever?"

"And ever... And ever after."

Harlequin Superromance

COMING NEXT MONTH

#366 UNTIL OCTOBER • Margaret Chittenden
Maddy Scott knew Dr. Nate Ludlow's type—fun-
loving, footloose, no commitments. But between
holding down a full-time job and caring for her
sister's kids, she welcomed some fun in her life.
Their relationship wouldn't last . . . unless Nate had a
change of heart.

#367 THURSDAY'S CHILD • Nancy Elliott
Sheltered since birth, Elise St. James knew nothing
about the world . . . or about men. Then Logan
Hunter became her bodyguard. Attorney by trade,
adventurer by inclination, Logan proved to be a
good teacher. Maybe too good. Soon Elise was
deeply in love, yet she could tell him nothing about
her past. . . .

#368 HONOR BOUND • Shirley Larson
The last time Shelly Armstrong had seen stunt pilot
Justin Corbett, she'd been overwhelmed by his good
looks and opulent life-style. She'd been a tongue-tied
teenager then. Now she was an accomplished pilot
with her own flight school, and equal to Justin in all
respects but one—she was still a novice at loving.

#369 CANDLE IN THE WINDOW • Suzanne Ellison
Gary Reid was imprisoned in a notorious California
correctional institution for a crime he refused to
name as such. Still, he refused to commit to fire
fighter and conservationist Carly Winston while he
had nothing to offer. And Carly had her own doubts.
Did Gary love her, or was she just his candle in
the window?

Harlequin American Romance®

Gull Cottage

The sun, the surf, the sand...

One relaxing month by the sea was all Zoe, Diana and Gracie ever expected from their four-week stay at Gull Cottage, the luxurious East Hampton mansion. They never thought that what they found at the beach would change their lives forever.

Join Zoe, Diana and Gracie for the summer of their lives. Don't miss the GULL COTTAGE trilogy in Harlequin American Romance: #301 CHARMED CIRCLE by Robin Francis (July 1989); #305 MOTHER KNOWS BEST by Barbara Bretton (August 1989); and #309 SAVING GRACE by Anne McAllister (September 1989).

GULL COTTAGE—because one month can be the start of forever...

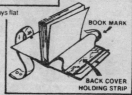

ANNOUNCING...

Harlequin
Romance
#3000

The Lost Moon Flower
by Bethany Campbell

Look for it this August
wherever Harlequins are sold

HR 3000-1